Praise for TURNING THIRTY

'Not just readable, fresh and witty but sophisticated in execution . . . funny but also poignant'
Independent on Sunday

'A lively take on growing older'
Guardian

'This is a warm, funny romantic comedy'
Daily Mail

'Mike Gayle has carved a whole new literary niche out of the male confessional novel. He's a publishing phenomenon'
Evening Standard

'Delightfully observant nostalgia . . . will strike a chord with both sexes'
She (Book of the Month)

'Mike Gayle manages to weave everything together with such a warm-the-cockles-of-your-heart manner that once you've finished reading *Turning Thirty* you want to turn right back to the beginning and start all over again. It's real life – but better than we know it'
B Magazine

'Funny and endearing . . . chuckle-on-the-bus readable'
Heat

Praise for MR COMMITMENT

Praise for MY LEGENDARY GIRLFRIEND

'Full of belly-laughs and painfully acute observations'
Independent on Sunday

'If you like *Gregory's Girl* . . . then this novel has your name on it'
Sunday Times

'Hilarious debut'
Cosmopolitan

'Comic . . . fizzy. Here comes the male Bridget Jones.'
Mirror

'A funny and frank account of a hopeless romantic'
The Times

'Wonderfully contagious, humorous and astute'
The Bookseller

'Can't help but win you over'
Company

'Gayle handles the tale impressively and in the almost-Biblically desolate Will, he has created a character who would cheer Holden Caulfield up'
GQ

'Bridget Jones for the boys'
Observer

'A fresh, funny debut for anyone with their roots in realism, but their souls desperately holding out for a movie life'
Birmingham Evening Post

Also by Mike Gayle

My Legendary Girlfriend

Mr Commitment

Turning Thirty

DINNER FOR TWO

MIKE GAYLE

FLAME
Hodder & Stoughton

Grateful acknowledgement is made for permission to reprint
excerpts from the following copyrighted works:

The lines from *Heartbreak House* by George Bernard Shaw reproduced with
permission of The Society of Authors on behalf of the Bernard Shaw Estate

Quotation from *Self Made Mann*, an interview with Aimee Mann by
Tom Shone for the *Telegraph Magazine* October 14 2001 with
permission of Tom Shone, c/o Carlisle and Co.

The lines from *The Apartment* by Billy Wilder © 1960
Metro-Goldwyn-Mayer Studios Inc. All Rights Reserved

The *Cosmopolitan* article *After The Beep* by Mike Gayle is reproduced with
permission of the National Magazine Company

First published in Great Britain in 2002 by Hodder and Stoughton
A division of Hodder Headline

A Flame Paperback

1 3 5 7 9 10 8 6 4 2

A CIP catalogue record for this title is available from the British Library

ISBN 0 340 82342 9

Set in pt Benguiat by
Rowland Phototypesetting Ltd,
Bury St Edmunds, Suffolk
Printed and bound in Great Britain by
Clays Ltd, St Ives plc

Hodder and Stoughton
A division of Hodder Headline
338 Euston Road
London NW1 3BH

For monkey one

Acknowledgements

Thanks to: my wife, Mum, Dad, Phil, Sheila, Andy, Jackie, Jenny, Phil P, Jane BE, Euan, Georgina (I told you so), Cath, Nikki, Math, Mike, Elt, Vic, Ruth, Ange, James, Dave, Maz, Lisa, Chris/John, Helen, Arthur, Charlotte, John, Nadine, Rod, everyone @ Hodder, everyone @ Curtis Brown, everyone @ The Board, the guy I was talking to about MLG at the Astor Place Barnes and Noble event in New York, February 2001 (sorry I lost your e-mail), David Kitt for writing such a 10/10 album in *Small Moments*, nice Natalie at Natmags and finally the magazines and newspapers where some of these articles originally appeared: *Cosmopolitan*, *B magazine*, *Living Etc*, *Express* and *The Times*.

I do believe that the drinks are on me.

DINNER FOR TWO

Prologue

Apparently (at least, so she told me) it all happened because her best friend Keisha had to stay behind after school for hockey practice. Usually she hated going home on her own because it was lonely. But that day she didn't even notice Keisha wasn't there because of Brendan Casey. Her obsession with him had developed to the point where she'd begun to semi-stalk him, watching him at lunchtime in the canteen, or positioning herself next to the classroom windows during English with Mr Kelly on Tuesday afternoons when Brendan's year had games because it was possible – if she squinted really hard – to just about make out his silhouette on the football pitch.

That day she'd determined that she was going to speak to him for the first time. Having thought about it a great deal she decided that the best way to do this was to be in his general proximity, smile at him a great deal and hope beyond hope that a conversation would spontaneously evolve out of nothing like some sort of conversational 'Big Bang' theory. The moment the end-of-school bell rang she'd raced out to the school's main entrance and waited.

She followed Brendan and his friends to the gates without being detected – which was more difficult than she'd anticipated. Brendan and his friends didn't walk anywhere fast, and each time they stopped she had to bend down and fiddle with her laces, or rummage in her bag, or sometimes she simply stood still and gazed into the mid-distance as if she were looking for inspiration. Eventually, her persistence paid off: the boys made it out of the gates and up the path to the bus stop. She positioned herself directly behind Brendan, a place that up until this moment she could only have ever imagined in her wildest dreams. Brendan, however, didn't pay her the slightest bit of attention no matter how much she smiled in his direction.

As the number 23A arrived and the double-decker opened its doors, the orderly queue disintegrated into a free-for-all and she was pushed to the back. By the time she got on Brendan and his friends had disappeared upstairs. She followed them but by the time she got there the top deck was full. She sighed, and made her way back downstairs.

Ten minutes later when the bus reached her stop she was so angry as she got off that she wanted to scream. She didn't, of course. As she stormed down the road she decided she wasn't even going to look back for a last glance at Brendan. Her resolve however melted as she imagined his face pressed up against the window, his eyes searching for her. She turned, but couldn't see him – and she hated herself for seeing hope where there was none. She hated herself for being so obviously devoid of self-respect.

It started to rain and she decided she was going to change – that she was going to take control of her life – and the first thing that she was going to do was change her mood by treating herself to something nice. She checked her Hello Kitty purse to see how much she had left – £2.70. Unsure exactly how she was going to treat herself, she wandered into the newsagent at the top of her road and found herself drawn towards the magazine racks. This was what she wanted.

She wanted a magazine that understood her feelings.

A magazine that understood her better than she understood herself.

A magazine that could simply make her feel better about being her.

She scanned the titles aimed at her age group: *Smash Hits, Mizz, 19, TV Hits, Top of the Pops, Teen Scene, J17, Bliss, Sugar* and *Looks* and she immediately felt better. It was as if they were friends all desperately vying for her attention. She knew she had to choose carefully. She couldn't afford to be disappointed. All of the covers looked the same: beautiful young girls or pop stars with flawless skin and perfectly proportioned features smiling serenely. As for the content, she could barely tell them apart: fashion, makeup, pop interviews, features about boys, features about friends.

After a few moments she made her choice. *Teen Scene*: 'the magazine for girls with go'. It was 10p cheaper than the others; she liked the purple eye-shadow the cover girl was wearing and hoped that they might say which brand it was inside; it had cover-mounted stick-on tattoos which although she considered a little bit babyish she thought might be a laugh; and it had the best advice column, 'Ask Adam'. Her friends laughed at the girls who wrote in to advice columns, but she knew that when it came to boys, she was as clueless as the girls in the letters. She loved problem pages: they made her feel she wasn't alone in the world. That she wasn't weird. That all the thoughts and fears that roamed around inside her head could be solved by 'Dear Pam', 'Ask Adam', 'Getting Personal with Dr Mallory', 'Boy Talk with Stephen', and 'Crisis Confidential with Dear Anne'. The list was endless. But 'Ask Adam' was the best.

She picked up the magazine and went to pay for it. The man behind the counter scanned the barcode, the till beeped, she gave him the exact money and left.

Chaos theory states that something as simple as a butterfly flapping its wings millions of years ago could have changed world events. Well, if that's so then for me, Dave Harding, a happily married music journalist, that was the moment at which a butterfly soared into the air and chaos theory became chaos practice.

PART ONE

(July–August 2000)

There they sat, those two happy ones, grown-up and yet children – children in heart, while all around them glowed bright summer – warm glorious summer.

Hans Christian Andersen, *The Snow Queen*

right

It's just coming up to midday and I'm at work when the phone rings.

'Dave Harding,' I say into the receiver. '*Louder* magazine.'

'It's me.'

My wife Izzy's at the other end of the line, calling from her office.

'Hey, you. How's your day?'

'Fine. What are you doing right now?'

'Nothing that couldn't do with an interruption.'

'Oh.'

'What's up?'

Silence.

'Are you okay?'

Silence.

'What's wrong?'

The silence ends. 'I think I might be pregnant,' she says, and bursts into tears.

tick

'You're pregnant?' I repeat.

'I think so.'

'You think so?'

'I haven't done the test . . . I wanted you to be there. But I'm late. Very late. In fact, late enough for it to be a foregone conclusion.'

'Why didn't you tell me?'

'I was kind of hoping it wouldn't be true,' she says quietly.

'I love you,' I say.

'This is so terrible,' she says.

'I love you,' I say.

'This is the end of everything,' she says.

'I love you,' I say.

'But what are we going to do?' she says.

'I don't know,' I say. 'But I love you.'

hello

Some people conceive their firstborn on a sun-kissed beach in the Caribbean, others on a stormy night in the Lake District, or in their own bedroom, by candlelight with a Barry White CD playing in the background. What do Izzy and I get? A slightly grumpy midnight coupling on a rainy north London Tuesday last June. Izzy and I try to work out when it might have happened and we can't help but laugh when we do – Izzy had spent part of that day editing an article on the decline of sexual activity among thirtysomething couples and had initiated our encounter as a token protest.

Like her, I make my living from writing for magazines and I know well enough that you should never believe anything you read in a magazine because it's all written by people like us – jobbing journalists who, at the end of the day, are as clueless and lacking direction as the rest of the world, the only difference being that we'd never admit it. Still, none of this changes the fact that *we* are pregnant and we hadn't planned to be so.

Am I annoyed with the magazine?

No.

Am I annoyed with Izzy?

No.

Am I even angry with myself?

No.

11

I am – to use a cliché – over the moon.

Ecstatic.

Overjoyed.

This is *the* best thing that has ever happened to me.

mistake

Izzy is crying on the phone because she doesn't want to have kids . . . yet. It's not as if Izzy doesn't like kids – we know loads of people who have them and she's forever cooing over them, making trips with their mothers to babyGap and pinning photographs of them on the cork board in the kitchen. The thing is, she wants them later rather than sooner.

'Maybe in a couple of years,' she'd said, at twenty-eight, when the first people we knew became pregnant.

'I just don't feel ready,' she'd said, at twenty-nine, when a whole herd of workmates, friends, cousins and neighbours produced infants.

'I'm not even sure I want them,' she'd said, at thirty, when she heard that her childhood best friend was expecting her fourth child.

To be fair to Izzy, her anti-baby stance is both publicly and privately supported by me. 'We're not a very child-friendly household,' I'd say, whenever the subject came up among friends. 'Me with a kid? You must be joking.' And then Izzy and I would laugh and joke about how bad we'd be at child-rearing. We even have a little routine to go with it:

Her: We can't have kids. We'd make terrible parents.
Me: We'd end up feeding the baby Budweiser instead of milk.

13

Her: Or leaving it on buses.

Me: Or in supermarkets.

Her: They'd be the unluckiest kids in the world with our gene pool to cope with.

Me: They'd inherit your huge ears.

Her: And your weird monkey toes.

Me: Imagine that – a big-eared, monkey-toed child clutching its bottle of milk without using its hands.

Her: And don't forget we're both short-sighted! So that's a short-sighted, big-eared, monkey-toed child.

Me: And you were asthmatic as a child and I'm allergic to just about everything: pollen, penicillin, shellfish . . .

Her: (Takes deep breath) An asthmatic, allergic to just about everything including pollen, penicillin, shellfish, short-sighted, big-eared, monkey-toed child. Incredible!

Me: It wouldn't bode well for a kid at all. (Pause.) So it's just you and me, then?

Her: Yeah, it's just you and me.

Even when the peer pressure was turned up to the max and all the babied-up couples kept pressuring us with their 'Oh, you *must* have a baby, it's so fulfilling,' mantra, I continued to back Izzy because I loved her. And she loved me. And I wanted her to be happy, whatever we chose to do in life.

But the truth was, I'd wanted kids from the word go. I didn't want to wait. If I could've had them the moment I met Izzy and kept on having them until we were old and grey I couldn't have been happier. But I kept it in. I didn't want to pressurise her. One day, I told myself, she'd change her mind and until then I'd have to be patient. So I was patient while we did the couple thing: installed kitchens, ripped out walls, holidayed in exotic locales far off the beaten track. We were poster children for the twin-income no-kids generation. We had it all and we had it now. But I would've swapped the lot for a pile of stinking nappies and the child that had filled them.

babies

'Which one shall we get?' I ask.

It's now a quarter to seven and Izzy and I are standing in the large Boots store on Oxford Street staring at a long row of pregnancy-testing kits – about which I know nothing. This is all new to me and I hadn't even been sure where they'd be located in the store. In Feminine Hygiene? Next to Haircare? Between Shapers sandwiches and refrigerated soft drinks? It turns out that they're in the same aisle as contraception, which I find amusing, on a shelf called, ironically, 'Family Planning'.

'We did a consumer test feature on them a few months ago,' says Izzy as we carefully study the row of tests. 'This one,' she points to a dark blue box, 'and this one,' a pastel green box at the opposite end of the row, 'came out on top.'

I pick one up and look at the price. I'm horrified. 'Is this a mistake?'

She peers at it. 'No, babe. That's how much they cost.'

'Because?'

'Because that's how much they cost.'

'Everywhere?'

'Everywhere.'

'You could buy a half-decent CD for the price of one of these,' I say, frowning.

'And *you* probably would,' says Izzy, smiling. She has a

wonderful smile, my wife. The kind that makes you glad to be alive. 'Which CD would you get?' she asks.

'Tindersticks, *Simple Pleasures*. Cracking album.'

'But haven't you already got it?'

'Yeah,' I reply. 'But it's so good I'd like to own it twice.'

home

On the journey home to our flat, 24b Cresswell Gardens, Muswell Hill, we talk about everything and nothing: how things have gone at work, what to eat when we get in, what to do at the weekend, real couple stuff. However, as soon as we reach the flat – the second-floor of a three-storey Edwardian conversion – we stop kidding ourselves that this isn't the biggest thing to happen in our relationship since the day we met.

Suddenly we're on a mission and only one thing counts. Even though our cat, a three-year-old egocentric grey Persian called Arthur, is mewing like a maniac and writhing on the floor for attention, we ignore him and head to the bathroom. I watch as she opens the kit and brandishes the test stick in my direction. I'm mesmerised. It's hard to believe that this piece of plastic can determine what kind of *rest of my entire life* I'm going to have.

'Okay,' she says. 'This is it.'

She looks at me and I look back at her. After a few moments of quiet, while we collect our thoughts, I give her the nod. 'Go for it,' I say.

She doesn't move.

'What's wrong?'

'I can't pee with you in the room. You'll have to wait outside.'

'Why not?' I'm not joking either. I think it's a ridiculous thing to say. 'Why do I have to miss out on all the good bits?'

'You're not going to miss out on anything,' she snaps.

I leave the room and she closes the door behind me. I stand directly outside, place my ear to the door and strain to make out the sound of my wife peeing on to the plastic stick. The cat joins me. He doesn't listen at the door, though: he weaves in and out of my legs purring loudly. I kneel down and scratch the back of his neck and he looks up at me, with his huge grey eyes. We have a Moment, my cat and I, but he doesn't know I'm not really there with him – I'm in the bathroom with Izzy.

'Are you done yet?' I call.

'Will you give me one *bloody* second, Dave?' yells Izzy. 'I've only just got going.'

There's a long silence, then the sound of intermittent peeing, the loo roll rattling, then a flush, and Izzy emerges with the test. 'Only a man could have invented that,' she says. 'Only a man would think it was a great idea to pee on something that requires the target skills of a sharpshooter.'

I laugh – that was a very Izzy thing for her to say. She spends all day helping to create a magazine that speaks directly to hundreds of thousands of women and one of the easiest ways to create a united sisterhood is to have a common enemy in 'useless men' in a 'Can't live with them, can't live without them' way. The truth is, though, that Izzy doesn't believe in sexual stereotypes. She believes in people.

'How long do we have to wait?' I ask.

She looks at the back of the box to check, even though she knows that I know that she knows. 'Three minutes.'

'Well, it's been at least thirty seconds since you flushed

the loo and started talking to me so it's two and a half minutes to go.' Before Izzy can object I take the stick from her, put it carefully on the floor, grab her hand, drag her into our bedroom and close the door behind us. Here we stand, with our arms wrapped around each other and our eyes stuck to our watches for precisely two and a half minutes. Then Izzy makes a break for the door. Although I'm not far behind her she gets to the test before me and by the time I catch up with her it's in her hand.

The tension is so excruciating that I can barely speak. 'What does it say?'

'I'm pregnant,' she says quietly. Tears are already rolling down her face. 'You're going to be a dad.'

I put my arms round her and hold her close. 'Don't cry. Everything's going to be all right.'

'I'm not crying because I'm sad,' she says. 'I'm crying because right now I feel like this is the best news I've ever had.'

readers

It's the following day and I'm at my place of work – the fourteenth floor of the Hanson building in Holborn, which is home to BDP Publishing, the small magazine empire that produces seventeen magazine titles covering pretty much everything people like reading about:

Interiors: *Your Kitchen, Bathroom and Bedroom* and *Metrohome*

Women's fashion and lifestyle: *Femme, It Girl* and *Fashionista*

Babies: *Your Baby and You* and *Mothers Now*

Computing: *Computer Gaming Now, Download* and *Internet Express*

Sport: *Football Focus* and *Tee Off*

Cooking: *Now Eat That* and *Food Review*

Music: *Louder*

I work at *Louder*, 'the magazine for people who live music'. *Louder*'s tag line always makes me laugh because it's just so accurate. Our readers don't *love* music they *live* it – eat it, breathe it. Just as I do. Or, perhaps, that should be 'did'. Though I love my job I'm also well aware that music journalism, like its more glamorous counterpart 'being a rock star', is by its very nature a young person's occupation. Of course, plenty of musicians churn out albums well into their thirties, forties and even fifties, but I have no desire to become the journalistic equivalent of any of them. Like my musical heroes, Buckley, Hendrix, Cobain, Curtis, Shakur, something appeals to me about the idea – metaphorically speaking – of dying young and leaving a good-looking back catalogue. As it is, I'm not only past the thirty mark but have reached the stage where I'm beginning not to 'get' a few of the new musical hybrids that the constantly evolving beast that is rock 'n' roll churns out. I hide my ignorance behind outrage at the bastardisation of music's purest forms, but the truth is, with a lot of music, I feel I've heard it all before. And I hate myself for feeling that.

For instance, one particular record that's been in the charts recently samples the theme tune to a well-known TV drama. Every time I hear it I want to smash my car radio. I've never felt like this before and it's unnerved me so much that I daren't tell anyone else at *Louder* – even though I can see that some of the other writers feel it too. Maybe that was why, over recent months, *Louder*'s circulation figures had been falling. Maybe none of us has realised how out of touch we are with our target audience – fifteen to twenty-six-year-old males with ridiculously large record collections who regularly go to see live music.

Maybe the music that makes me want to smash my car radio is intended to have that effect on me, a thirtysomething music journalist. Maybe as far as 'The Kids' are concerned I am the enemy – I'm no longer the rebel without a cause: I'm a rebel with a mortgage, a pension plan and a very large record collection. If I'd been fifteen years old I'd probably love the record that nowadays makes me want to smash my car radio. I wouldn't care that I'd heard it all before because I would feel it was talking to me about my life. This was one reason why music used to be so all-important to me. I can still remember how it used to mean everything – when it was in my head, in my heart and in my soul. But now I realise there's more to life than music.

When I'd been at school sitting in an empty classroom during my lunch-break proudly reading my copy of *NME* I'd never have believed that one day I would be a part of the glamorous world of rock 'n' roll. And yet here I am, sitting at a desk in front of piles of cardboard CD mailers with my name on them. Record company PRs take me to lunch to court my favour, I get to go on tour with bands and I've travelled all over the world all expenses paid to interview artists. It's a fantastic job. I often wonder what I'd have done if it hadn't happened. Plan B (which, of course, had once been plan A) had been to form a band but as I couldn't sing and my dexterity with the bass guitar was limited to the 'good bit' in Clapton's 'Sunshine of Your Love', I'd excluded myself from rock 'n' roll super-stardom. Plan C (which had once been plan A) had been to start my own record label, but as I had about as much business acumen as a five-year-old in a toy shop I knew, deep down, that this, too, would be doomed to failure. Music journalism (plan D) had risen to the top of the charts because it was the only one that I felt I might achieve.

The *Louder* office is not what you would call a normal working environment. In a staff of nineteen there are eighteen men – committed music snobs, the lot of them – who act like they hate each other, and one woman, the ever chirpy Chrissy, who is the magazine's editorial assistant. Few pleasantries are exchanged in the *Louder* office and little conversation is to be had unless it's directly related to music, work or abusing our rivals and the bands they're championing.

To a degree, working at *Louder* is a lot like joining the SAS: we don't take on just anyone and all members of staff have to be able to kill with their bare hands if the need arises. It is a cruel but comfortingly masculine environment to live in – like a prison, but without the razor blades in the soap. Women hate it. The first time Izzy left the *Femme* office on the eleventh floor to visit me she told me *Louder* looked like a cold, merciless and miserable place to work.

'You're right,' I replied. 'But you said that as if it was a bad thing.'

tock

It's hard for me to be at work today. I want to tell the entire office I'm going to be a dad. Because that's what you're supposed to do when this happens. You get to be proud. *I created life*, you want to say. *There will be one more human being in the world because of me!* But I don't, of course, mainly because the office probably wouldn't care. Instead I sit down at my desk, stare into space and the daydreams kick in: my kid's first Christmas, my kid's first birthday party, playing football in the park when my kid's a bit older. I do it all. And I do it now. On a whim I even type my foetus a letter:

11 July 2000

Dear Foetus,
Let me introduce myself: I'm Dave Harding and I'm your dad. So hello there. I'm a music journalist by trade – I work as reviews editor on Louder. *No doubt when you're a bit older (a couple of weeks maybe) I'll play a couple of my favourite albums to you (they're constantly changing but I can pretty much guarantee that there'll be stuff from the Rolling Stones, Mos Def, Public Enemy, Radiohead, Mazzy Star and Aretha Franklin).*
I know it's quite dark where you are and that

you're probably under water but you can hear in there, can't you? I'm pretty sure you can. By the way, the woman who is carrying you around at the minute is your mum, Izzy. We have been married for three years (we celebrated our anniversary a few weeks ago) and together for three years before that. We're very happy.

Anyway, I looked up some stuff about reproduction on the Internet (I'll explain that to you when you get out) this morning and once I managed to get through a plethora of bizarre triple xxx porn sites I found a web page that had information about your people (i.e. really, really small people). Apparently, right now you're 1mm long – which if you're not familiar with the metric system is not very big at all. Is an ant 1mm long? I don't know but at a guess you're probably a bit smaller than an ant.

Right, what else should I tell you? Your mum is deputy editor on a glossy women's magazine called Femme and she works very hard. She's thirty (I'm thirty-two) and she's a very smart, and very sexy woman (although the less said about her being sexy the better as I don't really want to contribute to any burgeoning Oedipal complex you might be working on in there if you're a boy).

As you probably haven't got a mirror with you, I'm guessing that you have no idea what you look like. Well, to help you along, here's what we look like and I suppose you'll be somewhere in the middle. Your mum is five foot nine, and a little over ten stone. She has jet black hair, hazel eyes, a smallish nose and slightly chipmunky cheeks. I know you're not familiar with any cultural references but she's best described as a cross between Minnie Driver in Circle of Friends *and Julianna Margulies before she left* ER. *As for me, I'm six foot two and a well-proportioned fourteen stone. I have short, black hair, dark brown eyes, a wide nose and, I like to think, a well-defined chin.*

Izzy's mum was born in South Wales, and her dad (who died a couple of years ago) was born in Poland; my mum and dad are from Trinidad. Izzy and I were both born in England, which means that you'll be of (cue drum roll) Anglo-Welsh-Polish-Trinidadian heritage and will probably have café-au-lait skin.

If it hadn't have been for my constant petitioning of your mum to change her name when we'd got married you'd have ended up with a double-barrelled surname: Small Foetus Lewandowski-Harding or Small Foetus Harding-Lewandowski, which I think you'll agree is a bit of a mouthful.

Anyway, this is just a short letter of introduction to say . . . welcome to the family.

Take it easy in there.

All the best

Dave Harding (your very proud dad)

on

Izzy calls me from work to tell me the good news. She's just been to see a doctor at our local surgery, who has confirmed that she is pregnant. Using the last day of her period as day zero the doctor tells her that she has in fact been pregnant for approximately six weeks. Something clicks inside me at this news. I feel like a man possessed. I can think of nothing except that I'm going to be a father. It dominates my thoughts, my life and Izzy's and my conversation over the following week.

Monday morning at work

'Hello, *Femme* magazine, Izzy Harding speaking.'

'Hey, you, it's me,' I reply.

'What's wrong?'

'What do you mean, what's wrong? Nothing's wrong. I just wanted a chat.'

'It's just that it's only ten past ten,' says Izzy. 'You never call me at ten past ten. In fact, there have been times that I've wanted you to call me at ten past ten and you've said, no, it's too early.'

'That was the old me. The new me can call you at work any time.'

'So?' says Izzy, expectantly.

'How are you feeling?'

'Okay.'

'Are you sure?'

'I don't feel any different. Do you feel any different?'

I laugh. 'I'm not the one who's . . .' I look round the *Louder* office and decide against saying the word, preferring to let Izzy fill in the blanks. 'Am I?'

'What are we like?' says Izzy. 'It's such early days and already we're obsessed. We'll drive each other insane by the time the . . . arrives. We should make some sort of pact to stop talking about it for a while.'

'Okay, but before we start let me ask you this one thing.'

'Okay, what?'

'Names.'

'Names?'

'Just wondered. What are your current faves?'

'*Please* tell me you're joking?'

'Can't.'

She laughs.

'I'm thinking Levi for a you-know,' I continue, 'and Lois for a you-know . . .'

A roar of laughter fills my eardrum. 'Let me guess,' says Izzy, still laughing, 'Levi because of the Temptations' Levi Stubbs and Lois because of . . . Superman's girlfriend?'

'You're absolutely wrong.' I say, even though she's scored two out of two. 'They're just names I like.'

'Yeah, right,' she says. 'It doesn't matter anyway.' She lowers her voice even more. 'You've got no chance of lumbering anything that comes out of my loins with the name Levi, I guarantee you that.'

'So what about you, then?' I ask, not bothering to pretend that Izzy hasn't been thinking about the same thing.

'Hang on a sec . . .' she says. I can hear someone asking

her what time the chromalins are due from the printer's. 'Okay, I'm back,' she says. 'Do you know what?'

'What?'

'I like it that you know I'm as demented as you,' she says, and there's real joy in her voice. 'Yeah, I have some . . . yeah, I know we're getting a little too excited but . . . well . . . you think, don't you? Whether you like it or not.'

'Agreed. But you can stop stalling – it isn't going to help your case in the least.'

'Okay,' says Izzy. 'Well, I dismissed all the usual suspects that have been floating around my head since I was about ten – you know, Molly, Polly, Chloë, Poppy, Lucy, the kind of names I secretly wished I'd been called because I'd read too many books about posh girls at boarding-school. Then I did that thing where you dismiss any name that might help the school bully so out went Gregory Pegory,' she paused to laugh again, 'Rossy Bossy and Jasmine Frasmine. Then I realised that was a silly reason not to choose a name so now I've sort of settled on Maxwell and Jasmine, but I'm open to persuasion.'

'Maxwell and Jasmine are good names,' I tell her. 'But so are Levi and Lois. Three names are going to have to go in the bin, unless . . .'

'Unless what?'

'Well, it could be quadruplets, couldn't it?'

Thursday evening in the kitchen

'Dave, are you sure about not talking about this thing that we said we wouldn't talk about?'

It's five past eight and we are in the kitchen. One of the work surfaces is covered with last Saturday's *Guardian* and there is soil everywhere because Izzy is planting a mixture of gerberas, hyacinths and pansies she's just bought from B&Q in a window box. A large bag of compost sits in the sink and she has her hands inside it.

'Yeah,' I reply, 'I don't think it's good for us. I think we're obsessing.'

'So we can't say anything about this thing that we're not talking about or the whole pact will be rendered null and void and pointless?'

'What? Do you mean, what if you were to ask me something like . . . "Had any interesting baby thoughts today"? Yeah, I think the pact would indeed be rendered null and void and pointless.'

'But you've just said it,' she says. She takes her hands out of the bag. They are covered in the rich black compost.

'I've just said what?' I ask playfully.

'The word that we're not supposed to say, the topic that we're not meant to discuss.'

'Damn. You're right.' I pause. 'Oh, well, then, had any interesting baby thoughts today?'

Friday mid-afternoon on the internal line at our respective places of work

'Levi,' I say.

'Maxwell,' says Izzy. 'Second choice?'

'Dave,' I say.

'Yeah, right,' she says. 'Vernon.'

'Sounds like "vermin",' I say. 'And for girls?'

'Still Jasmine,' she says.

'Still Lois,' I say. 'Second choice?'

'Adele,' she says.

'Izzy,' I say.

'That's nice,' she says.

'I know,' I say.

Saturday morning at my parents' in Streatham, south London

'Mum, Dad,' I say, 'Izzy and I have something to tell you.'

Izzy and I are round at my mum and dad's house to tell them the good news. 'We're . . .' I look at Izzy and squeeze her hand '. . . we're going to have a baby.'

My dad explodes. 'Congratulations! Well done!'

'That's such wonderful news!' says my mum. 'The best news I've heard in a long, long time.'

All the parties in the room stand up, shake hands, hug, kiss and generally congratulate each other. I revel in seeing my parents so overjoyed. They insist that we stay for lunch. The second we agree Izzy is whisked off to the kitchen by my mum under the ruse that she needs assistance with the food. I know full well that Mum won't let her so much as get her fingers wet in the washing-up let alone cook. I stay in the living room with my dad, watching TV and talking about the events of the day.

Sunday afternoon at Izzy's mum's in Oxford

It's just coming up to midday and Izzy and I are at her mum's in Oxford, standing in the kitchen. The original plan was that Izzy would ring her mum yesterday and tell her over the phone but each time she tried to dial she couldn't do it. When I had asked why not she'd replied, 'Because I want to see her face,' and I understood straight away. We arrived at Izzy's mum's under the pretence that we'd just dropped in, and she, too, insisted that we stay for lunch. Izzy's unsure when it would be best to tell her mum so she instructs me to stay with her at all times in preparation for the moment. It comes as Izzy is peeling potatoes and I'm standing beside her holding a kettle of boiling water in one hand and a packet of chicken stuffing in the other while carefully studying the instructions, and her mum is crouched down at the oven peering through the glass at the chicken inside it. That's when Izzy says, 'Hey, Mum, I've got some news for you. I'm pregnant.'

Her mum turns to face her and right away begins crying. Barely able to get her words out, she says, 'Your dad would've been so proud.' That's it. Izzy starts crying too and her mum cries even more, then hugs Izzy, and me, and finally she makes all three of us hug together. She really is that happy.

friends

Now that my parents and Izzy's mum know, the only other people we decide to tell at this early stage are our close friends, two couples: Jenny and Trevor, and Stella and Lee. I wanted to keep it quiet until we were a little more sure but Izzy says, 'They're the people I'd turn to if I had some bad news so why not tell them when the news is good?' I have no answer to that but I still have reservations. Friends can be funny about change. Especially *our* friends, who aren't in the kind of relationships where settling down, let alone having kids, would end in anything but tears.

them

Trevor is thirty-one and works for an IT company called C-Tec, installing software for financial institutions. His girlfriend before Jenny was Adalia, a Spanish student whom he'd met in a club in Hoxton. After a short and passionate beginning they had what can only be described as the most vicious break-up in history, but not before Adalia became pregnant. Trevor agreed that he would support the child as best he could but he and Adalia wouldn't be getting back together. Things were fine between them, even after the baby (a little boy she named Tiago) was born, until Trevor started his relationship with Jenny. Adalia claimed still to be in love with him and started using the baby as a way to get at him. She'd arrange for him to spend time with Tiago then be out when he arrived; she'd tell mutual friends that he wasn't helping with Tiago even though he was. Eventually she struck the ultimate blow: she returned to Spain. He tried to make her stay – he even said he'd get back together with her. But it was too late. Initially he flew out to see Tiago whenever he could but Adalia continued to make things difficult, so he took a hard decision and stopped going.

The other side of this partnership is Trevor's girlfriend Jenny, one of Izzy's best friends. Izzy and Jenny met in their early twenties when Jenny worked briefly on *Femme*. Now at thirty-one Jenny's doing the kind of job that is always a talking point at parties – she's editor of *Teen Scene*, 'the magazine for girls with go'. She loves her job and takes it very seriously, but I don't. I tease her constantly about it because, to my mind, it isn't a real job. From what I can gather she seems to spend most of her day lunching with advertisers, talking about *Dawson's Creek* with her staff and extolling the physical virtues of whichever boy band is in vogue. Trevor and Jenny have been together for eighteen months and sharing a flat in Ladbroke Grove for more than half of that. Quite often they acknowledge to us – but never to each other – that they moved in together too early. I reckon they're so unready to enter the world of parenthood that they use three methods of contraception at once.

Stella Thomas, of Stella and Lee, is thirty-three and works as a recruitment consultant for blue-chip companies. She's by and large an angry woman, who tends to take out her frustration with the world on her boyfriend Lee, whom she's been with for over a year. At twenty-four he is nearly a decade younger. While at first Stella thought it was the coolest thing on earth to have a toy-boy, things changed as she fell in love with him and that decade began to bother her. I like Lee: he's laid back to the point of being horizontal and treats life like it's all a bit of a joke. As long as he has enough money in his pocket to get a round in at the pub he's a self-proclaimed 'happy chappy'. He works as a runner on a cable programme called *The Hot Pop Show*, and gets to stand around all day smoking Marlboro Lights with other similarly attired young graduates, all delighted to be working in 'telly'. On the whole Lee and Stella are about as likely to have kids as the Pope. Maybe even less so.

talk

It's nine o'clock on the following Saturday night and Izzy and I are sitting at a candle-lit dining-table in our living room with our friends. Empty foil containers from the Chinese takeaway are stacked neatly to one side, small polystyrene tubs containing all manner of brightly hued sauces are scattered about the table, and flecks of fried rice and the odd beansprout lie abandoned on the tablecloth. Izzy clinks her fork against her wine-glass to get everyone's attention. 'We've got some news to tell you all. Some *really* exciting news.' She looks at me and I can't help but send her a great big cheesy smile. 'I don't know how to say this so I'll just come out with it – but this is absolutely top-secret, not to be divulged outside these four walls . . . They say you're not supposed to tell anyone in the early days because . . . well, you know, but we're way too excited to keep it in. We're pregnant!'

'Congratulations!' screams Jenny, who is the world's number-one expert at congratulating people enthusiastically: she makes the whooping noises, she squeals, she beams like a sunburst and kisses us like a game-show contestant. Following her lead, Stella joins in with the whooping, squealing, beaming and kissing and then, in one fell swoop, they rise and whisk Izzy away to the kitchen.

Later that night in bed, Izzy and I exchange notes on the

evening. I tell her about my conversations with Trevor and Lee and she tells me about hers with Stella and Jenny. While her friends had been less forthright with their opinions than mine – Lee wouldn't be following me into fatherhood at any time soon – Izzy thinks that she could sense varying degrees of resentment at our news. Not nasty stab-you-in-the-back resentment, but the kind that might instinctively spring from a generally good-natured child before good manners kicked in. Izzy thinks that Stella and Jenny were put out because it forced them to look at their own relationships. In direct contradiction to what Trevor told me, Izzy says that Jenny has never raised the subject of kids in all the time she and Trevor have been together: she knows the subject is off limits because of what happened between him and Adalia.

Stella went for a passive-aggressive comedy routine. 'You've activated my biological clock, Izzy,' she'd said. 'I'm a thirty-three-year-old woman who's going out with a twenty-four-year-old who's not going to want to have kids until my eggs are old and shrivelled.' Izzy thinks she'd only been *half* joking. After Stella had met Lee, Jenny and Izzy had acted as agony aunts to her while she hadn't been sure about the relationship. As good friends do, they didn't tell her the truth – i.e., that Stella and Lee were pretty much doomed from the start – because that wasn't what she wanted to hear. Instead they told her that opposites attract, love conquers all, and everything would be all right in the end.

All in all, our announcement had without question managed to upset and partially alienate every one of our four friends.

look

It's the following Tuesday, early evening. It's been really hot all day and it's still warm. Everyone's wearing short sleeves, and all the pubs and bars I pass are surrounded by alfresco drinkers. I'm on my way over to Covent Garden from Holborn to meet Izzy so that we can go out for the evening for the first time in ages. We decide we're going to be really cool parents-to-be even though all we want to do in the evenings after work these days is sit at home, firmly ensconced on the sofa in front of the TV. In short, nesting. So tonight we're back, just to show that we can still do it. The plan for the evening is to meet Lee and Stella for a few drinks at the launch party of a new bar on James Street, and after that the four of us will meet up with Jenny and Trevor, then head over to the Astoria for a gig – I'm on the guest list, plus five. Afterwards we'll probably spend half an hour or so at the after-show party then head home.

Izzy calls to say she's running late from a photo-shoot at a studio in Kentish Town and won't be with me for another half-hour. So I turn on my personal stereo and head towards Long Acre, hoping to lose myself in window-shopping to an old Elliot Smith album, *XO*.

Half-way there, I find myself drawn towards one shop window in particular and stop. I look at the sign above my head: babyGap. I glance furtively from side to side then I walk through the doors into a place that is, to all intents and purposes, on another planet. Strolling along the aisles are women of all ages, whom I guess are expectant mothers, mothers with children, mothers-in-law or friends of mothers. I am the only male who isn't attached to reins or being manoeuvred in a pushchair. I catch a glimpse of myself in one of the store's mirrors and realise I stick out like the proverbial sore thumb, but it doesn't bother me. My personal stereo gives me the illusion of detachment – a cloak of invisibility – allowing me to roam without embarrassment.

Suddenly I'm drawn towards a sky blue romper-suit for children aged six to eight months. I pick it up by its hanger and hold it up in the air in a similar fashion to many of the female shoppers in the store and again my imagination goes into overdrive. I picture my baby-to-be in it, then with an orange sun hat adorned with animal ears. My child is going to be the best-dressed kid in the crèche. Then I pick up a pair of lime green corduroy dungarees and I'm lost. Right there in the middle of the shop I conjure up my child from head to toe. Izzy, I decide, should be the main contributor as she has the kind of face, thoughtful, sweet-looking, that will take a child far in life. Perhaps I'll chip in with the ears or the chin, but on the whole I want the baby to be more her than me. Its personality should be split fifty-fifty between me and her. I'll contribute a relatively analytical mind, the ability to keep calm in a crisis and a love of music. Izzy can give it her generosity, the way she makes people feel good about themselves and just enough neuroses for it not to feel superior to its peers. Together we will give it a love of the written word, a sense of humour and a pretty good dress sense. What's left: the rest of the child can be made up of various parents, grandparents, uncles, aunts and maybe a little bit of the unknown thrown in for good luck. That's what a pair of dungarees is making me think about in the time that I hold them in my hands, they make me think that anything and everything is possible.

Ten minutes later my phone rings again and I think it must be Izzy calling to tell me she's in a cab and will be with me soon but it isn't. It's a woman from the photographic studio in Kentish Town where Izzy has been all afternoon. She tells me that Izzy has been taken to hospital with stomach pains. She says I should get there as soon as I can. I leave the shop and start running.

words

It's nearly seven o'clock by the time I arrive at the obstetrics unit in the Whittington Hospital. I tell a nurse my name and she asks me to take a seat while she finds a doctor to come and speak to me. I don't sit, I remain rooted to the spot, my eyes fixed on the door through which she has just left. In the cab on the way over I played out the worst-case scenario in my head several times. I told myself that if I anticipated the worst it couldn't possibly happen.

The nurse returns with a doctor at her side. He is tall and young, younger than me, and I tell myself that this is good: everything he's learned will be fresh in his mind. I tell myself that this is a man I can trust. This is a man who won't fail me. The doctor says hello, shakes my hand and takes me to one side. He explains that Izzy is fine but that she has had a miscarriage. He tells me that miscarriages are relatively common during the early stages of pregnancy, that they happen for any number of reasons, that it shouldn't stop us trying again in a little while. I ask him if I can see Izzy yet, but he says she's waiting to see a consultant. His pager goes off and he apologises: he is needed somewhere else in the hospital. I thank him for his time, then watch him walk away. I'm sure he did his best, I tell myself, because he looks like a man who would.

I know I should call people, Izzy's mum and my parents

especially, but I can't bring myself to tell them that after all this time and all this soul-searching, everything has been for nothing. The names Izzy and I have dreamed, the hopes we'd had for our child's future, the love that has filled our hearts – all wasted. It is this that I hate most of all: the loss of potential – the thousands of things that will never take place now because of what has happened. I can find nothing to take comfort from. No matter what happens in the future *this* child will never be.

Impatient for further news of Izzy I pace the waiting room. I buy myself some coffee from a drinks machine then let it go cold. I buy a Mars bar from the machine next to it, open the wrapper and throw it away, then finally spot a diversion: a wall display of hospital literature. I scan the dozens of leaflets for one that might help me. There it is. I take it down from the display and then, leaning against the wall, begin to read.

As I digest the contents I can't help but think about the person who wrote it. Was he or she a journalist, like me and Izzy? Did they make their living writing hospital pamphlets just as I make mine writing about music? I try to picture them sitting at their computer with a list of ailments and diseases that have to be translated into digestible chunks of normal-speak. Did this person ever imagine who their audience might be? Or did they just sit at their computer, working their way from A to Z of the things that can go wrong with the human body? When I finish reading I screw up the leaflet and throw it into the bin next to me, which is already overflowing with empty drinks cans and polystyrene coffee cups. Of the many facts in the leaflet only one remains lodged in my head: thirty per cent of first pregnancies end in miscarriage.

One in three people.

I look around the room and count out three people from the dozen or so with whom I am sharing it: a young girl reading a magazine; a middle-aged woman with a bandaged leg; I look down at my trainers and count myself.

Two people get away with it for each time that another doesn't. This time I'm the unlucky one. But it doesn't seem fair that it has happened. The fact that, as the doctor told me, 'Sometimes these things just happen,' didn't help me to understand *why* it had happened, clutching as I do to the eternally optimistic theory that bad things shouldn't happen to good people.

When I eventually get to see Izzy she doesn't look any different. She's still wearing the clothes I saw her put on this morning. This morning when everything was so different from how it is now. It makes me think – if only for a second – that this is a bad dream. That somehow everything will still be all right.

'I love you,' I say, holding her tightly. 'We'll be all right.'

'I didn't love him enough,' says Izzy, as tears stream down her face. 'That's why he's gone.'

'No.' I wonder why she's made up her mind that the baby would've been a boy. 'You're wrong. You did love him. You loved him more than enough for the two of us. And, if it was possible for him to know anything, he knew that. It wasn't anybody's fault, Izzy. It's just one of those things.'

past

When the news emerges everyone is incredibly supportive: Trevor and Jenny say they're available to help whenever help is needed, and Stella and Lee call constantly for updates. They're all really good friends to Izzy and me.

Several days after Izzy is discharged from hospital we decide to spend some time away from London and head for Izzy's mum's holiday cottage in Wales. I think we assume that somehow we'll be able to leave our problems behind if we aren't at home. All we want is to stop feeling what we're feeling but we can't manage that. Neither of us has the strength even to bring up the subject of the miscarriage. Neither of us wants to remind the other of the terrible thing that has happened. This is ridiculous, of course, because those key hours in hospital are our constant companions: we review them separately, time and again, wishing that the past hadn't happened.

long

When something terrible happens and you're in the middle of it you really do feel like you're never going to be the same again. You feel like every day of your life from now will have about it the same dull greyness. Sometimes you feel like you'll never smile again. Then, of course, the day arrives when the anger and bitterness are not as intense as they were the day before, and eventually the catastrophe seems like a distant memory from some other lifetime. You begin to feel . . . okay. Not great, not good, but not bad either. You can laugh without feeling guilty. You can smile without wanting to cry.

As things get better Izzy and I treat ourselves a million times better than we ever have before. We buy a new car – a 1964 white Mercedes 280 SL convertible that's in relatively good condition. The first weekend we have it, we drive to Brighton with the hood down. It makes us feel free. It makes us feel young again. The miscarriage made us feel like fully-fledged adults, which we both resent. The car gives us back our youth and returns to us our right to be carefree.

grand

It's a couple of weeks later and we're in the car driving to a restaurant in Ladbroke Grove to meet up with Trevor and Jenny. It's raining and one of the windscreen wipers is making a terrible screeching noise. The guy who we bought the car from had installed a CD player in it and we're listening to Rod Stewart's *Never a Dull Moment* because I think it's good driving music. Izzy and I are both singing along quietly to 'You Wear It Well,' which we both consider one of the best songs ever written. Just as it comes to the chorus for the second time Izzy turns down the volume. I'm about to ask her what she's doing but something makes me stop.

'Dave,' she says quietly, 'I've been thinking about kids. And I know that what has happened should make me want to have them more than ever – but it hasn't. And I have to be honest . . .' she begins to cry but manages to control herself enough to continue '. . . I'm not sure I could go through all this again. I really don't think I could. I'm sorry if that makes me a coward. I really am. But . . . at least for the foreseeable future, I'd like us to forget about it. I don't . . . I can't even think about it if it's going to fail every time. And before you say it, I know it won't necessarily happen every time. But even one more time is one time too many.'

I pull the car over to the side of the road and tell her I

understand. I tell her that I, too, am not sure. I tell her I think it would be best for us to forget about having kids for a while.

silence

This decision turns out to be a defining moment for Izzy. It's the moment she lets go of the past and decides to live in the future. It's the moment she moves on from being just okay to being her old self. Soon everything is back to normal.

Apart from me.

While I understand her apprehension about trying for another baby, and while I'm far from sure that I have what it takes to face that kind of disappointment again, the truth is that we've come to different conclusions about our future. Right now I want us to have a baby more than anything in the world. I want to be a father. I want it more than I've ever wanted anything in my life. And while I'm accomplished at hiding this knowledge from the world at large, it makes me feel a greater sadness and emptiness than I've ever known. But I don't tell Izzy. I don't tell anyone. It's going to have to be my secret.

PART TWO

(November–December 2000)

People say, 'All you write is about relationships.' I'm like, yeah, well, you got anything more interesting? There are a million variations. I could write a million songs about them.

Aimee Mann, singer–songwriter

worked

It's Monday morning, a little before ten o'clock when I settle down at my desk and turn on my computer, listening to its gentle harmonica wheeze of a 'good morning'. Like all good office workers I have no intention of using it for a good half-hour and have started it up merely to state my intentions to the world that I will be working soon(ish). It's taken for granted at *Louder* that we work late, so the boss doesn't worry too much if we're not in by ten a.m. – nine times out of ten we're sleeping off the previous night's activities (gigs, after-show parties, band showcases) endured in the name of work. I haven't been on such nocturnal outings for a long while, though. I just haven't wanted to.

My usual itinerary for the first half-hour at work is to have breakfast at my desk – a toasted bagel and coffee – then flick through the day's newspapers, but today the new issue of *Louder* is in the office so I read that instead – I like to double-check the sections I've edited. To my left Bill Reed, *Louder*'s features editor, is sitting with his feet up on his desk, listening to an advanced promotional tape of the new Busta Rhymes album on the office hi-fi; to the right of me Jon Cassidy, *Louder*'s staff writer, is going through his morning post; and at the desk opposite Mark Attwood, *Louder*'s assistant editor, is on the phone arguing with his girlfriend. All of the art department are at their computers at the back

of the office; the three members of the production department are at their desks in the middle of the office; and the
rest of editorial, Col Campbell, the news editor, and Liam
Burke, the junior writer, are deep in conversation by the
printer. The only person missing is Nick Randall, Louder's
editor.

I'm about to begin working my way through the new issue
when Chrissy hands me an old-fashioned office memo. I
receive dozens every day by e-mail, all of which I tend to
ignore because they're usually about tedious stuff like
stationery. The memo in my hand is a sign of bad news
though. It's a memo that says, 'Don't ignore me.' And as I
make my way to the boardroom along with the rest of the
team, as instructed by the memo, my stomach tightens. As
I've got a pretty good guess what kind of bad news I'm
heading for.

drop

Louder's new circulation figures are in and the news is bad. The magazine has suffered the steepest drop in readership not only among music titles but for the whole BDP group. Statistics like this, we're told by the deputy MD, can only mean one thing: *Louder* will fold immediately. Izzy has been telling me to jump ship for the last year because of our falling circulation, and I'd always assured her that it was happening right across the music industry. If major artists aren't releasing the kind of high-profile albums that people want to read about, it's no wonder that we've struggled to keep our circulation up. Despite this I'd been convinced that *Louder* could ride out the lull.

A magazine folding is no big surprise in this trade, and it had affected me more times than I cared to remember. Back in the summer of 1992 I'd got my first job as a music journalist freelancing for *Start*, a monthly magazine that had folded after eight issues. Then, determined not to do anything other than write about music I'd eked out a living doing occasional live reviews for the weekly music newspaper *Sound Clash*, before I swallowed my pride and freelanced for a number of titles that *never ever* made it on to my CV: *TV, Cable and Satellite Plus* and *Careers Choice*. Eventually I landed my first staff job as a junior writer on a new music magazine called *Compact* – which folded after two issues. Six months later I became a staff writer on *Up*, a music-and-lifestyle magazine aimed at the eighteen-to-twenty-five male market, which lasted two years. Then I did freelance stints in the offices of *Below Zero*, a unisex lifestyle title, which collapsed after a year. By this time, however, my reputation as a writer was strong enough to clinch me the senior writer's post on *Louder*. I'd been at the magazine five years, longer than I'd ever been in any other job, and now it was all over.

With the prospect of a relatively hefty redundancy package and the expectation that it wouldn't be *that* hard to find another job, I'm fine with my new-found unemployed status. Perhaps this is the push I need to do something new. The usual way out for the thirtysomething music hack is to move to more adult music titles, which to my mind is the equivalent of one of those horrible Eighties revival concerts where the balding remnants of a once great band parade around on stage unaware of the self-parody they've become. The other option is to join a national newspaper as one of those rock critics who have their picture next to their byline. Several music journalists I admired in my youth have done this and while it's an okay compromise I can't help but think that it's like admitting defeat. What's the point of writing about music for people who don't like it enough to buy a dedicated music publication? Why bother reviewing music when all your readership wants to know is what CD they should buy to accompany their next dinner party? If I'm going to continue to write about music I want to write about it for an audience who appreciate it the way it's meant to be appreciated: when it's in your heart, in your head and means more to you than life *and* death.

buy

It's now nine o'clock in the evening and I'm sitting on a stool in the kitchen drinking a bottle of Becks while Izzy makes dinner. I've spent the majority of my day of freedom with my former colleagues in the Eagle, on Charing Cross Road, drowning our collective sorrows. Izzy had called me on my mobile when the news had filtered through to her that *Louder* had closed. She'd been annoyed because I hadn't phoned to tell her straight away. We talked over our various options and soon realised things weren't too bad. Yes, there were mortgage, credit-card and bank-loan payments to be met but, thanks to the money Izzy had inherited from her dad, we had enough stacked up in savings plans and in various high-interest accounts not to panic immediately. I'd bounced back from this kind of thing before and, she assured me, I'd bounce back again. I'd just have to get myself some freelance work in the meantime and it was with this in mind that Izzy makes herself the first person to offer me work.

'Why don't you do some work for *Femme*?' says Izzy, who is washing her hands under the tap. 'You'd be good at it,' she continues. 'You could write one of those touchy-feely "what men are really thinking" pieces. You should see the guys we get to write those things: I doubt that any of them has had a girlfriend in a very long time, so who

cares what they think? You're a listening-to-serious-music-
on-your-serious-hi-fi-on-your-serious-headphones-because-
your-partner-won't-let-you-play-it-loud-because-she's-watch-
ing-*EastEnders* type of bloke. There must be millions like you
and I'm pretty sure that ninety per cent of *Femme* readers
have got one.' She laughs. 'You'd be good at it, Dave.
Women would love to know what's going on in your mind.
What am I saying? I'd like to know what's going on in it.'

While I have the greatest respect for what Izzy does for a
living, in my heart of hearts I only let her get away with it
because she's a girl. I really can't stand any of that women's
magazine nonsense. I hate the horoscopes and the health
columns. I hate the fashion spreads and the makeup tips.
I especially hate the sex advice of the 'how to have multiple
orgasms' type, and the endless features about making
relationships 'work'. To me, writing about music is writing
about the really important things of life, while writing about
relationships is a great way to persuade fashion houses,
cosmetics developers and calorie-controlled frozen-meal
manufacturers to part with millions of pounds in advertising.

'Thanks,' I reply, 'but no thanks. I'm a *music* journalist,
Izzy. That's what I do. I can't write about emotions. I can't
write about relationships. All that stuff's just too . . .' I don't
bother finishing the sentence.

Izzy laughs, clearly amused at the distress the thought of
writing for *Femme* has caused me. 'You're right, I suppose,'
she agrees. 'It was a terrible idea. I couldn't imagine you
writing a piece for us in a million years. You haven't got the
right mindset. I'd ask you for a piece about what men are
thinking and you'd write one word: "Nothing".'

'It's true,' I say. 'Other than the odd thought about naked
ladies there's absolutely nothing going on up here.' I point

to my temple. 'Men are visual creatures. If we're thinking about something, nine times out of ten it's something that's right in front of us. Like that,' I say, gesturing at the yucca on the kitchen TV. 'I can't begin to count the times when I've turned off the TV and thought about that plant – what it would think about if plants could think, whether it would die if it didn't have a pot to live in; how the word "yucca" came into existence and whether it sounds stupid or not; then finally I think about naked women and go to bed.'

'By naked women I presume you mean me?' asks Izzy, grinning. She's heard this particular rant of mine many times before and has previously confessed that she finds it quite endearing.

'Of course. But my point is, my dear wife, that there *is* nothing going on in my head, no secret thoughts; only thoughts of the extraordinarily vacuous variety about yucca plants.'

'Were you really thinking about yucca plants last night?'

I nod.

'And you can think stupid thoughts about yucca plants just because they're right in front of you and not spend that time more wisely, for instance, thinking about me?'

I nod again.

'You're right,' says Izzy, turning off the heat under the pan of pasta, 'you *should* keep that kind of stuff to yourself. I'm *so* glad I was born a chick.' She kisses me and drains the pasta. 'Dave?'

'Hmm?'

'What are you thinking about right now?'

'Right now?'

She nods.

'I'm thinking about the guy who invented pasta, how he came up with such a great idea and whether, you know, there were failures along the way – things that could've been pasta but didn't make the cut.'

'Do you know what?' she says, smiling. 'Sometimes I really hate you.'

'Yeah, I know.' But the truth is, I hadn't been thinking about pasta. I was thinking – and still am – about Izzy: what a great woman she is, what a fantastic wife, and what a wonderful mother she would have been.

dream

It's a Saturday morning several weeks later, there's snow outside and the flat is freezing because the central heating has been playing up. Izzy and I are in bed, working our way through the morning papers: the *Independent*, the *Guardian*, *The Times*, the *Telegraph* and the *Mail* and all their attendant supplements. As with most magazine journalists, these are a major habit because first thing on Monday most of us have dreaded features meetings where we're supposed to come up with ideas for the next issue. Nine times out of ten, however, no one has any, which is why we steal them from the weekend papers. Ironically, most journalists working on weekend newspapers have no ideas for their features meetings either, other than those they've stolen from magazines – it's symbiosis at its most carnivorous.

'Will you look at this!' I say, waving the newspaper I've been reading for the last half-hour in front of Izzy's face.

'Will I look at what?'

I point to a picture of a Grade 2 listed farmhouse in Cumbria on page five of *The Times*' property section. What's strange is that I never usually read the property sections and neither does Izzy. We usually keep them piled up in the kitchen because they're exactly the same size as Arthur's litter tray.

'See this farmhouse?' I say, indicating the picture with my

nose because I'm still holding the newspaper with both hands. 'It's only a little bit more than we paid for this flat.'

'And?'

'Well, we could sell up and move there, couldn't we?'

She peers at it. 'It says it needs a lot of work doing to it.'

'We could do that.'

'Dave, we don't do that. We get *men* in to do that sort of thing for us.'

'We could leave London for good. Simplify our lives.'

'All this just by buying a farmhouse?'

I nod.

'Let's do it,' says Izzy.

'Really?'

'No,' she says, tersely. 'I was joking.'

'I'm serious. I think we should consider moving to the country.'

'Why?'

'Why not?'

'But what would we *do* in the country?' she says, rolling over on to her side to return to her article.

'Anything we wanted to. You could write a novel, I could freelance at something or other . . . I don't know.'

'Have you noticed that the only reason we can afford the mortgage we've got is *because* we live in London?'

'Sure. We live here to earn good money but life here is too expensive. If we move out we'll get more for our money but earn less.'

'Exactly.' She pauses, waiting for me to say something more. I don't. 'Is that it, then?' she asks. 'Are we agreed that we're staying in London until we're old and grey?'

'I suppose,' I reply, but my eyes have flitted across to a

sixteenth-century manor house in Ayrshire, a snip at £1.4 million.

There's a long silence from Izzy and then, with a sigh, she turns towards me. 'You know I love you, don't you?'

'Yeah.'

'You know we have this little thing called a mortgage, don't you?'

'We have?'

'Yeah, we have. Apparently the way it works is that every month we pay the bank a certain amount of money not to take away our home from us. It's a relatively simple arrangement – well, except that it requires us to have money in the bank in the first place.'

'You want me to get some work?'

'That's exactly what I want.'

'I shouldn't worry,' I reply nonchalantly. 'I'll get some work. I mean, think about it. Between us we have enough friends working in the business – one or two will throw a bit of freelance stuff my way.' I think for a moment. 'Tell you what, just to show you what a good sport I am, I'll even have a go at writing a relationship feature for you.' I wink at her in a manner clearly intended to wind her up. 'Something nice and touchy-feely about men. I mean, how hard can it be?'

'Harder than you think,' she replies.

'What do you want me to write about?'

'Anything you want.'

'How much do I get?'

'Three hundred and fifty pounds. That's the standard rate for new freelancers.'

'I'll do it for four hundred.'

'Three hundred and fifty. Take it or leave it.'

'Okay, I'll take it on one condition.'

'What?'

'I get to sleep with my commissioning editor.'

type

I begin to write the feature late on Sunday afternoon while Izzy is working her way through the Sunday papers. At first I don't take it seriously and my early drafts are terrible but then I add more to it, editing and deleting copy that no longer fits. By the time I finish it, on Monday afternoon, it's 1200 words too long because I've got so carried away with it. It feels strange to write this kind of article for this kind of audience: I feel like I've been using a different part of my brain. It's such a relief not to have to search for some pompous alternative to the word 'crap', and not to be transcribing the utterance of some dreary musician and trying to make them sound interesting. In fact, for the first time in a long while I'm genuinely excited about the work I'm producing. By about three o'clock I've managed to trim the piece to roughly 800 words. I entitle it: 'The Art of Talking Without Talking', and e-mail it to Izzy at work.

speak

To: izzy.harding@bdp.co.uk
From: dave_atch01@hotmail.com
Subject: Femme article

Dear Babe,
Here's the article I promised you enclosed as an attachment. It is
to be truthful a little clichéd and not at all me. I'm not a big fan
of invoking sexual stereotypes but I reasoned for this kind of
thing I had to be a little extra blokey, and while you've never
been much of a practitioner of the art of talking without talking
I've known plenty of women who are.

love you

Dave X

PS You'll notice that I've used anecdotes from our friends to
illustrate the various points. I thought about changing the names
to protect the innocent but it's a lot funnier if I don't . . .

The Art of Talking Without Talking

Here's the scene: my mate Trevor is standing in Wax
Lyrical with his girlfriend when he gets the Look.
    'What?' he responds.

'You know,' she replies.

'I don't know,' he protests.

'If you loved me you'd know,' she says. Then Trevor's girlfriend storms off leaving him holding a box of scented candles.

When, days later, he shares his story with me and the rest of our mates down the pub we all nod in silent recognition. 'It's the female art of talking without talking,' I say. 'It can really bugger up your day.'

The art of talking without talking (henceforward known as ATWT) has long been a source of fascination and fear for mankind. I remember when a group of us were at the pub when one of our friends (a woman) came in crying. She exchanged one glance with my better half, then disappeared to the toilets.

'What was that about?' I asked my good lady.

'She's split up with Tony, she's just had an argument with her mum, her cat's sick, she can't make her mind up about a strappy floral print dress she saw in Kookaï . . . oh, and she hates her job.'

'You got all that from one look?' I asked.

'Of course,' she replied. 'Isn't it obvious?'

Okay, so that might be a slight exaggeration of what happened but it wasn't far off. When the ATWT is used for the power of good it's amazing, but when it's used for the power of evil (i.e., against me) it's truly scary.

My first encounter with the ATWT came in my teenage years while I was hanging out in the park. I was minding my own business when a random girl appeared from nowhere, stood next to me, without saying a single word for half an hour, then disappeared. Next day at school

I discovered that Melanie Chissock and I were now officially 'going out'. How did this happen? The ATWT, that's how. In her world, standing next to me was a declaration of love, while in my world it meant that she was either lost, bewildered or waiting for a bus. It was all very confusing.

In the last fifteen years I'd like to think I've become more worldly wise, but when it comes to the ATWT I'm as hopeless as the teenage me. For example, I was at a party recently with the woman in my life. I'd chatted to a few people I didn't know, had a bit of a dance and we'd disappeared home just after two. All in all I'm thinking it was a good night. In the car, however, I got the silent treatment. After much begging and pleading on my part I discover I'm guilty of being flirted with.

'Who was flirting?' I asked.

'That trollop in the boob tube.'

'Which one was that?' I asked.

'You don't even know?' she cried.

The thing you have to realise about us men is that we're very simple creatures: what you see is what you get. When it comes to reading between the lines we can't – we're illiterate – which is why having a go at us for not understanding why you're upset when you refuse to tell us is both cruel and mean. It's like smacking a puppy for leaving a deposit on the carpet when you had clearly stated in a seven-page document left in the kitchen drawer why it's not the done thing. Men, like puppies, can't read seven-page documents or find anything located in the kitchen drawer and, most of all, they can't read women's minds. Which is why if you ask us to guess what's troubling you we will invariably get it wrong. We don't do this on purpose: what we do is work on the assumption that, mentally speaking, you're a bit like us. This means that there's not a great deal on your mind to 'read' other than endless lists of top-ten favourite things, pictures of naked women and fluffy clouds. Even if we tried to put ourselves in your shoes there'd be problems. Have you ever tried walking in a pair of kitten-heeled mules that are several sizes too small? Exactly.

The answer to the problem is, I'm afraid, a little obvious. In a straw poll of my mates down the pub six out of six of us agreed that the one thing we'd love the women in our lives to do is just tell us what's wrong rather than us having to guess all the time. As my mate Trevor put it, 'We're reasonable people. If they just talked to us with their lips instead of their brain waves we'd know exactly what to do.' So, there you have it. Save the guessing games for Christmas Day at your gran's, the psychic exchange for Uri Geller and start talking to your man like a regular human being.

post-it

Izzy likes the article. In fact, she likes it so much that she forwards a copy to everyone in the *Femme* office for their amusement. Apparently it's a job so well done that it's going to be used in the next issue. I feel good. I feel like this is the beginning of something new. I'm so inspired that over the following week I make all the calls to friends in the trade that I'd promised Izzy I'd make. I'm offered a reasonable amount of freelance work: a couple of gig reviews for a national newspaper (which I accept), a couple of shifts' holiday cover next week at *Loop*, a music magazine that used to be one of *Louder*'s main rivals (which I turn down out of pride) and endless offers to help out on ailing music websites (which I also turn down). None of it really interests me in the way that writing the article for *Femme* had. It all seems so dry and overly familiar – so seen-it-all-before – that I can barely motivate myself. I'm even thinking seriously about a career change – something different from music journalism, such as becoming a secondary-school English teacher or going back to university to do a postgraduate degree. Anything seems to appeal, apart from what I've been spending the last ten years doing.

select

It's eight o'clock on the following Friday night and Izzy, our friends and I are standing in our local video shop: Blockbuster on Fortis Green Road. The shop is full of people like us: a slightly older crowd for whom staying in and watching a video has become the new going-out-clubbing-and-drinking-too-much. We've been here for over half an hour without reaching a consensus. Lee has seen everything in the entire shop. Stella and Jenny had seen *Gladiator* twice when it came out at the cinema and say they want to see it again. Izzy is voting for *Perfect Storm* because it has some of the best cinematography ever seen and *not* because, as she points out to everyone with a smirk, she fancies the idea of ogling George Clooney in a wet T-shirt. Trevor, who is a huge fan of Hollywood gross-out comedies, can't make up his mind between *There's Something About Mary* and *American Pie*, but says he's not bothered either way.

The only person who hasn't voiced an opinion is me. I haven't decided yet because I've been wandering around the shop looking at the shelves housing all the videos that came out years ago, making a mental shortlist of how many I can find about babies. So far I've counted: *Three Men and a Baby, Raising Arizona, Look Who's Talking, Nine*

*Months, Rosemary's Baby, She's Having a Baby, The Rug
Rat Movie.*

My list would actually be funny if it wasn't quite so sad.

day

Later that night, after an evening of *Gladiator* and Domino's pizza I can't sleep. I'm trying to get to grips with why I'm so desperate to be a father. I conclude that perhaps it's less to do with the ticking of an imaginary biological clock – although that would make *some* sense – than my relationship with Izzy. After all, it's classic TV-movie-of-the-week fodder: woman gets pregnant in the hope that it will bind her closer to her husband – but in this scenario I'm the woman. As far as I'm aware there's nothing wrong with my relationship with Izzy. I love her. She loves me. We row occasionally about stupid things but always make up. Where's the problem?

I wonder if I'm bored because I've been with one woman for so long. But, again, the answer is no. I'm happy with her. I'm happy with just the two of us. We have what many people tell us is an enviable lifestyle. We both have (or had) cool careers, and, thanks largely to the money Izzy inherited when her father died we've got a foot in the property market without mortgaging our souls. In a lot of ways we have it all – but it doesn't seem to mean anything any more.

It isn't that I think our life together is pointless without a baby. It's rather that I feel having a baby would give us an extra reason to get out of bed, an extra reason to make things work. Some people don't need that extra reason for their lives to be okay. I know this because I used to be one of them. But somewhere along the way I've switched sides: I'm now one of those who *needs* to have children, like I *need* to breathe. I've never been a big fan of the word 'need'. I've never liked to need anything or anyone too much. One of the things that had first attracted me to Izzy was that she was so strong, so independent. Maybe this is my problem: after all this time as individuals I want us finally to be one.

youth

It's Tuesday morning and I'm sitting at the kitchen table with my laptop, writing up a gig review from the previous evening, when my mobile rings. The display says: *number withheld*.

'Hello?'

'Hi, Dave, it's me.'

It's Jenny.

'Hi, Jen. What can I do for you?'

'What are you up to?'

'Writing a gig review.'

'Were they any good?'

'The band?'

She laughs. 'Yeah, of course I'm talking about the band.'

'They were okay,' I reply. 'A bit derivative.'

'Is that what you're going to put in your review?'

I laugh. Jenny never asks me anything to do with music unless she wants something. 'What are you after?' I enquire.

'I need to ask you a massive favour.'

'Go on.'

'I've just seen that article you wrote for Izzy and, well, I was wondering if there was any chance you could do something for me?'

'On what?'

'It's only a short piece. Four hundred words or so. I think you'd be really good at it. It's easy money.'

I can hear desperation in her voice.

'It's a teeny-weeny article about the lies teenage boys tell,' she continues. 'It won't take you long and I know you've always made fun of what I do and everything but . . .'

'I'll do it,' I say.

'What?'

'I said I'll do it. I've just got this gig review to finish. It'll take me half an hour and then I'll start on your thing.'

'Dave,' says Jenny, 'you are an absolute life-saver.'

write

To: Jenny.ottaker@peterborough.publishing.co.uk
From: dave_atch01@hotmail.com
Subject: Teen Scene boy lies article

Dear Jen,
Here's the piece you wanted. I am pleased with my words of
wisdom. Teenage boys won't know what hit them when girls
armed with my inside info lay into them! You'll be pleased to
know that I'm now taking myself off for a well-earned lunch at
Café Crocodile on the Broadway. Mail me back when you've had
a read.

Yours with an invoice

Dave H X

Live and Let Lie – the top five tall tales boys tell

Lad Lie: 'It's just a scratch'
The Total Truth: Boys are immune to pain. We stare
anguish in the navel and tweak the chest hairs of
affliction. From the lethal dangers of paper cuts to the
touch-and-go nature of carpet burns, we'll wince a bit
and grit our teeth, but never ever admit we're actually

hurting. Why? Well, by pretending it doesn't hurt we're informing you by way of pantomime that we're on the verge of blacking out from the pain. The result is that we get to look manly while you lavish love and sympathy on us like latter-day Florence Nightingales.

Lad Lie: 'My last girlfriend broke my heart'
The Total Truth: Sometimes this is a lie and sometimes it's more a bending of the truth. For instance, maybe his last girlfriend hurt him because she caught him kissing her best friend and whacked him in the shins. These are the kind of boys who think that if they say this type of stuff you'll be extra nice because they'll seem cute and vulnerable. The truth is that even if his last girlfriend did hurt him there's a pretty strong chance that he hurt her too.

Lad Lie: 'I don't care what I look like'
The Total Truth: The messy hair, the untucked T-shirt, the smell of Polo Sport in the air – boys spend five minutes getting ready and they still manage to look great, right? Wrong! Welcome, girls, to the latest fashion trend in boys: The 'I don't care what I look like' look. Boys spend hours in the bathroom scrubbing, cleaning, dousing and shaving. Then they take ages deciding what to wear. The result is a very studied state of cool. And you fall for it every time.

Lad Lie: 'I'll phone you, honest'
The Total Truth: This has to be the oldest untruth in the book of Lad Lies. Boys were using this one even before the invention of the telephone. In the Dark Ages

knights out on a date with a damsel would say, 'I'll
carrier-pigeon you, honest,' only for the damsel never
to hear another word. Any boy who uses it knows that you
know that it really means: 'Thanks and everything, but
I WILL NEVER SEE YOU AGAIN.' No boy who really likes
you will ever say it. And if a boy does say it, the best
way to counter it is to respond: 'That's sweet of you,
but I think you ought to know that I'm busy for the rest
of my life.'

Lad Lie: 'It's not you, it's me'

The Total Truth: It's not you. It *really* is him. It's
the fact that he's a useless lump. It's the fact that
he's always eyeing up your best mates. It's the fact
that all the little things he used to do that you
thought were charming are actually annoying. Yes, all
these things are his fault. He knows this. Which is why
he's using the classic double bluff to make you think
that it's all your fault. They say, however, never
bluff a bluffer – so bluff back. Tell him you know that
it's his fault, and that's precisely why he's being
dumped.

more

When I return to the flat after lunch there's a message on the answerphone from Jenny. I call her back and her assistant puts me through. 'Hi, Dave,' she says. 'I absolutely love your piece. It's really good stuff.'

'Cheers,' I reply. 'Is that all you called to say? I thought for a minute there might be something wrong with it.'

'No. It was perfect.'

I can hear an element of uncertainty in her voice. 'So what's the problem then?'

She sighs lightly. 'The thing is I've got *another* favour to ask you and I feel bad asking because we're friends and I don't want you to think that I'm emotionally blackmailing you into doing it, even though I will really be in the crap if you don't.'

'But, Jen, you *are* emotionally blackmailing me.'

'I know,' she says, laughing. 'By any means necessary, eh? Okay, I'll just lay it on the line, shall I? I'm massively short-staffed here, and this morning I had an increase in the marketing budget of the magazine, which means that the next three issues will have cover-mounted free gifts, which means—'

'That all your issue deadlines are being brought forward. We used to have the same thing happen whenever we slapped a free CD on the cover of *Louder*.'

'Exactly. So the thing is I need help in the office on the editorial side of things for a few weeks. It would be perfect for you, Dave. It'd be freelance so you could come and go as you please, as long as the work gets done. And it's just basic stuff really: sorting out a few album and singles reviews, doing a couple of celebrity interviews with various teen pop stars and at a push, maybe, the odd think piece like the one you've just done. It's the kind of thing you'd do standing on your head.' She pauses then adds, 'So, will you do it?'

I think for a moment. Jenny's right. This kind of thing is easy enough. The only thing I'm not too sure about – and I know I'm being a snob – is the distinct lack of cool in writing for teenagers. It's a long time since I've been the kind of jobbing journalist who'd write about anything as long as he got paid.

My fear is that when word gets out that my first job after the closure of *Louder* is working on a teen mag, and that I've done the think piece for *Femme*, people will think I've gone a bit soft. That I'm no longer serious. Because if there's one single requirement you need to be a music journalist, it's *seriousness*. On the other hand, I'm reminded that I want to write about music for an audience who appreciate it. And there's no audience in the world who feels about music as intensely as teenage girls. Maybe their enthusiasm will rub off on me. Maybe I'll get my passion back for music. Or maybe it will be a nightmare from start to finish.

less

'I don't get it, Dave,' says Izzy, when I call her at work and tell her what I've agreed to do. 'Why teen mags? You know enough people to get yourself some freelance work with proper music mags. You'll hate it. You couldn't have picked a weirder mag for a thirty-two-year-old man to work on. You don't know anything about teen pop music. You hear a catchy chorus on the radio and you act like it's going to permanently damage your hearing. I'd never heard of a good sixty per cent of the bands you used to write about in *Louder* and I consider myself quite up to date. In short, you know *nothing* about teenagers.'

Izzy's right. Apart from catching ten minutes or so of kids' TV on Saturday mornings, I've paid little attention to the teen world. Occasionally record companies sent various pop offerings by mistake to the *Louder* office and I'd never even take them out of the Jiffy-bag in which they arrived. Instead I just piled them up next to my desk and when the tower of bubblegum grew tall enough to topple over I'd take them to a second-hand CD shop in Soho and exchange them for cash.

'I'll be all right,' I tell her.

'Fair enough,' she says, resignedly. 'But if you're going to compromise on this, you should compromise on all your other no-go zones. Ever since you wrote that piece for

Femme my boss has been on about me getting you to write a regular "men's point of view" column for us. I said you wouldn't do it in a million years but you bloody well can do it now.'

'How regular is regular?'

'Every month.'

'That's a bit steep, isn't it?'

'And the column's going to be called Male Man – you know, as in postman only not quite – and will feature a picture of you looking sufficiently fanciable.'

I laugh and cringe at the same time. 'You've got to be joking – me? Male Man?'

She adds: 'This is my revenge for all the time you've spent thinking about that yucca plant.'

welcome

It's nine fifty-five on the following morning and I'm standing in front of the revolving glass doors of the Palace Building, 112 Tottenham Court Road, which is home to Peterborough Publishing. A couple of people are outside having a cigarette. They look like journalists. I enter the building and walk up to reception to sign in. There's quite a big queue of people ahead of me, most of whom I overhear are freelancers waiting to sign in because they haven't got full security passes. I take a moment to study all of the magazine covers on the wall by the lifts. Peterborough isn't as big a publisher as BDP but they have quite a few well-known titles. Apart from *Teen Scene* there's *Stylissimo* (women's fashion), *New You* (women's health), *Top Wheels* (motoring), *Burn* (Heavy Metal), *Metrosoundz* (dance music and lifestyle), *Gloss* (unisex fashion and lifestyle), and finally *Grow* (urban gardening).

I receive my pass and take the lift to the third floor then walk along a short corridor. I know when I've reached the *Teen Scene* office because the door is plastered with stickers that say things like: 'Kiss Me Quick, Snog Me Hard!' and 'Wow!' and my least favourite, 'Hello, Big Boy.' In the middle is a large poster of Leonardo di Caprio taken from *The Beach*. Someone has scribbled, 'Love god,' across his chest. I feel threatened.

I take a deep breath, open the door and step inside the office. No one looks up. Ignoring strangers in magazine offices is pretty much standard industry so I don't take offence. Anyway, being ignored allows me to get my bearings. The *Teen Scene* office is busy: telephones ring, printers spew out pages of copy, and the music of some boy band is playing in the background.

During my survey I notice two things: first, that I am the only man here, and second, that I'm the only person over twenty-five. All the *Teen Scene* staff, from editorial to production, art and picture research, are dressed as if they're part of some impossibly trendy twentysomething secret army: hair up, hair down, big thick black 'media' specs, sunglasses on head, numerous hybrids of army trousers, designer jeans, denim skirts, T-shirts emblazoned with logos and slogans and top-brand sports footwear.

Feeling distinctly out of place, I approach a girl sitting at the desk closest to the door, staring intently at her computer screen. Like the others, she's in her early twenties but she seems young in a way I can only just about remember being. She's wearing a T-shirt with the American hip-hop label Rawkus Records' logo across it, a long denim skirt and blue and white Adidas trainers. I can just make out a small indentation on the left side of her nose where she must have had a piercing in her student days and then thought the better of it. She's pretty in a delicate way – the sort of girl that a younger version of me would definitely have found attractive. As it is, her small stature and air of fragility stir up in me feelings towards her that are more brotherly than sexual.

'I'm Dave, the music bloke,' I say to her, by way of introduction. 'Jenny the editor's expecting me.'

She turns and stares at me. 'Hello, Dave the music bloke,'

she says. 'I'm Fran Mitchell, the junior writer. Jenny the editor . . .' her eyes flit to the back of the office '. . . is in meetings all morning.'

Her manner makes me smile. Sarcasm with strangers. I like her style.

'I'll just wait for her, then, shall I?' I ask.

She pulls a Post-it note from the screen of the computer next to her desk, reads it then hands it to me.

'It says I should make myself at home,' I announce.

'I thought that's what it said.' She points to the desk next to her. 'This is where freelancers live when they're in the office. Pull up a chair and I'll show you the ropes.' Her phone rings. 'Hello?' She nods, listens, then covers the mouthpiece. 'I'm going to have to take this call. Do you mind? I won't be long.'

'No problem.' I sit down at my desk, switch on the computer in front of me out of habit rather than a desire to do any actual work and look around me. The *Teen Scene* office is more modern than I've been accustomed to at *Louder*. All the editorial staff are working on brand new colourful i-Macs, the pale grey desks are ungraffitied and the carpet isn't coffee-stained. The office seems brighter too: a line of huge windows runs along one side of the room flooding the space with natural light; along the other there are huge shelves filled with books, magazines and folders. All in all, this seems like a nice place to work.

'Sorry about that,' says Fran, putting down the phone. 'It's a reader's real-life story I've been chasing for the last three weeks. Basically it's this fourteen-year-old girl is so obsessed with a certain soap star that she's spent weeks camped outside his house. Anyway, about a month ago, by means that I'm still not sure are legal, she managed to get a pair of his underpants from his washing line. It's such a great story.'

'It is?'

'Our readers love that kind of stuff. It reassures them that they're not completely alone in the world. You know – that they're not utter basket cases. Because the thing you have to remember about teenage girls is that, at the end of the day, they're all only a few steps away from basket-casedom. I should know. I used to be one.'

'Teenage girls,' I repeat, scribbling down the words on the back of my Post-it note message, 'total basket cases.' I underline the last two words.

'You think I'm joking, don't you?' says Fran, smirking.

'No,' I deadpan. 'And do you know what? That's what really unnerves me.'

wait

I'm left alone to wait for Jenny for over an hour before she drops by briefly, says hello, then disappears to another meeting without telling me what to do. To amuse myself I begin work on my next column for *Femme* but don't make any great inroads. I'm torn between writing about why it's a man's fundamental right to leave the toilet seat up and why it's impossible for men to do more than one thing at a time. I'm thinking about taking myself off to the nearest newsagent's for a packet of crisps when Fran, who has been tapping away at her computer for the last half-hour, asks, 'So, tell me, Dave the music bloke, what are you doing here? Not that being here is a bad thing but . . . you know, you don't exactly fit in, do you?'

'I don't?'

'Don't get funny with me. I know for a fact that you're a proper music journo. I used to read your stuff in *Louder* when I was at university but only because my then boyfriend bought it every month religiously. So come clean: what are *you* doing *here*?'

'I'm a friend of Jenny's. She wanted me to help her out and as I wasn't doing anything better here I am.'

'What about *Louder*?' Her eyes widen and she looks scandalised. 'Have you been sacked?'

'Nothing so glamorous. The mag folded a few weeks ago.'

'I didn't know. I haven't bothered with music mags since I stopped going out with muso types. Anyway, they're all staffed by po-faced boys who think that the more obscure a band is the cooler they are.'

'So I guess there's no point in me talking to you about my collection of limited-edition seven-inch Sub Pop singles, then,' I say. 'You should count yourself lucky. But there were an awful lot of writers on *Louder* who were infinitely more po-faced than me. I'm just mildly po-faced.'

There's a long pause while Fran peers into her screen, concentration written all over her features.

'So you're married?' she says eventually, and looks across at the third finger on my left hand, which is currently resting on my mouse.

'Three years,' I reply. 'Why do you ask?'

'I don't meet many married people.'

'You don't?'

'No. And you don't *look* married either.'

'How am I supposed to look?'

'Less down-with-the-kids,' she says, looking me up and down. I was wearing jeans, my Nike trainers and an ancient bootleg Beastie Boys T-shirt from the year they'd toured with the Rollins Band. 'You look like you should be shacked up in a crap flat in Ealing with a girlfriend who has long since decided she hates you.'

'That could well have been me ten years ago,' I say, and she laughs. 'So what about you?' I peer over at the third finger on her left hand. It's naked.

'Am I married? No way. One very crap, very sullen boy-friend.'

'Is he nice?' I ask.

'He's okay,' she replies.

I can't really think of a follow-up boyfriend-related question but I like talking to her and I don't want to stop yet. 'So how did you end up here?' I ask rather unoriginally.

'The usual way,' she says, shrugging. 'Went to university. Came out with an English degree. Moved to London with a bunch of friends. Decided I wanted to be a magazine journalist. Did work experience here at *Teen Scene* for a month and got offered a job when Daisy over there' – she pointed to a ridiculously skinny girl wearing a bright red long-sleeved top – 'got promoted to a senior writer's position. It's all just a big game of musical chairs, really. I love this job, though. It's the best thing in the world. People think it's easy just because we're writing for teenagers but I've written for supposedly *grown-up* magazines and this is the hardest thing I've ever done.'

I'm not convinced, and I make sure my face says so.

'Tell me this,' she says, in response to my frown, 'would a *Louder* reader stop reading an article after three lines because it was boring? Would a *Louder* reader write you a seven-page letter telling you why they hated one of the features you wrote on their favourite pop star? Would a *Louder* reader threaten to stop reading *Louder* because you were rude about their favourite TV programme?'

'No,' I reply. 'They were quite a quiet bunch, really.'

'Exactly,' she says. 'Welcome to the world of the most demanding readership that you will ever encounter. Welcome to the front line.'

I'm amused by the idea that, after nearly ten years in music journalism, working in teen mags is considered 'the front line'. The phone on my desk rings several times and I look at it as if I've never seen a phone before.

'It's a phone,' says Fran.

'I know.'

'Well, aren't you going to answer it?'

'Yeah,' I nod. 'I'm not really expecting anyone to call, are you?'

Fran laughs, and I pick up the phone and clear my throat. 'Hello, *Teen Scene*. How can I help you?'

'Is that you, Dave?'

It's Izzy.

'Yeah,' I reply. 'That was my first "Hello, *Teen Scene*". Did you like it?'

'It was great,' says Izzy. 'Very well delivered.'

'How's it going, sweetheart?'

'Same old, same old. Had a couple of meetings. Had a shoot fall through for this afternoon but on the whole everything's been okay. But never mind me. How are you coping with the world of teens? You hate it, don't you?'

'Actually I don't,' I say, looking at Fran, who's now on the other side of the office standing by the network printer with her hands on hips waiting impatiently for something to come out of it. 'I quite like it.'

'That's great. I'm really pleased for you – even if it does mean I lose the bet.'

'What bet?'

'I bet Jenny a slap-up meal you'd be out of there by the end of the day.' She laughs. 'Made any new friends?'

'Not really. They're all girls.'

'No boys?'

'No boys.'

'What *are* you going to do?' she says, teasing. 'Who are you going to talk man things with? Who are you going to impress with your encyclopedic knowledge of obscure bands?'

'I know. I'm a right Billy-no-mates.'

'What about Jen? Can't she play with you?'

I adopt a suitably childish sulky tone. 'She's like you. She's in *meetings* all day, doing important stuff.'

Across the office Fran is now angrily fiddling with the printer's paper drawer. I like this. I like the fact that she can make me laugh without using words. 'Actually, I have kind of made one friend.'

'Who?'

'The girl who sits next to me. Her name's Fran. The only thing is, I think I might've annoyed her by implying that she was wasting herself writing for teen mags.'

'The scathing sarcastic school of making friends,' says Izzy. 'I know it worked with me, Dave, but I'm not sure it works with all of us *birds*. You should make it up to her.'

'I can't,' I explain. 'You know how I don't like to have women as friends.' I'm not exaggerating: I really don't have any female friends who aren't friends of Izzy's or in a relationship with one of my male friends. I've never been a big fan of having women as friends: it makes life too complicated. The only one I've ever had I married.

'So who are you going to have lunch with?' asks Izzy.

'No one.'

'Oh, Dave, that's so pitiful. It's like the first day at school.' She laughs. 'D'you want me to get a cab over and meet you somewhere?'

'No, honest, I'll be all right.'

We speak for a while longer about nothing in particular, and this makes me feel good. Talking to Izzy on the phone from work is one of the things I've really missed in the time I've not been in an office. It's not the same when the time's your own. There isn't that frisson of pleasure to be gained when you really know you should be working. We chat for five minutes or so, say our goodbyes and I hang up. Seconds later Fran's phone rings and she races across to answer it. After a moment in which she says little but laughs a lot she puts down the receiver.

'That was your wife,' she says. 'She's just made me promise to look after you at lunch-time in case you're lonely.'

bloke

Fran and I talk haphazardly, lurching from one topic of conversation to another all the way from the office to the magazine's local watering-hole, a wine bar called Hampton's. She'd invited some of the other girls to join us but they all declined. *Stylissimo* was having a beauty sale – selling off the various products that cosmetics companies had sent in to be reviewed. Apparently a huge pile of cheap beauty products is more alluring than three-quarters of an hour being nice to the new boy in the class. So it's just her and me. Me and her. I feel very uncomfortable.

'I'm sorry about my wife,' I say, as we settle down to bottled beer and prawn cocktail crisps for two. 'She's very protective of me.'

'It's no problem,' says Fran. 'I didn't realise you were married to Izzy Harding. I'm a big fan of her stuff. She used to write that column in *Femme* a few years back, didn't she, "Girl About Town"?'

'Yeah,' I reply, and I know exactly what her next question's going to be.

'Does that mean you're "The Bloke" she always used to mention.'

'I should hope so.'

Fran drums on the table with delight. 'I feel like I know you already!' she says, clearly delighted. 'Izzy's one of the reasons I went into journalism in the first place. I remember one column she wrote about the sub-duvet shenanigans of an old boyfriend and it had me in hysterics for ages. All her observations about men and stuff were so spot-on.'

'She'll be impressed when I tell her that. Izzy loves people who say nice stuff about her work. There's only one thing, though . . .'

'What?'

'That column you were talking about. That ex-boyfriend's bedroom habits were mine.'

'You're kidding!' says Fran, stifling a fit of giggles. 'Doesn't it bother you that she puts all these intimate details of your life in her column and features?'

'Not really. She makes half of it up and what she doesn't make up she exaggerates for "comic effect". No one could live as glamorous a life as she used to make out in her column, and no boyfriend or husband could be as annoying as she makes out I am. Anyway, I'm very thick-skinned about that kind of thing.'

'You're a very blokey kind of bloke, aren't you?' observes Fran. 'That's the sort of response I'd expect from a blokey bloke.'

'Well, there you go.'

'I bet you don't talk about relationships either, do you?'

'I don't mind. Just as long as you don't start crying.'

Fran laughs. 'One man in an office full of girls. It's going to be a lot of fun having you around. Relationships are all we ever talk about.' She pauses. 'Well, relationships – and the state of our hair.'

For the rest of our lunch-break, in a concerted effort to show how girly she can be, Fran talks mostly about her boyfriend, Linden. They've been an item for two years but don't live together. He's slightly older than her and works in a clothing shop in Camden. I like the way she talks about him, with a mixture of pride and adoration, even if he sounds like a bit of an idiot. He has a cool group of friends who do cool things in cool places. I begin to wonder whether she's with Linden to make a fashion statement rather than because she's in love with him. However, she seems content to talk and I'm content to listen. It's the perfect match.

love

Over the lunch-times that follow my first day at *Teen Scene*
I eat a sandwich at my desk and work on my next column
for *Femme*. Izzy says no to both the toilet seat and why men
can only do one thing at a time. I suggest a column about
my lack of DIY skills and she laughs – she knows what I'm
going to write about because she lives with the results – and
says yes. By Friday lunch-time I finish my piece so I e-mail
it to her.

chocolate

Dear Babe,
Here is my very first Male Man column.
The idea came to me when I was thinking about the time the
bathroom radiator leaked all over the floor . . . Exactly. Bit of
truth. Bit of fiction. But a cracking column all around I'm sure
you'll agree.

Dave XXX

Man About The House

There's one phrase I dread hearing more than any other
in the English language. In my book it's worse than such
spine-chillers as: 'It's not you it's me,' 'Is this
your vehicle, sir?' and 'The bank has instructed me to
cut your credit card in two.' Only my wife has the power
to utter the phrase I fear so much, and then only when
some catastrophe has befallen the house – like, for
example, last Saturday when the kitchen radiator pre-
cipitated a scale version of Lake Windermere across
the kitchen floor. Just as I began searching for the

biscuit tin that constitutes my toolbox, my wife disappeared and returned, *Yellow Pages* in hand, and
uttered the words I loathed so much: 'I think we'd
better get a man in.'

I know that in this day and age, when Calvin Klein
makes a unisex perfume, sexism is considered uncool by
all but a few dinosaurs, and gender roles are no longer
set in stone, such things shouldn't matter, but I feel
incredibly threatened by the thought of 'getting a man
in'. 'I'm a man,' I tell myself, 'I don't need to get a
man in!' The truth is, however, that fixing stuff
appeals to the five-year-old that dwells within every
bloke and I don't see why I should pay someone to have
all the fun.

When I lived in rented accommodation, I wouldn't
even have changed a light-bulb without making a huge
song and dance about it. Instead I'd be the first on the
phone to the landlord. The minute my wife and I bought
a place of our own, we drew up a long list of things that
needed fixing. It suddenly dawned on me that, without a
landlord, I'd have to take on the mantle of Mr Fix-it.
The prospect of doing all the DIY things I'd watched
my dad do when I was a kid had me so excited I literally
didn't know what to do.

Received wisdom has it that home improvements – like
football and Claudia Schiffer's vital statistics – are
something men know how to do instinctively. Unfortu-
nately, somewhere in the mists of time, one of my ances-
tors must have suffered some sort of genetic amnesia
because while I'm okay on Liverpool FC seasons
'82-'87, have a fondness for Mercedes soft tops and
German supermodels, I know NOTHING AT ALL about HOME

IMPROVEMENTS. This, however, doesn't stop me having a go. And before I know it I'm lying on the floor, monkey wrench in hand, refusing assistance of any kind.

My wife, much to her credit, is extremely patient and holds off with the *Yellow Pages* until I admit defeat or have made the situation so dangerous that she is in fear for our lives. Then, and only then, I make the call. That done, I sit and wait to be emasculated and curse the education system. What use is a degree in English when you've got a leaking radiator? My constant wish is that, one day, a man in overalls will call me up on a Saturday morning (double time) and ask me to come round and explain the works of Shakespeare to him in front of his despairing wife. It'll never happen. Instead when The Man arrives, I compensate for my inadequacies by standing over him while he's working to give him the impression that I understand the basic principles of central heating. When the humiliation is all but over, my wife will insist that I offer him a cup of tea and a biscuit while he charges me an exorbitant amount for ten minutes' work, tells me my DIY skills made the situation worse and then, finally, adds, in a jokey sort of way, 'With a bit of know-how, mate, you could've saved yourself a load of money.'

please

It's the morning of my last day at *Teen Scene*. I've been here for two weeks and I feel like a completely different person. I've learned all the names of all the members of the Backstreet Boys; I no longer feel the urge to smash my car radio when I hear the record that sampled the TV-drama theme tune because from doing my singles reviews I've been made aware that a lot worse music is out there; I've got so deeply into *Dawson's Creek* that I now actually care about whether Dawson and Joey will ever get it together properly. In short, I've enjoyed my second adolescence, but not enough to contemplate staying at *Teen Scene* any longer. Five days ago Gary Robeson, editor of *Selector*, which is a kind of cross between *Rolling Stone* and *NME*, offered me a job as deputy editor for a lot less than I'd earned at *Louder*. I haven't said yes to him as *Selector*'s circulation is so low that it might fold before the end of the year.

At about midday Jenny sends me an internal e-mail, asking me to come and see her for a chat. I'm in the middle of setting up a photo-shoot and interview with a new UK girl band, and it isn't going well. They can't make any of the dates when the photographer is available and I'm trying to come up with viable alternatives. Talking to Jenny is just the break I need.

Her office is a real teen treasure trove. The wall behind her desk is plastered with *Teen Scene* front covers dating back to 1994. Along the wall next to it are shelves of American teen and entertainment magazines, and stretching halfway across the wall facing her desk is a large cabinet overspilling with paraphernalia from the teen world: boy-band T-shirts, abandoned TV merchandising, CDs, logoed sweatshirts, and a thousand and one promotional gifts and freebies.

'I can never believe just how much stuff you have in here, Jen,' I say, gesturing to the cabinet as I sit down opposite her.

'It's only here because I feel bad about chucking it out,' she replies. 'There are kids out there who would cut their arms off to have some of this stuff, but Trev won't have it in the flat.' She laughs. 'Feel free to help yourself to anything that catches your eye.'

'I'll take this,' I say, reaching down to pick up a *Dawson's Creek* novelisation sitting on top of a pile of *Teen Scene* back issues. 'Something to read on the tube. So, what's up, then?'

'You know I've asked you a couple of favours in recent weeks? Well, now I need to ask another.'

'Go on.'

'You must have read the magazine by now, and you must have seen the advice pages . . .'

'You mean the "Your Confession" section? Four pages of teenage girls yapping on and on about boys and acne and boys and periods. Yeah, I know that.'

'Scoff all you like but it's the mag's most popular section.'

'And?'

'Well, the thing is I'm thinking about revamping it and I'm

going to get rid of our freelancer Adam Carter, who wrote the "Ask Adam" column.'

'No more "Ask Adam"? I'm gutted.'

'Not as gutted as he'll be, I suspect. I've never really liked his column – he was way too old-school.'

'So why is he here, then?'

'I inherited him from the last editor and was always too busy to make a change. Anyway, I was talking it over with the editorial director at lunch and we decided that the section needs a young, fresh, funky approach to agony-uncling.'

I can't help but laugh. Only in her world did adults use the words 'fresh' and 'funky' without the faintest degree of irony. 'So, what's this fresh and funky approach, then?'

'You,' she says, pointing at me. 'You're perfect for the job. You're young. You're good-looking. You're cool. Our readers would love to take advice from you.'

All I can do in response to this is laugh. I laugh so much I can't stop.

'You're not taking my misery seriously, are you?' says Jenny. 'Just think about it, will you? We're keeping on "Dear Dr Liz", to deal with all the "technical stuff" of problem pages: periods, pregnancy and the like, and we'd have you for the fun side of things. And we're going to expand it. Six whole pages every month.'

'I can't, Jen. I'm really grateful for the work, honestly, but you know I was only doing this until I found something else.'

'But you haven't found anything else yet, have you?'

'Not exactly. *Selector* have offered me a job but—'

'You reckon it will fold just like *Louder*.'

'How do you know?'

She gives me a sly wink that she knows is incredibly annoying. I put two and two together. 'Izzy told you.'

'She was just trying to give me a bit of ammunition to help me out. Listen, please take the job I'm offering. It's not just me who thinks you'd be great at it either. Fran suggested it at a features meeting ages ago. She said you'd been giving her tips about how to handle her boyfriend.'

This is true. She'd come into the office crying on the Friday morning of the previous week because she and Linden had had a massive row and he'd said that he didn't want to see her any more. She'd wanted to know if she should call him and apologise, even though it was always her who called and apologised when they rowed. I bet her ten pounds that if she didn't call him all day and went out with her friends in the evening she'd have an apology from Linden by ten o'clock that night. At half past eight she'd called me on my mobile, while Izzy and I were watching TV, to tell me that Linden, who had never before begged for anything in his life, had begged her not to end the relationship. She'd never been in such a strong position with him in all the time they'd been together and she nominated me as her 'relationship guru of choice'.

'You can't take Fran's opinion on anything. She's a bit strange.'

'Come on, Dave,' says Jenny, 'aren't you bored with all that music stuff yet? Proclaiming some band to be the best on the planet one month only to slag them off the next? We'll pay you decent money for what amounts to very little work. You won't have to come into the office every day and even if you did get a new job you could carry it on. What do you say?'

'How much are we talking?'

She scribbles a figure on a Post-it notepad and pushes it across her desk towards me.

'Not bad,' I say to the pad. 'I take it that it has occurred to you that I haven't got any formal advice-giving qualifications.'

'Doesn't matter. I like the stuff you've already written for us and for Izzy. Fran thinks you're the best thing in the world. All that matters is that, once upon a time, you were a teenage boy, which means you know what they think about. That's all our readers want: someone who used to be a teenage boy explaining to them the mindset of the teenage boy. Our readers can't work them out at all. You'd be a kind of big-brother figure, explaining the complicated species that they see regularly at school but don't understand.'

'Can I give it some thought?'

'No. Tina, the deputy editor, has been lobbying desperately for me to give it to her boyfriend who works on the second floor at that men's magazine that always has semi-naked female TV presenters on the cover. I said I'd get back to her by the end of the day. Don't make me give it to him, Dave. I can't stand him. He's a real idiot. A sexy idiot but an idiot all the same. You'd do a million times better job. So, what do you say?'

Briefly I review my career over the past few months: lose job as music journalist, get freelance work with a women's glossy magazine, write a couple of gig reviews for a newspaper, write a feature for a teen mag then go and work for said teen mag. What is life trying to tell me? I don't know, but I find myself saying okay to Jenny.

'That's fantastic,' she says. 'You are now officially Dave Harding – Love Doctor.'

'Love Doctor?'

'Yeah. I came up with it during a brainstorming session a

while ago. You're an agony uncle for the twenty-first century.'

'And what about the music and celeb-interview stuff? Who's going to be writing that?'

'Good point,' says Jenny, winking knowingly. 'I was kind of hoping that, until we find someone permanent, you'd do it too.'

smile

'Congratulations,' says Fran, when I arrive back at my desk.

'This is all your fault,' I tell her.

Fran looks thoroughly pleased with herself. 'I think you'll make a great agony uncle. Much better than Adam, who was just a few strides away from being a bit creepy.' She pats my shoulder. 'Well done, mate. First thing to do is have a cheesy photograph taken for the top of your column.'

'Why?'

'You have to have one if you have a column in the mag – the readers like to know what you look like so they can pretend you're their best friend.' She handed me a picture of herself smiling impishly. 'I had it done last summer and I look about twelve in it, don't I?' She giggled. 'They'll probably have to do a lot of work on yours, though.'

'Why?'

'It's not a veiled insult, honest. It's just that Daisy told me they had to get the photographer to shoot eight rolls of "Ask Adam" before they got a single shot where he didn't look like a serial killer. They were even toying with the idea of using a male model as a front but Adam wouldn't have it. He said it would compromise his integrity.'

'That's a lot of effort for one photograph.'

'Not really. What you've got to remember is that, well, blokes are a bit scary, aren't they? Especially when you're a girl and you're only fourteen. That's why teens like boy bands so much. They're a nice non-scary introduction to the delights of older boys. They've got smooth cheeks and they're sort of girly-looking – just the kind of boy a girl likes at that age. So, the photographer will turn you into the boy-band version of an agony uncle, the perfect non-threatening male role model.'

'You're enjoying this, aren't you?'

'Of course,' says Fran. 'Can you think of anything funnier than a former cooler-than-cool music journo dispensing words of wisdom to a bunch of teenage girls? I certainly can't.'

call

'The Love Doctor!' exclaims Izzy, when I call her at *Femme* later that afternoon and tell her the news. 'You have *got* to be kidding.'

'It's true,' I say. 'It was Jenny's idea. She said calling the column "Dear Dave" wasn't "fresh and funky".'

'And "Love Doctor Dave" is?'

'Apparently.'

'Hats off to Jen for persuading you to do it, though. When she told me about it I said there was no way you'd do it. Not even because we're all friends. And there you are, an agony uncle. You should start reading up about all this advice stuff, you know – try some of those Oprah-endorsed books. I could probably steal a couple from work.'

'Hmm, maybe. The thing is I was thinking about taking the organic instinctive approach to agony uncling.'

'Which is?'

'Making it up as I go along.'

Izzy laughs. 'That's it,' she says. 'I'm going to round up everyone and we're going to celebrate tonight. It's not every day a girl's husband becomes a doctor of love.'

peroni

Trevor, Jenny, Stella, Lee, Izzy and I are sitting together in a crowded Pizza Express in Soho. We've been at our table for over fifteen minutes and have sent away the waitress twice as we're all too busy talking about my latest career move to concentrate on ordering.

'You do know that being an agony uncle on a teenage girls' magazine isn't a normal occupation for a man of your years?' says Trevor. 'Not normal at all.'

'You'd be hard pushed to find yourself on a weirder mag,' says Stella.

'*Yachting Monthly*?' suggests Izzy. 'Dave hasn't been near the sea in his life. I think that would be pretty weird.'

'No,' says Trevor. 'Boats fall into the category of "things a man can fake an interest in even if he isn't that interested". Along with golf, any kind of vehicle that has a motor . . .'

'Anything technological – computers, video cameras, etcetera,' adds Lee.

'Basically anything that's really *manly*,' says Trevor.

'Leave him alone, you lot,' says Jenny. 'Dave's going to be brilliant at giving advice. When he used to come over to the flat that Stella, Izzy and I shared in East Finchley we were always asking him for advice about men.'

'She's right,' says Stella. 'But that's what you do with a

friend's boyfriend, isn't it? You treat them like they're your big brother.'

This is true. I didn't do much except listen to them talk incessantly about the men they were interested in. I didn't think of it as giving advice – it was more a way of keeping my girlfriend's flatmates amused while I waited for her to get ready to go out.

'He was more like your flat's resident eunuch,' says Trevor. 'And, anyway, Dave's advice to Jenny when she was thinking about going out with me was that I was the love-them-and-leave-them-type.'

'I was just messing with your head,' I say, laughing. 'You're all right by me, Trev.'

'Enough of the squabbling,' says Jenny. 'The question is, Dave, are you ready?'

'For what?'

'Your first-ever agony-uncle letter.'

agony

Jenny has thoughtfully brought a carrier-bag full of 'Ask Adam' letters with her to the restaurant. As if I were selecting a winner for one of those TV competitions of my youth, I root around in the bag and pull out an envelope. It is pastel green with the *Teen Scene* address painstakingly scrawled across it in silver metallic ink. The letter itself is written on yellow paper in the shape of a dog. I read it aloud:

> *Dear Ask Adam,*
> *I am a fifteen-year-old girl. I have liked this boy at school called Peter since the start of term and I think he really likes me. The only problem is Peter is my best friend Liz's boyfriend. He lives three doors down from me so we quite often end up walking home after he's walked Liz home. He's really nice. And this isn't just a crush. I think he feels the same way. But I'm not sure. Should I say something? Should I risk my friendship with Liz? What should I do?*
> *Yours*
> *A Puff Daddy fan*
> *Bristol*

'What's your gut reaction?' asks Stella.

'I don't understand,' I reply. 'Why's she signed it "A Puff Daddy Fan"?'

'Because she likes Puff Daddy!' says Izzy, and rolls her eyes.

'And this is relevant because?'

'You're being deliberately obtuse, Dave,' warns Izzy. 'She's signed it "a Puff Daddy fan" because she doesn't want anyone she knows to recognise her and, well, the only other option – "anonymous" – is just a bit square, isn't it?'

'Okay, okay.' I focus on the letter again. 'So she fancies her best friend's boyfriend and she wants to know if he fancies her and if it's ethical.'

'*Good*,' says Jenny, encouragingly. 'What's your answer?'

'My answer? Well, it's bad news, isn't it? She shouldn't steal her best mate's boyfriend because that's going to cause a whole heap of trouble.'

'And?'

'And the boyfriend might not fancy her anyway.'

'Exactly,' chips in Trevor. 'From what she says in the letter, do you think the boyfriend does like her?'

'Probably.'

'Really?' says Stella. 'I thought he was just being friendly.'

'No,' I reply firmly. 'He fancies her. If he didn't fancy her he wouldn't be walking along the street with her. Believe me, having once been a teenage boy I know I wouldn't have been seen dead talking to a girl I didn't fancy in case my mates saw me.' I look over to Trevor and Lee for support. 'Am I right or am I right?'

They nod and grin enthusiastically.

'That's so shallow!' says Izzy.

'Fifteen-year-old boys *are* shallow,' says Lee. 'That's why they're fifteen-year-old boys.'

'Maybe you should leave that bit out of your answer in the mag, eh?'

'I'm enjoying this. Let's see what else is in there.' I search around in the bag again. The next letter is in a small white envelope; the handwriting appears youthful but masculine.

Dear Ask Adam,
I'm a thirteen-year-old boy. I don't normally read
girls' magazines but I picked up my sister's copy
and it seemed okay. My problem is that I really like
this girl at school called Charmaine. She really
likes me too. The thing is I've never had a girlfriend
before but I know that she's had at least three
boyfriends. I'm really scared of looking stupid in
front of her especially as I've never kissed a girl
before. Is it easy? Where should I put my hands?
I've heard that some girls like you to use your
tongue and others don't. How can I tell which kind
of girl she is? This is all very confusing.
Yours,
A Manchester United fan, Essex

'What a sweetie!' enthuses Jenny. 'Let me have a look at his letter.' I hand it to her and she examines it carefully. 'Why can't all boys be like this?' She adopts a look of mock-menace for Trevor's benefit. 'All nice and sweet and vulnerable instead of being the nasty, leering creatures they usually are.'

'Are you talking about teenage boys or men in general?' asks Lee.

'All of you,' chips in Stella. 'All men could learn a thing

or two from a sweetheart like that. You should definitely put him in your first Love Doctor column. I'll bet you'll have loads of *Teen Scene* readers gagging to introduce him to the delights of kissing. I tell you what, if I was ten years younger I'd probably have a go myself. What are you going to tell him?'

'About kissing?'

'Yes! About kissing.'

'Honestly, I can't even remember this being an issue.'

'That's such a lie,' says Izzy. 'How can your first ever kiss not have been an issue? Who was it with?'

I think long and hard. The details are foggy. A fourteenth-birthday party. A game of Spin the Bottle gone out of control. A darkened room. An alien tongue tasting of Pernod and blackcurrant.

'Amanda Reddington at a party,' I confess. 'Chunky girl with huge glasses. Kind of took me by surprise.'

'Did you fancy her?' asks Lee.

'Not really,' I reply.

'So why did you kiss her?' asks Jenny.

'She offered.' I tell her. 'It felt rude not to.'

'So what did you know about kissing before that moment?' Izzy interjects.

'Nothing.'

'And what had you learned after you'd kissed her?' asks Stella.

'Not to go into a darkened room with Amanda Reddington.'

'So what advice are you going to give this poor boy?' says Izzy, pointing at the letter.

'I'll tell him to do it like they do in films. Go in gently, keep his eyes closed, head angled to avoid a clash of noses.

117

He could hold her hands, and he shouldn't even attempt to put his tongue anywhere it doesn't belong for the first ten minutes unless invited to do so.'

'What about lubrication?' asks Stella.

'*What* about lubrication?'

'Dave, as someone who was once a teenage girl, let me tell you that teen boys have a major problem with lubrication. They're either so dry it's like kissing sandpaper or they're foaming at the mouth and you want to gag. Mind you, the worst thing they can do – and, believe me, this used to happen to me a lot – was lick their lips then wipe them on their sleeve!'

Jenny lets out a shrill scream. 'That is *so* horrible.'

'I always thought the lick 'n' wipe was quite a sexy manoeuvre,' I tell her. 'You know, like, "Here I am, babe, limbering up for the kill." Izzy used to love it when we first started going out.'

Izzy laughs. 'You can bet your life that wasn't me you're talking about,' she says. 'He is *so* lying.'

'So I've got to tell him all this?' I ask Jenny.

'Exactly,' she says. 'It's not as easy as you thought, is it? Pick one more, then let's order some food because I'm starving.'

The final letter I pull out is a brown manila prepaid envelope to British Gas, only the address and prepaid symbol have been crossed out with a thick black marker pen then replaced with the *Teen Scene* address. I hold it up for the entire table to see.

'Looks scary,' says Lee.

'I think you're right,' says Trevor, who is studying the letter. It's written on a page torn from a school exercise book.

Dear Ask Adam,
I'm eleven. I love boys. I want one to be my
boyfriend. All my friends talk about boys all the
time. They say I am boy obsessed. How do I get a
boyfriend? Please, please, please.
  Yours
  An eleven-year-old desperate Teen Scene *reader,*
Leicester

'The pre-teen contingent,' says Jenny knowingly. 'Explains everything.'

'It does?'

'Pre-teens haven't got the faintest clue about real teen *angst* so they have to make it up. They read in the problem page about all these teens with real worries and feel envious so they make stuff up.'

At this moment the waitress arrives at our table with a look of determination. We order six beers and when they arrive Jenny takes the tray from the waitress and hands them round. Raising hers in the air, she addresses the table loudly enough to get the attention of the whole restaurant: 'Will you all be upstanding for Dave Love Doctor Harding, the nation's number-one agony uncle!'

And they all stand up and give me a round of applause.

post

'Which one of you is Dave Harding?' says the guy from the post room, not noticing that, other than himself, I'm the only man in the office.

It's now four o'clock on the following afternoon and I've been waiting all day for the rest of the 'Ask Adam' postbags to arrive. Keen to get on with my new job, I'd called several times and been told that the bags would be up in 'twenty minutes'. It isn't until my fifth call that Fran explains to me that the post room's 'twenty minutes' could be anything from half an hour to an entire day, depending on what they're watching on their portable TV.

The post-room guy drops three huge green plastic post-bags at my feet, then leaves the office without another word.

'What's up with him?' I ask Fran, as she helps me untie the bags.

'It's nothing personal,' says Fran, grimacing in the direction of the door. 'All the post guys are a bit surly when you ask them to do their jobs. When they're eyeing up my arse as I go into the lift or having a fag outside the office, they're the nicest people in the world.' She struggles to open her bag while I search around for a pair of scissors. 'We're in,' she says eventually, having severed the cords with her teeth. She leaves me to wade through hundreds of pages of love, self-hatred, self-loathing and self-doubt. It's amazing. I can't believe how complicated a teenage girl's life can be.

PART THREE

(January–March 2001)

'You know, I used to live like Robinson Crusoe – shipwrecked among eight million people. Then one day I saw a footprint in the sand and there you were. It's a wonderful thing, dinner for two.'

Baxter, in Billy Wilder's *The Apartment*

lift

It's raining heavily and I feel as if steam must be rising from my soaking clothes as I wait in the lobby for the lift. The first issue of *Teen Scene* with me as agony uncle has been out in the shops now for two weeks and I'm quite proud of it – apart from the photo at the top of the column. Just as Fran had said he would, the photographer has made me look like a (slightly haggard older version of a) boy-band member and Izzy has been having a field day teasing me about it. I press the lift button repeatedly and, as one of the building's two lifts finally begins its descent, Fran appears next to me. 'Morning,' she says brightly.

'Hey, you,' I reply. 'What did you get up to at the weekend?'

'I stayed in for most of it and had a massive row with Linden.'

'About?'

'Everything.'

'Where did it begin?'

She half smiles. 'I think it might have been when I opened my mouth to say hello when I dropped round at his flat on Friday night.'

'I've said it before and I'll say it again,' I tell her, 'he's a waste of space.'

'I know,' says Fran, as the lift arrives. 'But I *like* him. He's a very sexy waste of space. What's a girl to do?'

I'm about to reply when I realise we're no longer alone. A couple of women – all perfect lipstick, perfect hair, perfect dress sense, who obviously work on *Stylissimo* – have arrived and are standing to the left of us and a young casually dressed guy is next to me. I do a double-take and realise I recognise him just as he realises he recognises me.

'Dave Harding?' says the man, as we get into the lift.

I smile politely. It's all coming back to me. He'd done quite a bit of work experience at *Louder* about a year ago but we hadn't been able to give him a job. I feel myself shrink.

'I thought it was you,' he continues. 'How are you, mate?'

'Okay,' I reply. 'How about yourself?'

'Excellent, actually. You know how it is, a bit of this and a bit of that. I DJ at a couple of bars in Soho, and then I do a bit of stuff for a couple of underground labels and on top of all that I'm working at *Metrosoundz* on the top floor. Features editor, actually. Just got promoted.'

'Congratulations,' I say, in a tone that I hope doesn't sound churlish or needlessly genuine. 'You must be really pleased.'

'Sorry to hear about *Louder*,' he says. 'It was a great mag *in its time*.'

'Cheers,' I reply, aware of the thinly veiled insult. Out of the corner of my eye I notice that Fran is wearing the look of someone who is desperate to be introduced. 'This is my mate Fran,' I say grudgingly. 'Fran, this is —'

'Steve Jackson,' he interrupts, then corrects himself. 'Stevie J.'

It said it all.

'Hi,' says Fran to Stevie J. 'I've seen you about in the building.'

He smiles widely. 'I've seen you too.'

I sigh. I don't really care that Fran is flirting with him but I don't understand why she's doing it in front of complete strangers.

'Which mag do you work on?' he asks Fran.

'*Teen Scene*,' she replies. 'I'm a writer there.'

'I've always thought it would be a good laugh to work on a mag like that.'

'It is,' she says, grinning like an idiot.

'And what are you up to at the minute, Dave?'

'This and that.'

'Dave's *Teen Scene*'s agony uncle,' says Fran. 'Aren't you, Dave?'

There's a long uncomfortable silence.

Stevie J looks at me in disbelief. 'You've stopped writing about music?' he asks.

'Not stopped,' I tell him. 'Just taking a break.'

'Dave's really good at it,' says Fran. 'If you've got any relationship problems you should go and see him.'

Stevie J and Fran laugh and I have to join in. Fortunately I don't have to endure this torture for long as the lift arrives at the third floor.

'Nice talking to you,' says Stevie J, as Fran and I step out.

'See you around,' says Fran.

'Yeah,' he replies. 'Definitely.'

As the lift door begins to close behind us Stevie J calls out, 'If you're looking for some writing work, Dave, you should give me a call and pitch some ideas to me.'

Before I can muster a reply the door closes.

'That was nice of him,' says Fran. 'I can't tell you how long I've been dying to talk to him. He's very, *very* sexy.'

'That *wasn't* nice of him,' I snap. 'He was having a laugh

at my expense. He did work experience for me once. He used to make *my* coffee. Open *my* bloody post for me. And there he is asking *me* to pitch *him* features ideas. I should've . . . I should've—'

Fran, highly amused by my anger, grabs me by the arm and pulls me into the *Teen Scene* office.

bag

It's midday and I'm at my desk. Jenny has been in meetings
all morning and Fran's now out of the office overseeing a
reader photo-shoot with the fashion editor at a studio in
Fulham. Together they're making over a bunch of girls to
look like their favourite female pop stars. Even though I
have loads of work to do by the end of the day – some
singles reviews and a telephone interview with a new Irish
boy band to write up – I decide to take a break with a little
light reading from my Love Doctor postbag.

According to Fran, I'm officially getting more post than
'Ask Adam' ever had. I grab a handful of letters from the
pile I've been sorting through and begin to read:

Dear Love Doctor Dave,
Why is it that, given a choice between a big-chested
but stupid girl with the personality of a wet
envelope and a flat-chested but really funny girl,
boys always without fail pick the stupid girl with
the big boobs? I only ask because there's this guy
at school who I really like and who I know likes
me but rather than going out with me he's decided
he only wants to be friends and has started dating
a girl with a big chest who laughs like a hyena.
A confused Janet Jackson fan (14), Aberdeen

Dear Love Doctor Dave,
My dad caught me and my boyfriend lying on my
bed kissing and he went ballistic. The thing is my
dad didn't even know this boy was my boyfriend
because I'd told him that we were just friends. Now
he says that I'm grounded for 'the foreseeable
future', he's banned me from using the phone and
on top of all that he says I'm not allowed to have
anything to do with my boyfriend any more. I'm
so upset and this situation is driving me crazy.
What can I do to make him see that I'm not in the
wrong?
  A desperate Dawson's Creek *fan (16), Cheltenham*

Dear Love Doctor Dave,
My boyfriend keeps treating me like I'm the
Invisible Girl all the time. Whenever we're on our
own he's as sweet as anything but the moment
we're out in public he barely talks to me and
refuses even to hold my hand. All my friends say I
should dump him but they don't know how lovely
he is when we're on our own. Why is he acting like
this and what can I do to make him stop?
  Anonymous (15), Liverpool

I flick through another pile of letters. Some are written in felt-tip pen, others thick black marker pen, glitter pen on black paper and in some the ink has been smudged by the tears of the author. Their topics cover everything from unrequited love and dumping techniques to love bites and hand holding. I decide to read one final letter before getting down to work again. It's in a bright yellow envelope and inside are three pages of light blue paper accompanied by two photographs. The handwriting is neat but unmistakably that of a teenage girl.

Dear Love Doctor Dave,

It's been a couple of weeks since your first column in Teen Scene *and I've been meaning to write to you for ever (in more ways than one). I know you may think this is a bit strange but I've got a really strong feeling that you might know my mum. Her name is Caitlin O'Connell. You met her in Corfu in a nightclub, in a place called Benilses on 11 August 1986 and spent the night with her. Mum said that if things had been different (that she didn't live in Dublin and you didn't live in London) the two of you might have tried to make a go of it and seen each other after the holiday. All this should be old news to you.*

What you don't know is that Mum got pregnant with me. My name is Nicola O'Connell, and I'm thirteen (I turn fourteen in four months' time). Anyway, if you're slow on the uptake this all means you're my dad and I'm your daughter.

I couldn't believe my eyes when I saw your photo in Teen Scene. *I thought I was going mad but then I compared it to the only photo I've got of you and I just know it is you. Even though the picture was taken before I was born I can tell you're my dad because when you've spent the majority of your life looking in the mirror trying to imagine one of the two most important people in your life you know exactly what you're looking for.*

*I haven't told anyone about you (not even Mum).
And I don't think I will as it will cause too much
upset. But I'd like to meet you just once, if you
don't mind. Mum and I live in London (Wood Green)
so it should be pretty easy to arrange.*

*I've enclosed the only photograph I've got of you
and one of me taken at Christmas. I've written my
mobile phone number on the back of it. So please
call me if you can. Please.*

Yours faithfully

Nicola O'Connell

*PS Don't ring during school hours, though,
because you're not allowed to have them on.*

shake

I read the letter several times but nothing's going in. I look round the office to check I'm not dreaming: Lisa, the production manager, is putting a new CD into the office hi-fi; Daisy, the senior writer, is talking loudly to a friend on the phone; Jessica, the junior designer, is standing by the colour printer in the far corner of the art department. Everyone's going about their business. No one's looking at me waiting to go 'Ha! ha! Had you fooled there!' I'm alone on this one.

I check the postmark on the envelope several times – it has been posted in London. I study the enclosed photos and one definitely features an eighteen-year-old me. If it wasn't for that I wouldn't believe the content of the letter for a second. But the thing is, I've never seen this photo in my life.

I look at the letter again, the letter that is trying to tell me that, for the past thirteen years, I've been a dad and haven't known it. Is this the answer to my unspoken prayers? How can it be that while I'm still feeling the pain of loss for a child that never was, I should discover that there's a child in the world who is mine all along?

I just can't take it in.

I can't think straight.

None of this is happening to me. It's happening to the person who is responsible for it – the eighteen-year-old Dave Harding – a person I haven't been for over fourteen years.

sun

Corfu. August 1986. It was the summer before I went to university to study English. I'd been working part-time in the warehouse of a frozen-food supermarket to earn enough money to pay for the holiday. Four of us went: me, Jamie Earls, Nick Smith and Ed Ellis. All friends from school. We'd been looking forward to the holiday all year. Everything was planned down to the last detail and we had even bought a tourist guide to the island that listed where all the bars and clubs were so that we could work out where we wanted to go on our first night out. None of us had girlfriends; Jamie had been seeing someone for a few weeks but he dumped her because he didn't want to be the only one of us who was attached.

The bravado of four eighteen-year-old boys together on a foreign holiday was intoxicating. We soon established a regular daily pattern – get up at midday, slope to one of the many roadside cafés for an 'English breakfast', then go to the beach, lie down and stare at girls. About four o'clock in the afternoon we'd wander back to the apartment to sleep and at about eight o'clock we'd go out to get something to eat, usually burgers, then head for the various bars and clubs Benitses had to offer. We never arrived back at our apartment before five a.m. if we could help it.

Our success rate with the opposite sex wasn't high.

Despite this, though, we'd stand each night in a group in the corner of whichever bar or club we were in, watching girls. Eventually one of us would declare that someone was 'giving us the eye' and walk over to try to chat her up, only to return shame-faced minutes – or seconds – later. Rejection, however, is part and parcel of what being an eighteen-year-old male is all about.

On the final night of our holiday, however, something strange happened. We pulled.

It happened exactly as the letter said. I'd been in a beach bar with my friends when a group of girls about our age walked in and ordered drinks. We thought they were English from the way they were dressed but when we sent Jamie on a reconnaissance mission to the bar we discovered they were from Ireland and they'd just arrived in Corfu. So there we were, four lads from south London on the last night of our holiday in one corner and four girls from Ireland, determined to kick off their holiday with a real party, in the other. It was the perfect match. We started talking to them immediately. Jamie and Ed were chatting up a girl called Caitlin. Nick was chatting up Brenda, and I was trying to entertain Colleen, whom I fancied, and her bored friend Sarah-Jane, whom I didn't.

It was a scattergun approach to seduction: we indicated which girl we were attracted to and, after a decent interval, they indicated whether we were in with a chance. As it stood we'd got nearly everything wrong. It turned out that Sarah-Jane liked Nick, Brenda liked Ed, Colleen liked Jamie and Caitlin didn't really like any of us, which left me as the odd one out. Within half an hour of the who-likes-whom information going public Brenda and Ed had left to go to another bar, Colleen's tongue was lodged down Jamie's throat, while

Nick and Sarah-Jane had tucked themselves away in a corner of the bar, laughing and giggling.

The bar was filling up now, a DJ had begun to play a variety of chart hits and people were congregating on the dance floor. The entire world seemed to be having fun, apart from me and this fantastic-looking girl. Caitlin and I spent half an hour or so alternately staring emptily into our drinks and at each other. Then she shrugged, as if she'd come to a major conclusion. 'I'll dance with you,' she said, in a lilting Irish accent I could've listened to all night, *'but that's all.'* Although her voice was soft it carried a hint of menace that unnerved me, but I followed her on to the dance floor.

The DJ was playing any old stuff to get people to dance – Madonna, Michael Jackson, Abba and some cheesy Italian house music – and Caitlin kept going all the way through it. I thought, as she seemed exceptionally cool, that she'd sit down when they played Abba but she carried on. A few times – even though it must have been clear to everyone in the bar that I was dancing with her – guys tried to edge their way in right in front of me and each time she manoeuvred herself deftly back to me.

At about eleven, I'd realised nothing was going to happen between us and was contemplating going back to the apartment to pack my bags in preparation for the flight home. 'Listen, Caitlin, I'm off,' I said. 'It was nice to meet you.'

She smiled at me for the first time that evening, and said, 'Don't go.'

No explanation.

No additional information.

Just 'don't go.'

So I didn't.

Soon after that we left the bar, headed down to the beach,

sat on the sand and watched the tide come in. It was like she was a completely different person. She apologised for being offhand with me, and explained she'd only come on the holiday under pressure from her friends because she knew they'd spend the whole two weeks 'chasing lads' and she wasn't 'into all that'. I asked her what she was into and, without pausing for thought, she said, 'Music.' She named some bands she liked. I nodded and named some bands I liked. We passed each other's first round of tests. I named some more bands I liked, more obscure ones, and she did likewise. We passed each other's second round of tests. Finally I named some obscure tracks by the obscure bands I liked and she did likewise. We passed each other's final round of tests. And everything changed.

When we got cold, we walked back to the apartment she and her friends were renting. None of the others was there, even though it was three o'clock in the morning. We talked more about highlights in our record collections and a little later we began to talk about ourselves. She told me she was seventeen and had lived her whole life in a place called Sutton on the outskirts of Dublin. Because of the way the education system worked in Ireland, even though she was a year younger than me she was going to university in Dublin that October. I told her about life in London and attempted to make Streatham sound marginally more interesting than it was. She was impressed that I was from London. She had relatives there, she told me, and she planned one day to spend a summer with them.

She made coffee and we sat on the balcony, which overlooked the swimming-pool. On a whim she picked up a camera and said she was going to take a photograph of me. I hated having my photograph taken so I suggested we take one of the two of us. We sat on her bed and I put one arm around her waist and held the camera as far away from us as I could. And with the lens pointing at our faces and laughing like idiots, I took the picture.

I can't recall how we started kissing. One minute we were talking, the next kissing. Even that was different, though – it wasn't frantic in the way I was used to, where my eagerness had less to do with passion and more to do with a suspicion that the girl might change her mind. We kissed as if we had all night – which we did.

The following morning when we woke up, we were awkward but comfortable at the same time. Neither of us talked about the night before. I think we both felt that we'd had a perfect night with a perfect person and that the time we'd spent together would lose its perfection if we tried to make any more of it. So we didn't say anything about swapping addresses or telephone numbers or even that we were unlikely to see each other again. I remember feeling so grown-up as I got into the taxi that took me back to my hotel. Like I was a real man. Like I'd finally made it.

photo

There's a part of me that isn't even bothering to question whether the girl who has written the letter is my daughter: that night with Caitlin had been the first time I'd played reproductive roulette but it wasn't the last. The occasions (all before Izzy) were few and far between: a one-night stand with a girl I'd met at a party in Liverpool, a reunion with an ex-girlfriend in Glasgow, a girl from Austria when I was on holiday in Ibiza.

I wasn't proud of them.

I knew my actions were stupid at the time.

But this knowledge hadn't stopped me for a second until now.

I pick up the photograph of the girl who has written to me. Her dark brown corkscrew curls are held away from her face by a blue hairband, and she is wearing small gold hoop earrings, a dark blue hooded top, unzipped, and underneath it a light grey T-shirt. It's her face, however, that holds my attention. She's got beautiful light brown skin, but even more fascinating are her features. Initially I'm convinced that I can't see myself in her but slowly, like a photograph developing in a darkroom, I see flashes I think I recognise: certain aspects of the shape of her face have echoes of my mum when she was younger and I notice her grin – broad-toothed – and I think if only for a moment that perhaps it's mine.

do

I decide to keep a tight rein on my thoughts. Worst-case scenarios can wait. First of all I have to deal with the problem at hand: this girl wants to meet me, but do I want to meet her? I weigh up the pros and cons but I know the answer will be the same at the end as it was at the beginning.

Yes. I am curious.

But, no, I do not want to see her because I can't afford the risks involved.

My main fear is of losing Izzy. After all our time together I know how she will react in any one of a million different situations except this one. I go through all the rational arguments several times. It happened a lifetime ago. I hadn't known the child existed. No one tried to contact me until now. *It's not like I can change history, is it?*

No matter how I look at it, no matter how liberal, fair-minded or forgiving I think Izzy might be, there's always the chance that she won't accept this, that she'll hate me, that somehow it will signal the end of us. Because after the mis-carriage I can't be sure how something like this might affect her. I tell myself that I'm doing the right thing. I tell myself that I'm protecting her from a truth that would hurt her more than anything in the world.

What I fail to consider is that I'm denying her the chance to make up her own mind. And if I can't tell the person closest to me, who else can I talk to? I go through potential confidants one by one until the only person left on the list in my mind is the one who's normally sitting right next to me.

Indeed

'So,' says Fran, as we sit down, beers in hand, in our favourite seats in Hampton's for an after-work drink, 'what's up
with you?'

'Nothing,' I say.

'Yeah, right. You've been acting strange ever since I came
back from the reader make-over shoot. What's up, Doctor
Love?'

I look at Fran carefully, weighing up whether or not to
trust her – and whether I have what it takes to betray Izzy
like this. Izzy and I never talk about our relationship with
anyone else. Never. And it's not one of those cases where
I think Izzy doesn't gossip with her mates about me when
secretly she really does. I know because she told me that
sometimes she feels a bit left out when Stella's telling her
stuff about Lee, and Jenny's going on about Trevor. I told
her she could if she was desperate, but she said she didn't
want to. She said our relationship wasn't like that and I
understood what she meant because our relationship *isn't*
like that. I'm the only person in the world she needs to
confide in about me and she is the only person in the world
I need to confide in about her. Until now. Although it feels
wrong wanting to confide in someone I barely know, I need
the opinion of someone who doesn't know me inside out,
who doesn't know me well enough to judge me, who won't

get upset and who will see the situation for what it was and not what it would mean to her. It might sound harsh but it's true.

'Listen,' I begin, 'it's serious.'

'How serious?'

'You have to promise me that you won't breathe a single word of this to anyone. And I do mean *anyone* and not just anyone I don't know because you know how things work in this industry – even if you don't know them directly you always know someone who knows someone else.'

'Okay, okay. Anyone would think I'm the world's biggest gossip when I'm not even *Teen Scene*'s worst gossip. That has to be Linda Bell, the freelance sub-editor, you know the girl with the bright red hair, she's got a gob on her like no one else. There's no way I'm that bad—'

'Fran . . .'

'Sorry. Go ahead with your secret. It's safe with me. And don't worry about how I'm going to react either because I'm pretty unshockable.'

'This morning I got a letter in my Love Doctor postbag only it wasn't that kind of letter.' I hand it to Fran and watch her face as she reads it.

'I don't know what to say . . . I mean . . . do you think . . . Is it possible?'

'Maybe.'

'Does Izzy know?'

'No.'

'And the photos and the details all add up?'

'Yes.'

'And you haven't met her – this girl, I mean?'

'No.'

'Are you going to?'

146

'No,' I pause. 'I don't know. Maybe.' I pause again. 'Probably not.'

'What are you going to do?'

'I don't know. Do you think if I knew I'd be telling you all this? It's a big one, isn't it? Do I meet this girl or do I try to forget all about her? Do I tell Izzy? If so, when? And how will she take it? I want to tell her, I really do, but I just can't. I've gone over it a million times and the answer is always that she deserves to know but when and how?'

'This might not be what you want to hear but I'd tell her right now. Believe me. I'm speaking as a woman and I know that if Linden had a kid and I didn't know about it I'd have to kill him. On the other hand you must be feeling so confused. And who can blame you? It's a lot to take in, and when you add on the whole thing about telling Izzy, well . . .' She doesn't finish her sentence. 'I suppose it's not like there's anything you can do about it now.' She pauses and picks up the photograph of me and Caitlin. 'She's very pretty,' she says. Then she picks up the photo of Nicola. 'And *she* is absolutely drop-dead gorgeous.'

I shrug, unsure whether to take credit for Nicola's good looks. I opt for not. There's a long and awkward pause.

'I haven't told anyone else,' I say, after a few moments.

Fran smiles. 'I don't know whether I should be flattered or not. You're the one who's supposed to be the problem solver.'

'Some agony uncle I've turned out to be.'

'Do you want another drink?' she says, pointing to my empty beer bottle.

I nod.

'Same again?'

'Yeah.'

She disappears to the bar and when she returns her face is animated. 'I've got a question that might help sort things out a bit,' she says, as she sets two bottles of beer on the table. 'I know this might sound a bit obvious but are you one hundred per cent sure this girl's your daughter?'

'As sure as I can be. It's too much of a coincidence for her not to be mine.'

'*If* she's telling the truth.'

'Why would she lie?'

'I don't know,' says Fran. 'Teenage girls can be weird like that. They get things into their head and it's hard to get them out. You just think of yourself as a jobbing journalist, but to *Teen Scene* readers you're a celebrity. Your face is in the magazine they spend their pocket money on. You interview the bands they have plastered over their bedroom walls.'

'She doesn't seem like that.'

'Maybe she is, maybe she isn't. I don't know her and neither do you. What do you know, though? That you're the guy in the photograph and that you did sleep with the girl who's also in it. Those are the facts, Dave. And none of them means for sure that you're this girl's dad. There are too many variables. You probably can't see them because you're too close.'

'What about the fact that she looks a little like me?'

Fran picks up the girl's photograph again and studies it. 'It doesn't prove a thing, Dave. If it did people wouldn't have to go to court to prove paternity cases. They'd just look in the mirror, wouldn't they?'

'But how could a thirteen-year-old girl make up a story like this?'

'Maybe she didn't,' says Fran. 'Maybe it's not her fault. Her mum might've made it up years ago and never bothered changing it. Imagine this: you're a seventeen-year-old girl. You sleep with some guy and immediately you have regrets because he's married, or he's your best friend's boyfriend or maybe he's just plain stupid – I don't know. Everyone wants to know who their father is and you don't want to tell so what's the easiest thing to do? Pull out a photograph of some random guy that you had a holiday fling with and have no way of contacting just to get everyone off your back.'

'But I'm not some random guy. I did sleep with her.'

'Even better. Gives the story authenticity. All her mates believe her because they were there, her parents believe her because her mates believe her and the guy who is actually the father is just grateful he's off the hook.'

I take a long swig of my beer and look at Fran in disbelief. 'How do you come up with this stuff? I'd never have come to those conclusions in a million years.'

'My wasted youth. Big fat airport novels with gold lettering, American TV mini-series, the whole lot. If it's trash I've either read it or watched it.'

'So you definitely don't think she's mine?'

'Not definitely but I think it's unlikely. Whatever the answer, the fact remains that you do not know for sure that you're this girl's dad, and short of having DNA tests I don't think you could.'

'I don't know how you go about having a DNA test. Boots don't sell kits, that's for sure.'

'I bet you can get them on the Internet. You can get anything on there or failing that, maybe you should get yourself on *Jerry Springer* or *Ricki Lake*. Every time I have a sickie and turn on the TV they always seem to be doing paternity tests.'

'That's useful to know.' I pick up my beer and finish it in

several gulps then put the bottle firmly on the table. 'I'd better get home.'

'I'm sorry, Dave,' says Fran quietly. 'I know you think I'm being flippant about this thing but it's all just so unreal that I'm finding it difficult to get my head round it.'

'You're right. And this is the first time I've seen how ridiculous the situation is. There's every chance that the girl isn't my daughter. There's every chance that she's lying or her mum's lied to her. There's every chance that this is some horrible freak coincidence. But there's also every chance that she *is* mine, that she's *not* lying, that this isn't about coincidences but real life. And the thing is . . .'

Fran looks at me and for a second I think she knows what I was going to say. I haven't told her about the miscarriage but maybe she's guessed how much I want to be a dad.

'The thing is?' she says quietly.

'Nothing,' I say, putting on my coat. 'Nothing at all.'

answer

At home I don't know how to behave around Izzy so, in classic male behaviour pattern, I opt to avoid her. When she's in the kitchen I go into the living room. When she comes into the living room I go to the bedroom. When she comes into the bedroom I head for the spare bedroom that we use as an office, which also doubles as home for my second hi-fi and my CD and record collection. This place is my comfort zone. The wall opposite the door is lined with custom-made shelves for thousands of CDs, vinyl albums and twelve-inch singles. I had to get in a carpenter from Crouch End to build them – and the strange thing is he turned out to have been in a band a few years ago that I'd reviewed several times for *Louder*.

There's a large desk under the window where I work at my laptop. Sometimes Izzy comes in here too but she prefers to work at the kitchen table because there's more light. On the table are a lamp, a fax-machine, and a mini-palm that Izzy bought last week from Safeway in Camden Town because she said I needed some oxygen in here. In the corner is a battered brown leather armchair I inherited from an ex-girlfriend, and on the floor are hundreds of back issues of magazines including *Femme* and *Louder*. There are no posters because I think posters are studenty but there's a large white wipe board, which was an impulse buy one day when I was walking along the Broadway. I don't use it much. Five weeks ago I wrote a twenty-five-item to-do list on it, and only four things are crossed off. I pick up a dry marker pen and cross off 'Buy a plant', at number twenty-two and add 'Sort my life out' at twenty-six.

I take Nicola's letter out of my bag and wonder what to do with it. I feel guilty for even having it in the house but I can't risk leaving it at work and I can't risk carrying it around with me either. I think several times about destroying it but that feels wrong. Hiding it is the only option. I scour the room for the perfect place then head to the shelf with the twelve-inch singles and pull out one. It's a three-song EP called *Maybe I Can Wear Your Jacket* by a band called the Parachute Men. I bought it over ten years ago after hearing it at two o'clock in the morning at an Indie night in a small club in Camden Town. At the time it was so absolutely and incontrovertibly everything I wanted from a record: passion, yearning and a female vocalist who sounded a bit like Debbie Harry. I'm pretty sure it only sold a few thousand copies but to me it was worth more than a mono-only copy of *Blonde on Blonde* or any of the multitude of rare Japanese-only pressings of Beatles seven-inch singles for which people like me are supposed to sell our souls. It was my all-time favourite record. If there was a fire in the flat and I could rescue only three things they'd be (in this order): Izzy, this record and the cat, mainly because Izzy would make me drop my hi-fi to go back and get him. I slip Nicola's letter and the photographs inside the dust sleeve of the record and put it back on the shelf.

Normally, given a problem, my first action is to drop a CD into my hi-fi, put on my headphones, sit back in the leather armchair and leave everything behind for forty minutes or so. When the album I'd selected for company finished, I may not have solved my problems but I would at least feel better about being in the world. Today I know that there's no point in doing this. Scott Walker doesn't have an answer for what's going on in my life, and neither does Lauryn Hill, Mark Eitzel, Chuck D, Beth Orton, the GZA, Björk, Al Green, D'Angelo or Roddy Frame or any of the hundreds of artists who can fit into my CD player. For the first time in my life I'm lost without music instead of lost in it.

locked

It's later in the evening, and the small lamp on the desk is on but the main light is off. I'm still in the armchair listening to the sound of nothing. Izzy knocks on the door, comes into the room and turns on the main light, making me blink.

'Sorry,' she says.

'It's okay,' I reply.

'What are you doing?'

'Nothing much. I'm still on lots of PRs' mailing lists so I've got this lot to work through.' I point to a large pile of CDs in Jiffy-bags. 'I could be up most of the night listening to this lot.'

Izzy nods but she's not convinced, I can see. 'What's wrong, babe? You haven't said a word all evening. You've been avoiding me.'

'I'm okay.'

'You don't look okay.'

'Well, I am.'

Without saying another word she leaves the room. I listen to the sound of her footsteps across the hardwood floor of the hallway, the familiar getting-ready-for-bed noises of taps running and the toilet flushing, the click of the hallway light and the bedroom door closing. Then I allow the tears of anger, frustration and disappointment I've been holding back all day to run freely. This is the moment at which I know I don't have it in me not to contact the girl who has written to me. I take out the photograph with her number from its hiding place, search for my mobile phone and dial. Her phone is switched off, so I breathe a sigh of relief and half smile as I listen to her voice: 'Sorry, I'm not available right now . . .' The message, in typical teen style, rambles on much longer than necessary. In contrast the message I leave is more succinct: 'Hi, it's Dave from *Teen Scene*. You wrote to me. I think we should talk. I'll try you again some time.'

right

It's just approaching ten o'clock as I reach work. I was up so late last night, thinking about the girl in the letter, that I overslept this morning, even though Izzy woke me several times with stern reminders that I'd be late if I didn't get up. She made no reference to last night's lack of conversational skills, which made me feel even worse. I knew I owed her an apology so once she'd left the flat I called her office number and left a message on her voicemail: 'It's me. Why do you put up with me? I love you. Speak to you later.'

When I arrive at work there's a message on my voicemail from Izzy: '*Women have a very complicated relationship with the telephone. But the intriguing question for* Femme *readers is what boyfriends think of the messages women leave on their answerphone. The usual amount of words. End of this week, please. And by the way, I love you too.*'

below

I e-mail her to say I'll do it for my next column and then I
receive a message back telling me to ring her immediately
because she has news for me. I dial her number and wait.
She answers on the second ring.

'Hello, *Femme* magazine.'

'It's me.'

She laughs. 'Guess what?'

'What?'

'Kara's leaving *Femme*. She's been poached to launch a
new title in Australia.'

'And you're excited because . . . ?'

'You know why I'm excited!'

Izzy has always wanted to be the editor of a women's
magazine. From the first day I saw her on our journalism
course it has been her number-one goal.

'They've offered you the job?'

'Not exactly. They're making me acting editor as of the
end of this week. You would've loved it – I was really cool.
I said I wasn't interested unless they were seriously con-
sidering me for the job – you know how they are here, they
get you to look after a magazine for half the pay of an editor
then wonder why you're annoyed when they get someone
else in who's got "more hands-on experience".'

'So what did they say?'

'That my name was at the top of the list. They want me to go for the job. Even Kara wants me to go for it and I tell you I'll get it!'

'My wife, the editor of a magazine with a massive circulation. How fantastic is that? I'm really proud of you, babe.'

'I knew you would be.'

'And I'm sorry about last night. I was just in a crappy mood. You should've just ignored me.'

'I can't. I love you. That's what being in love means. Is anything bothering you?'

'No. Not really. Just the usual. Nothing for you to worry about.'

'But I do worry.'

'Well, don't. After the end of this week you'll have enough to worry about with the magazine. Does this mean you're going to start power dressing for meetings?'

'A little bit of Prada never hurt anyone.'

'Will I have to speak to your PA to arrange what time to meet you at home for dinner?'

'You might.'

'Will you be ashamed that your husband is called the Love Doctor?'

'Never.'

We speak for another half-hour, during which she makes me promise to come out for a drink with her and some of the *Femme* crowd to celebrate. I can't say no even though I don't feel like being sociable. Then we suddenly remember we're at work. She has a million and one meetings to sit through and I have a telephone interview with a Swedish pop band, a couple of three-line album reviews to write and some pop gossip to sort out.

eat

It's just coming up to one o'clock and I've been working
solidly for most of the morning. The interview with the
Swedish pop band went well, mainly because it was the
complete opposite to the kind I used to do for *Louder*. No
in-depth autobiographical details. Instead I just cut to the
really important stuff – who their first kiss was with, what
size underwear they wore, and ten things about Sweden that
they thought *Teen Scene* readers wouldn't know.

'I'm going to get a sandwich,' I announce to Fran. 'Fancy
coming?'

'Can't,' says Fran. 'I'm being taken out to lunch with Ellie.'
Ellie is *Teen Scene*'s six foot tall and ridiculously attractive
beauty editor. 'There's a makeup launch or something and she
wants company. The deal is we eat lunch at a posh restaurant,
the makeup PR tells us about their range, we listen attentively
then drink ourselves silly. It's a three or four-bottler for defi-
nite.' She giggles and adds, 'This is such a great job.'

'You're choosing a "three or four-bottler" over Coro-
nation Chicken on rye, a Snapple and a packet of crisps
with me?' I say, laughing. 'It's your loss.'

Fran reaches into her bag, pulls out her purse and hands
me a pound coin.

'What's this for?'

'Have a Snapple on me.'

walk

I step outside and discover it's raining, but I pull out my personal stereo anyway and put on the headphones, press play and begin listening to the Swans' version of 'Love Will Tear Us Apart'. I was feeling in a bit of a retro phase this morning as I got ready for work and had dug out an old compilation tape I'd made when I was a student. I'd listened to it so many times that I knew it inside out. After the Swans there was Dinosaur Jnr's 'Freak Scene' and then Public Enemy's 'Public Enemy No. 1'.

There's nothing on my mind as I walk along Tottenham Court Road towards the deli where I usually buy my sandwiches. For one quiet moment I forget all the turmoil of the past few days. I'm not thinking about the girl in the letter, her mother, Izzy, being a father, an agony uncle on a teenage girls' magazine or even my career. I'm enjoying living in the moment with the music in my head. But then an oddly familiar-looking teenage girl in a rain-sodden dark blue school uniform appears in my line of vision and, suddenly, living in the moment isn't an option any more.

where?

The two of us stand and stare at each other, struck dumb. There's no doubting that this is the girl who sent me the letter. She's wearing a black pea coat, a dark blue V-necked jumper, a blue and white striped tie and a matching blue skirt that comes to just below her knees. Corkscrew curls of hair are tied back from her face, her light brown skin is without a blemish and across her nose is a light dusting of barely noticeable freckles. Her deep brown eyes are gazing at me unflinchingly. She still has a lot of that awkward charm of early youth in her face and although she's biting the corner of her lip, which makes her mouth look crooked, I can see that she is the kind of girl who in a few years will be breaking a lot of boys' hearts. That's what I think about in the twenty or so seconds while we stand and stare at each other in the middle of Tottenham Court Road.

'Dave Harding?' she says eventually. 'Are you Dave Harding?'

I don't speak. This isn't what I had planned for the next half-hour, I tell myself. I left the office to get a sandwich. I was going to go back to the office and eat it at my desk. *That* was what I had planned. I'm not prepared for this. I haven't had enough time to think about this properly so it can't be happening.

'I'm sorry,' she says, still looking at me. 'I shouldn't have come, should I? You're at work. I should've waited for you to call me, like you said you would. It's just that when I got your message I couldn't wait.'

She looks like she's going to cry. I can't stand the thought of her crying.

'It's okay,' I say softly. 'Honestly. Don't worry about it. I'm really glad you came . . . Nicola . . . Nicky . . . Nicola. Which do you prefer to be called?'

'Nicola,' she says. 'Mum sometimes calls me Nicky, but I prefer Nicola.'

'Okay, then, Nicola,' I begin, then realise we're standing in the middle of the pavement. 'I think we're in the way here,' I tell her, and point to a newsagent's with a large awning under which a number of people are waiting for the rain to stop. 'Shall we stand over there?'

Nicola nods and follows me. We stand at the edge of the crowd and look out into the rain rather than at each other.

'Have you got a day off school or something?' I ask.

She shakes her head.

'You've bunked off?'

She nods.

I laugh gently in an attempt to put her at her ease. 'I did that once when I was about fourteen,' I tell her. 'Not even for a particular reason, really. I just wanted to see if I could do it. I liked school.'

She doesn't say anything.

'How did you find me today?' I ask.

She bites her lip. 'I looked in the magazine for the address,' she tells me, 'and saw that it was on Tottenham Court Road so I thought I'd come and meet you. I've been waiting for you since about half ten, sitting over there.' She points to a bench across the road outside a row of electrical stores selling discount TVs and hi-fis. 'I didn't want to disturb you. I thought the best thing to do was to see if you came out for lunch.'

'What would you have done if I hadn't?'

She shrugs. And I join her in a brief silence of my own and watch the cars and taxis go by.

'This is weird, isn't it?' I say. 'I'm not sure what we're supposed to do now.'

She shrugs again.

'Well, how about this?' I say, trying to make my voice sound a bit less scary and a bit more cheery. 'How about we go to McDonald's or Burger King or wherever you want just to get out of the rain? Are you hungry?' She shakes her head. 'Thirsty, maybe?' She shakes her head again. 'You don't have to eat if you don't want to but if you change your mind I'll get you some food.'

'There's a McDonald's at the top of Oxford Street,' she says quietly. 'Mum and I go there sometimes.'

'Okay, we'll go there.' I step out into the rain but she's still standing under the awning. 'What's wrong?' I ask.

At first she doesn't reply. She still looks tearful but now she looks apprehensive too. Then she says, 'I don't know what to say.'

'About what?'

'Anything.'

I smile, trying to reassure her. 'That's okay. You don't have to say anything. We'll walk down to McDonald's and, well, we won't say a word. What is it? A five-minute journey? That's plenty of time. You think of all the questions you'd like to ask me. I'll think about all the questions I'd like to ask you and, hopefully, by the time we get there we won't have forgotten any of them.'

'Okay,' she says, and steps out to join me.

stare

We reach McDonald's and I ask her if she's changed her mind about eating and she shakes her head. I ask if she's vegetarian and she laughs for the first time, then tells me she just isn't hungry. I offer to get her a coffee or a tea or any kind of drink she wants, but she refuses everything. I nod in what I hope is an amiable fashion to show her it doesn't matter. Because I don't know if she's genuinely not hungry or just being polite I order a Big Mac, fries and a strawberry milkshake as well as my chicken sandwich in case she changes her mind.

When the food is ready I take the tray from the guy behind the counter and look around to see where we might sit. The restaurant is packed with lunchtime trade, which consists mainly of tourists, so we make our way downstairs and find a booth in a far corner. I set down the tray on the table and sit down while she slides in opposite me. I place the tray with the Big Mac, fries and milkshake in front of her and arrange my meal in front of me. Then, once again, we stare at each other wondering what to say.

'This is still weird, isn't it?' I say, opening the polystyrene container with my chicken sandwich in it.

She nods and looks at the fries. Maybe she's hungry after all, I think. 'You can have one of those, if you want. In fact, you can have them all – the whole thing's yours.' I laugh.

'Did you think I was going to eat two meals by myself?'

'I don't know,' she says.

I take a bite of my sandwich. I can't remember the last time I had a McDonald's. I only suggested it to Nicola as a knee jerk reaction – assuming that McDonald's was the type of place a teenage girl might like to go. Judging by the way she's warming to the food in front of her – dipping her fries into the ketchup and rearranging the contents of her Big Mac (neither the lettuce nor the pickled gherkins made the final cut) – I reckon I've made the right choice.

'So,' I say, when we've consumed about half of our lunch, 'I think that us eating has made this whole thing a lot less strange. Now we're just two people eating, aren't we?'

She nods carefully.

'It must have been a bit of a shock seeing me in *Teen Scene*.'

'I didn't know what to think,' she tells me. 'It was like something out of a film.'

read

She'd had a rough day at school and had wanted something to read to cheer her up. She'd saved *Teen Scene* until after her dinner because she liked to read it all in one sitting undisturbed. She'd begun in her bedroom lying face down on her bed with a pillow under her chin and the magazine propped against the headboard.

She liked to read magazines by flicking through from front to back to get an overview and then head to the articles and features that had caught her eye. She'd flicked past the contents page, the letters, the bits of celebrity gossip, a couple of features, the horoscopes and the fashion and makeup pages. When she'd got to the problem pages she'd stopped. 'Brand New Look Extra-sized Confidential Confession', the headline read. She'd searched for 'Ask Adam' only to discover that he'd been replaced by a new agony uncle called 'Love Doctor Dave'. She'd read my column and when she'd finished her eyes had been drawn back to the photo of me at the top of the page.

She thought she recognised me, but she couldn't think where from and then something clicked. She ran into her mum's room and searched the bottom of the wardrobe, scattering shoes and clothes around her, until she found what she was looking for: a photo album. She returned to her own room and flicked through the pages until she found

the photo of the young man with his arms around her mum.
She compared it with the picture in the magazine. Then she
looked through the contributors list in the magazine for a
Dave Harding.

And that was it.

She'd found me.

fame

I don't interrupt her as she speaks. The deeper into her narrative she gets, the more she seems to come out of her shell. By the time she concludes her story her whole manner has changed and she has relaxed. But then she suddenly becomes aware that she's dominated the conversation, withdraws into her shell and begins to chew her lip again.

'Can I ask you a question?' I say.

She nods.

'You said in your letter that you haven't told your mum about me and I was just wondering why not.'

'I just didn't.' It seems that that is as much of an answer as I'm going to get. 'Was it strange getting my letter?' she asks.

'Yeah. Very. If it hadn't have been for the photos I don't think I would have believed it.'

Immediately she looks uncomfortable. 'I don't want anything from you,' she says. 'I didn't get in touch with you to get things.'

'I didn't think you did.'

'I just want you to know that.'

'I do,' I reassure her. 'Have you thought about what you'd like to ask me?'

She shakes her head.

'Maybe we shouldn't ask any more questions then,' I say.

'Maybe we should just talk like two normal people eating in McDonald's.'

She nods and, to change the subject, I ask her what kind of music she likes.

'Anything really.'

'Pop, death-metal, hardcore rap, classical?'

'I don't think I know what those are,' she says seriously.

'Me either,' I tell her, 'but people like me spend ages making up new musical categories: Brit-pop, Shoe-gazing, Hard House, UK Garage, Drum and Bass, Jungle, New Wave of New Wave, Nu-Soul, Nu-metal, New Acoustic Movement – how ridiculous is all that? It's just music at the end of the day. But we're not satisfied until we've slapped a label on it so we can dismiss it once we've got bored of it.'

Nicola looks at me blankly. Obviously she hasn't got a clue what I'm talking about. 'I like pop stuff, really,' she says. 'The stuff you hear on the radio. Things you can sing along to.' She looks at me earnestly. 'What music do you like?'

'I like anything, really. Apart from pop music – can't stand it – dance music too – can't stand that either or death-metal and classical.'

She laughs. She has a nice grin and a nice laugh. 'So what does that leave?'

'I don't know.'

'But don't you write about pop music in *Teen Scene*? How can you write about it if you don't like it?'

'I know. It's terrible, isn't it?'

'You interviewed two of my favourite bands in this issue.' She proceeds to name two cheesy UK pop acts. 'It must be fantastic meeting famous people all the time. What are they like in real life?'

'Like me and you. Only less so. They're nothing special.'

'They are to me,' she says. 'I think they're the best bands in the world.'

Her reply is so earnest that momentarily I'm lost for words. I was right, I tell myself, teenage girls *do* know what music is all about.

'You're right,' I say. 'They probably are the best bands in the world.'

'You used to write for a magazine called *Louder*, too, didn't you?'

'Yeah, I did. How do you know? You weren't a *Louder* reader, were you?'

'The Internet. We have it at school. I put your name into a search engine on one of the computers in the library when I was supposed to be doing a geography project.'

'And you came across the *Louder* website?' She nods. 'I thought they'd shut it down.'

'The pages and links are still up there,' she says. 'You used to write about a lot of bands I've never heard of. Were they any good?'

'Some of them were good. Most of them were rubbish.'

'Is that why you became an agony uncle?'

'Sort of. *Louder* closed and a friend offered me this job as a stop-gap.'

'Did you have to go to university to learn to be an agony uncle?'

'Not really.'

'So what did you do to get the job?'

I have to think hard before I answer this question. It feels wrong to admit that I'm just a jobbing journalist. I don't want to shatter the illusion that I know what I'm talking about. 'I had some special training. But mainly I'm just a bit of a natural when it comes to relationships and stuff.'

'Have you got any other kids?'

Her question takes me by surprise but it's a fair one to ask, given the circumstances. A shadow of sadness falls over me but I refuse to let it stay. 'No,' I tell her. And then I wonder if she wants me to add the words 'apart from you'. She doesn't look like she has a secret agenda of any kind but I don't say it anyway.

'Are you married?' she asks.

'Yeah, I am.'

'What's your wife called?'

'Izzy.'

'Is she pretty?'

'Yeah, I think so.'

'What does she do . . . for a job?'

'Have you heard of *Femme* magazine?'

'It's the glossy one that's for "women who know what they want", or something,' she says, paraphrasing the magazine's strap line. 'Mum sometimes reads it.' She giggles to herself and adds, 'I'm not too sure she always knows what she wants though.'

'Well, Izzy works on that magazine. She was deputy editor there. Today she found out that she's going to be acting editor.'

'Does she get paid a lot?'

'She does okay,' I say, 'but the world of magazines sounds a lot more glamorous than it really is. Basically they're just a bunch of people sitting in an office all day answering the phone and typing at a computer.'

'Does she get to interview celebrities?'

'A few.' I name three who I think might impress a thirteen-year-old girl.

'I've heard of all of them,' says Nicola. The earnestness is back again and she is awestruck. 'It's amazing she's met them. What were they like?'

'I don't know,' I tell her, which is true. 'I think they were all right.'

'I've never met anyone famous,' she says, then adds, 'Apart from you.'

'But I'm not famous.'

'Your face is in a magazine,' she says. 'Girls at school have read your column. That's famous to me.'

'Oh,' I say. 'I suppose you're right.'

'bye

By the time we're ready to leave (the remains of Nicola's strawberry milkshake having melted to a pink slush at the bottom of the cup; the few remaining French fries having gone cold and hard; the odd bit of lettuce and abandoned gherkins having gone even more limp) I still haven't come to terms with what has just happened. Nicola, the daughter I hadn't known existed until yesterday, is sitting right in front of me. And we've just eaten lunch in McDonald's as if we're on a first date. It all seems too unreal for words and yet there she is. It's all I can do to stop myself leaning forward and prodding her arm to check that she's real.

'Have you got to get back to work?' she asks, as we stand up. 'You must have loads of letters to read.'

'Yeah, I have,' I reply, as we tidy away our trays and rubbish.

Together we make our way up the stairs and out of the restaurant on to Oxford Street. Sitting in the bowels of the restaurant I'd been oblivious to the world outside and had focused all my attention on this one person. Now suddenly I'm in a different environment and the adjustment seems to be taking longer than usual. It is no longer raining and the traffic seems louder, the sky brighter, the people around us busier.

'What are you going to do now?' I ask.

She shrugs.

'You could go back to school,' I suggest.

'I don't think I will, if that's all right,' she says, looking down at her shoes. 'I think I'll just go to the library and look at some books.'

'Have you got enough money to get home?' I ask.

'I'm fine, thanks. I bought a Travel Card.'

'And you'll be all right getting back to Wood Green?'

'I've been to Oxford Street on my own loads of times,' she tells me. 'I'm usually with my friends, but I'll be okay.'

'Listen, how about I give you the money for a cab? I don't want to spend the rest of the afternoon worrying about you.'

'I'll be okay.'

'You're sure?'

'I'm sure.' She looks at her watch. 'I'd better go.'

'Okay, then. Well, it was really good to meet you.' I think about shaking her hand but it doesn't seem appropriate. 'Your mum must be really proud of you.'

She half smiles in acknowledgement but avoids eye-contact. 'It was good to meet you too . . . Oh, and thanks for the McDonald's.'

Neither of us moves. A bus roars by and several taxis and cars exchange heated debate via their horns.

'I'd better go,' she says again, and begins to walk away.

She's only taken a few steps before I call out her name. She stops immediately and turns round.

'I know we haven't had much time today,' I tell her, 'but how about meeting up again? If you want to, that is.'

'Really?'

'Yeah, really. When shall we say?'

'I don't know,' she says. 'I'll have to think about what I'm going to tell Mum. I don't want to lie but . . .'

'You can tell her you know about me if you want. I don't think you should keep secrets from her.'

She stops and thinks. 'I want to tell her but not yet. Do you mind?'

'It's up to you. I just want you to be okay.'

'I am.'

'Also, I think that today should be the first and last time you bunk off school and the last time you come into London on your own. Maybe when we meet again I'll pick you up? Shall I call you and we'll arrange something?'

She nods. 'I'll see you, then.'

'Yeah, I'll see you soon.'

She turns and walks away from me, and I watch her until she has disappeared into Tottenham Court Road tube station.

oh

It's just after three and Fran's coming into the office with Ellie.

'Good lunch?' I ask her, as she sits down at her desk.

'Great lunch,' she replies. 'Best lunch ever. Shouldn't have had the last glass of wine, though. All I'm fit for is a long nap.' She laughs. 'How was your sandwich?'

'Nothing to write home about.'

'Made any decision about what to do about the thing?' she asks quietly.

'I'm not going to contact her,' I say, and wonder why I'm not telling her about my meeting with Nicola. I suppose it's because it feels too private, too recent. I need to get my head straight first. I need to decide what I'm going to do.

Fran gives me a half-smile as a show of solidarity but doesn't say anything.

'It's for the best,' I add, a touch guiltily. 'It's the right thing to do.'

'If you need to talk—' she says.

'No, thanks,' I interrupt, even though I do. 'I'm okay,' I add. 'I'll be all right.'

perform

It's seven o'clock in the evening and I'm standing at the entrance to Denim on St Martin's Lane. I walk past the bouncer on the door and scan the room for Izzy. The bar is busy with after-work drinkers, and mellow dance music is playing in the background. All afternoon all I've done is think about Nicola, and now I'm going to have to put her to the back of my mind. I can't afford to let Izzy detect the slightest trace of anxiety. I spot her and her impeccably dressed friends at a table to the rear of the bar, take a deep breath and prepare myself to have a good time on the outside even if inside I'm heading for chaos.

'Dave!' screams Izzy.

I smile and wave. As I reach the table she stands up and launches herself at me, wrapping her arms around me in a hug. She isn't drunk but she's getting there. 'How are you, gorgeous?' She looks right into my eyes when she says this with an intensity that feels like it could pierce my soul.

I laugh to cover my nervousness. 'Okay, thanks. No need to ask how you are, is there?'

'Don't you worry about me.' She smiles. 'I can drink you under the table.' She almost drags me over to meet the 'girls'. 'Everybody,' she says, waving her hands to get her friends' attention, 'do you know that my Dave is the agony uncle on *Teen Scene*?'

At this everyone sitting at the table giggles, laughs, whoops and mock-gasps, clearly titillated at the thought of having Love Doctor Dave in their midst. I am this evening's entertainment. And over the next half-hour I enter into an impromptu question-and-answer session as, one by one, Izzy's drinking companions introduce themselves, if they aren't known to me already, and then their love ailments, of which until now I've definitely been ignorant.

'Let me go first,' says a curly-haired girl of about twenty-five, who I'm told is freelancing in the *Femme* office. 'Hi, Dave, I'm Davina. I'm a designer.' I shake her hand. 'My boyfriend Nick is a lawyer and he's going to work in Hong Kong – for six months. How likely do you think it is that he'll cheat on me?'

Izzy's friends proceed to bang on the table rhythmically, chanting, 'Love Doctor!' at the top of their voices, clearly pleased with the fun they're having at my expense. Getting into the spirit of the evening I hold up my hands to silence them.

'Quiet please!' says Izzy, getting into her role as mistress of ceremonies for the evening. 'The Love Doctor speaks.'

'I'm afraid the Love Doctor's going to need more information,' I tell Davina.

'What like?' she asks.

'How long have you been with him?'

'Eighteen months.'

'And . . . well . . . this is a difficult question but has he . . . er . . . cheated on you before?'

'Only once,' says Davina, sheepishly. 'It was ages ago when he went on holiday with some of his mates.'

'And he told you?'

'I found out from the girlfriend of one of his best friends.'

'And you took him back?'

She nods.

'And he hasn't cheated on you since?'

'Not as far as I know.'

'So you think he might have cheated on you but you haven't found out?'

'Well, there was this girl in his office who kept calling him a while back but I couldn't prove anything.'

'What do you think, Love Doctor?' asks Izzy.

'I'm sorry, Davina, but I say, sack him. He sounds like a loser.'

The whole table erupts in a round of applause and whoops.

'Me next!' says an auburn-haired girl to my left. I recognise her. It's Becca, one of *Femme*'s junior designers – I've met her before. 'Okay, here's my dilemma: I fancy this guy who's a junior designer on one of the mags upstairs.'

'It's that boy Jake from *Download*,' says Izzy, matter-of-factly.

'How do you know?' asks Becca, surprised.

'Everyone knows,' says Davina, in a tone that indicates she's sulking about my solution to her love problem.

'Okay, okay,' says Becca, going crimson. 'You're right.' She casts a withering glare in Izzy's direction. 'Anyway, my question, Love Doctor, is how do I find out if he likes me without letting on that I like him? I don't want him to know if it's not a mutual thing. But he does keep looking at me whenever we get into the lift together.'

'You've probably just got toothpaste on your chin,' says a blonde dreadlocked girl to whom I have yet to be introduced.

Everyone laughs, apart from Becca.

179

'Why don't you ask him out?' I suggest.

'Because that would make me look desperate,' she tells me seriously. 'And I'm not desperate.'

'I take it you've been stuck in suspended animation since 1954 when that kind of attitude was all the rage.'

Becca laughs. 'I just don't ask men out, okay?'

'What have you got to lose?'

'My dignity.'

'And will your dignity be taking you out on Friday night and showing you a good time?'

She doesn't reply.

'Thought not.'

'What says the Love Doctor?' says Izzy, still camping it up.

'I say, next time you're in the lift try talking to him. If that works, ask him if he wants to get lunch some time – because lunch won't sound like a date. If he says yes and arranges a date, odds are you're in. If he says he's busy, move on to bigger and better pastures. Next!'

'Okay, here's a tricky one,' says the blonde dreadlocked girl. 'I'm Olivia, *Femme*'s art director and here's my question: I've been friends with this guy since college—'

'Is this Jeremy?' says a glamorous-looking redhead I recognise as Milly, *Femme*'s assistant fashion editor. 'You guys are perfect for each other!'

Olivia shrugs. 'I'm not so sure.'

'What's the background?' I ask.

'We've known each other since college, best mates and all that, seen each other through a lot of hard times, but nothing's ever happened between us until last Saturday when we—'

'You didn't tell me any of this when I asked you how your

weekend was!' says Izzy. 'You said it was okay. I'm meant
to be one of your best mates at work! And I'm pretty sure
you getting off with the bloke that you've been best friends
with since college is a bit more than okay. It's front-page
news.'

Olivia laughs. 'We just kissed.'

'So what's the problem?' I ask.

'I don't know . . . I suppose I want to know if we should
take it further.'

'Do you fancy him?'

'He's cute, and plenty of girls fancy him, but I'm not
sure.'

'That doesn't sound good,' said Becca.

'So you're not sure if you fancy him?'

She takes a sip of her drink. 'I feel comfortable with him,
and I love him to bits.'

'What does he think?'

'He really wants to go for it.'

'He would,' says Milly. '*He's a man*.'

'He's not afraid of jeopardising the friendship?'

'He says if it doesn't work out we can go back to how we
were before. But I'm not sure we'll be able to.'

Izzy looks at me. 'What says the Love Doctor?' she asks,
even though she knows exactly what I'm going to say
because Olivia's situation is how ours was when we first got
together.

'It all depends on how brave you are,' I say, holding Izzy's
gaze. 'It will always be easier just to cool off and let things
go back to normal. And, yeah, it might be that things go
wrong and you could fall out for good, in which case you'll
lose a good friend. But if you get it right, if you take your
time and don't rush into things, you might get more than you

ever dreamed of. You might get someone who will always be on your side, someone you never tire of looking at, someone who's your perfect soul-mate.'

I get a standing ovation.

On a high I get in a round of drinks, and when I return some more girls from *Femme* have arrived and insist on being 'Love Doctored'. This is nothing like my nights out with Trevor and Lee or any of my male friends. This is fun. I'm suddenly 'one of the girls', listening to all the gossip, the bitching about boyfriends and, for the first time today, I forget how complicated my life is and instead just dish out advice, left, right and centre. To Katie, *Femme*'s senior writer, I explain that her problem is that she's a thrill-seeker who likes the fact that her boyfriend Sol cheated on her because that makes him slightly more interesting. I warn Jessica, *Femme*'s production manager, that any ambiguity in her attempt to dump Jonathan, the trainee architect, would result in him following her around like a dog for the rest of her life; and to Debbie, one of *Femme*'s freelance writers who has a list of grievances about her boyfriend as long as her arm, I say: 'He never pays you enough attention, he rarely says anything nice to you, you say you're not even sure you fancy him any more and that there's a strong chance he's been seeing someone else. What are you doing? You're beautiful, intelligent, and you're wasting your-self on this guy who doesn't deserve even a minute of your time.'

I get my second standing ovation.

Izzy puts her arms round me and whispers a simple but heartfelt, 'I love you, Love Doctor.'

I return her kiss. 'I love you too.' And then I remember Nicola, and how heavy this secret weighs on my heart and

Dinner For Two

I'm almost on the verge of telling her everything. But then I pull back and regain control.

I can't tell her. I can't tell her because I'm sure it will destroy her.

locate

It's nine forty-five in the morning and I've just stepped out of Goodge Street Tube and I'm heading up the road towards work. I turn on my mobile. I have one message: 'Hello, Dave, it's me, Nicola O'Connell . . . er . . . and the time is eight forty-five. I've been thinking . . . I . . . I . . . I don't think I'm going to be able to see you again. It's nothing to do with you, honest. It's just that . . . that . . . I think it's for the best. It was a mistake. I should never have got in touch with you like that. You've got your own life. I'm sorry if I've upset you. I'm really sorry. 'Bye.'

want

As I continue up Tottenham Court Road it occurs to me that I should feel relieved to have been handed a Get Out of Jail Free card, that I've been let off the hook. Nicola doesn't want to see me again, Izzy is none the wiser, my life can go back to normal. But I know that 'normal' isn't possible any more because I don't want to be free of Nicola and I'm not sure she wants to be free of me. It's clear from her message that she's more worried about me than she is about herself and, if anything, this makes me want to see her more.

When I reach the office I decide to call her on her mobile and leave a message. But then, just as I pick up the phone, Fran comes into the office and disturbs my concentration. 'You're *so* going to be freaked out by this,' she says, waving a magazine in front of my face.

She holds up the front cover. I can see now that it's an old copy of *Femme* featuring an airbrushed former A-list female TV presenter next to her equally famous musician boyfriend. 'Last night I started rooting through some of the millions of magazines that clog up my bedroom, trying to work out which ones I was going to throw out, when I came across this old copy of *Femme* and you'll never guess what I found in it.' She flicks through the magazine until she reaches the page she's looking for, then hands it to me. I scan the headline: 'Does Your Partner Have A Secret Love

Child?' The article has Izzy's name in the byline and my heart races. I turn to the front cover to check the issue date: January 2000.

'I shouldn't read too much into this,' says Fran, matter-of-factly. 'You know that this kind of topic is regular women's-mag fodder, along with "Is Your Partner Cheating On You?" and "How To Get Your Man To Give You A Sixty-minute Orgasm" but . . . well, it is a weird coincidence, isn't it?'

Izzy's article consists of three women's case histories, which detail how they came to discover their partner's children. The first woman was in her early twenties and had only found out her boyfriend had cheated on her when the other woman appeared at her front door carrying a baby. The second was in her late twenties and discovered by accident that her husband of two years had fathered three kids by three separate women. The third, in her early thirties, was pictured with her two-year-old daughter, claiming that the father was an unnamed married pop star.

A fact box running down the side of the article really catches my interest. According to statistics, in England and Wales in 1998, of 240,611 births outside marriage, 49,960 had no father's name on the birth certificate – a strong indicator that the father was either unknown or no longer present in the child's life. A family law expert explained that the only way a father in the UK could have a child DNA-tested was with the permission of the mother, which she could refuse. This same lawyer also stated that a man discovering he has a child has no legal rights over it unless they are awarded to him by the child's mother or, failing that, a successful application for a Parental Responsibility Order (PRO). This involves a court hearing at which a judge decides whether the child's best interests will be served by having the absent father in its life.

The child's best interests. I have no idea what they might be. Is it in Nicola's best interests never to see me if I really am her father? Would it be better for her if I stayed out of her life? Should I try to contact her mum and get things out in the open, or should I try to continue to see her on my own so that we can get to know each other on our own terms?

More so now than ever, I need to talk. Once again I choose Fran, but the office isn't the place to tell her. I ask her if she wants to go for a lunch-time drink and she agrees. It might be one of the biggest clichés in the book but I tell myself that a problem shared really might be a problem halved.

things

Fran's bored of Hampton's so she's taking me, rather aptly, to Freud, a small below-street-level bar in Covent Garden. As we walk we talk office gossip – which means Fran talks office gossip while I listen: Tina is thinking of dumping her boyfriend, Ellie apparently pulled a C-list soap star after a photo-shoot last week and Gina is getting married.

We reach the bar and go downstairs. There are three staff behind the counter and a number of couples and small groups of people drinking and eating. Fran and I order Cokes and a bowl of olives, then retire to a table opposite the bar.

'So?' says Fran. 'To what do I owe the pleasure of your company this lunch-time?'

'No reason.'

'Yeah, right. Come on, out with it.'

'Who says I want to talk about anything?'

'*I say.*'

'Okay, okay, okay. There is something I want to talk about but not yet. I need a while to warm up. In the meantime, what about you?'

'What about me?'

'I'm the Love Doctor, aren't I? Haven't you got a love dilemma? How's things with Linden?'

'He's all right.'

'Good.'

'He's asked me to move in with him.'

'Congratulations.'

'I said no.'

'Why?'

'Loads of reasons.'

'Like?'

She sighs. 'I don't really want to talk about it.'

This isn't like Fran. 'Are you all right?' I ask.

'I'm fine.'

'Are you sure?'

She laughs. 'I can't believe you're the same grumpy music journalist who walked into *Teen Scene*.'

'It's just that—'

'There's nothing wrong, Dave,' she says firmly. 'I'm fine. I know I usually talk about everything but sometimes I talk too much. So I think it's back to you. Come on, I know it's to do with that letter. Has she contacted you again?'

'I've got a confession about that. I've met her.'

'But you told me—'

'Yeah, I know. I'm really sorry. I suppose I'm a bit like you, really. It was okay talking about it when it was all theoretical but then suddenly I met her and . . . well, I couldn't tell you. I couldn't tell anyone.'

'No one else knows at all?'

'Apart from her, me and you.'

'When did you meet her?'

'Yesterday lunch-time.'

'I thought you said you were just going out to get a sandwich. I'm pretty sure I would've remembered if you'd said' – she lowered her voice to a hoarse whisper – '"Fran, I'm going out to meet my long-lost thirteen-year-old daughter."' She laughs. 'So come on then, what's she like?'

'She was absolutely amazing. I mean there she was sitting across the table from me . . .'

'What table?'

'The table in McDonald's—'

'I thought you were getting a sandwich?'

'I was and then she was outside waiting for me.'

'And so you took her to McDonald's? The first time you meet your estranged daughter and you take her to – *and I'm guessing here* – the McDonald's at the top end of Oxford Street?'

I nod.

'You really know how to treat a girl.'

'I wasn't thinking, was I?'

'You can say that again. So what *was* she like?'

'Amazing. Really amazing. And so smart, funny and sharp. Listen to me, I'm already sounding like a doting father.'

Fran smiles. 'And she looks like you?'

'I don't know. Sometimes I thought I saw flashes here and there, but who knows? On the other hand she told me she was obsessed with music. I was, too, when I was her age—'

'A teenage girl obsessed with pop music? Now *there's* something she couldn't have achieved on her own!'

'Okay, sarky, you've made your point.'

Fran looks at me. 'Why do you want her to be yours, Dave?'

'What do you mean?'

'Most guys in your position would be looking for a million and one different ways to find out that the kid wasn't theirs but you seem to be doing the opposite. Why?'

'It just seems right.'

'I still don't understand.'

'In July Izzy was pregnant.'

'Oh,' says Fran.

'It didn't work out. And, well, we decided that maybe kids aren't for us, at least for the moment, but the thing is—'

'You want to be a dad,' says Fran.

'It's not as simple as that,' I tell her. 'It's more complicated. It's hard to explain . . .'

My hand is on the table and Fran puts hers on top of it. 'You don't have to explain anything,' she says. 'If you're happy about Nicola then I'm happy for you, Dave. But as the only person you've told about this I think I wouldn't be much of a friend if I didn't rein you in a bit.'

'What do you mean?'

'Well, from what you've told me you still haven't met her mum.'

'No.'

'So, as far as I can see, you're no closer to being sure Nicola's yours than you were when you first got the letter. And, well, I think you have to be sure. Not just for Nicola's sake but for yours too.'

Fran's right, of course. Once again I've got way ahead of myself. I did need reining in. Maybe that's what Nicola realised – the essential madness of our situation.

'The thing is,' I say, 'Nicola called me today and said that she doesn't want to see me again. I think . . . I know it's because she thinks she's messing up my life but she's not.' I take a sip of my Coke. 'What do you think I should do?'

'So you haven't already made up your mind?'

A smile spreads across my face. 'Yeah, I have, actually.'

'So what are you asking me for?' says Fran. 'You've got to do what you've got to do.'

191

kids

It's five past three – just before the end of school on a crisp, sunny winter's day. I'm standing by Nicola's school gates. As comprehensives go, Wood Green appears to be no better and no worse than the one I'd attended when I was her age. I look around me at some of the mums and dads sitting in cars waiting for their kids. It's hard to believe that at thirty-two I have anything in common with the type of people who do the 'school run', and yet here I am and here they are. I even spot a couple of women who look my age and wonder what their story might be.

At quarter past three I hear a bell ring and seconds later kids are flooding out of the school's doors and along the path towards the gates. Soon I'm surrounded but I spot Nicola well before she reaches the gate. I call her name and she looks up but doesn't see me. I call again, and she notices me, but as she walks over to me I have to ask myself again whether I'm really acting *in the child's best interests*.

'What are you doing here?' she asks quietly. 'Have I done something wrong?'

'No. Of course not. It's just that I got your message and I wanted to talk to you about what you said.' She nods. 'I understand this is all a bit weird for you. I really do. I mean I'm this strange guy who works on a magazine and you're a schoolgirl. And you think I'm your dad—'

'I *know* you're my dad.'

'You do?'

She nods again.

'But how?'

'Because of what Mum told me years ago. Because you're the guy in the photograph. And because of what Mum told me last night.'

'What did she tell you last night?'

'I asked her about you again – she's used to that. When I was younger I used to ask about you all the time.'

'So what did she say last night about me?'

'I asked her if she saw you again whether she'd recognise you.'

'And what did she say?'

'She said yes. She said even though you'd probably changed quite a bit the one thing that would be the same was your eyes. She said you had really beautiful eyes. And, well, you have, haven't you?'

I want to laugh. This seems too ridiculous for words but Nicola believes it: my eyes are her evidence.

'So, why don't you want to see me any more if you know I'm your dad?'

'All I wanted to do was meet you. I've done that now and it was nice. You were nice. But I don't want to cause any trouble. You've got your own life and . . .'

'If the reason you don't want to see me again is because you're worried about me then *don't* worry. I mean it. I really do want to see you if you want to see me.'

'But you're married . . . you don't want me messing it up.'

'You're wrong,' I tell her. 'I *do* want to see you.'

'What will your wife say when you tell her about me?'

'The same thing your mum will say when she finds out, probably.'

'Are you sure?' she says.

'Absolutely. But, more importantly, are *you* sure? Like I said, I reckon this must be pretty weird for you.'

'It must be weird for you too.'

'Yeah, but I'm thirty-two. Weird is pretty much normal when you're my age.'

'What do you think we can do to make this not weird?' she asks. 'Last time we had a McDonald's but we can't keep doing that – we'll get fat.'

'I suppose it would help if we came out in the open and told Izzy and your mum what was going on. At least then it wouldn't feel like we were doing something wrong. That's what's making us feel so strange – the secrecy. I'm really terrible with this kind of thing. And I'm sure it can't be easy for you either.'

'So you mean you *want* to tell your wife?'

'And you know you should tell your mum,' I say.

'Yes, but the thing is . . .'

'What?'

'If I told Mum, everything would change. It wouldn't be about me getting to know you, it would be about Mum being angry with me and, well, I haven't done anything for anybody to be angry at, have I?'

'No, I suppose you're right.'

'I will tell my mum about you – I *want* to tell her about you – and I know you'll have to tell Izzy because it wouldn't be nice not to . . . but wouldn't it be nice just to have a bit more time? You know, just to hang out and stuff? All I want to do is get to know you better first.'

'How long do we give ourselves, then? A day? Two days? A week?'

'I don't know. Whatever you think's best.'

'Okay. How about this? We leave it open. We'll know when the right time to tell people is, won't we?'

She squints at me and half nods, which I assume is a sign that we've reached an agreement. 'What shall we do now?' I ask her.

There's a long silence and then she asks me if I'm hungry. I say I am and she tells me she's going to buy me a burger. She takes me to Burger King on Wood Green High Road. The restaurant is crowded with post-school parents, prams and kids from Nicola's school. Nicola insists on paying because she says it's only fair as I got lunch last time. It's really very sweet of her, even more touching because I have to help her out with a small loan as she's fifty pence short. She orders a flame-grilled Whopper for herself and a Chicken Royale for me. I ask her if she's going to get them to do it without all the salad and stuff in it. She shakes her head and tells me that she likes to take it out herself. When our food is ready we set down in the middle of the restaurant. Nicola unpacks her burger and removes all of the vegetable matter within. I watch her out of the corner of my eye with a big grin on my face.

We sit there talking for just under an hour, during which I learn more about Nicola's likes and dislikes (including such highlights as how she likes blue but not orange, isn't keen on books but loves magazines, has always wanted a horse but is scared of ponies because they were 'a bit creepy-looking'). She tells me about her mum, how she'd deferred her place at university until the year after Nicola's birth, then did a degree in music. After graduation she had moved to London with the then four-year-old Nicola and stayed with her aunt while she did a teacher-training course. She is now head of music and drama at Highfields Community School in Hackney.

I want to ask Nicola if her mum is in a relationship but as she doesn't mention a step-dad and only talks about her mum or her grandparents in Dublin, I presume she must be single – which depresses me. I can't imagine it's all that easy to conduct a regular relationship when you've got a kid to raise and a full-time job. In the end Nicola mentions in passing a guy called Francis, a doctor, who had been her mum's boyfriend until the previous summer. The relationship had lasted two years and then one afternoon her mum had asked how she'd feel if Francis didn't come round any more. Nicola had replied that she'd miss him. Her mum explained to her that things hadn't been going well between them and that sometimes 'two people can be in love but want different things'. I ask Nicola if she still misses Francis and she says, 'Sometimes.' I think this is all she's going to say but then she suddenly seems unsatisfied with her answer and adds: 'He had a big car and he sometimes used to let me play his Ministry of Sound DJ mix album I've got as loud as I wanted.'

band

The following evening I have to review a gig at the Astoria
– a new US guitar band who are supposedly the next big
thing. I get to the venue just as I hear the support act
coming on stage and I think about going straight to the
stage but then I realise my need of a beer is greater than
my need to watch support acts so I head for the bar. As
I order a Holsten Pils, I spot a music journalist I know,
Karen Gibbons, and I get her a beer too. Karen works
for *Selector* and I've known her since the mid-1990s. In
all that time we've only ever spoken about music. This
evening, however, our music-related conversation is reduced to the act we're reviewing (Me: Have you heard their
album? It's terrible. Her: It's a real dog, isn't it?) and then
she asks if it's true that I'm working at *Teen Scene* as an
agony uncle. Within minutes of me confirming the rumour,
she's telling me how she's been two-timing her boyfriend
of four months with the drummer from a semi-famous
band.

This is not a one-off event: so far I've dispensed relationship advice to most of the *Teen Scene* staff as well as a few
at *Stylissimo*. The thing is, I feel as if I'm still the same
person I was when I wrote about music but now my words
and advice appear to carry weight. Do Karen and all the
other people who ask my advice really believe I have some

sort of insight into the world of love that they don't? The longer I'm an agony uncle, the more people seem to trust my judgement. If only they knew.

quite

Monday: Jenny over lunch

It's one thirty and Jenny and I are sitting in Wagamama in Lexington Street. We've been talking about life at *Teen Scene* for the previous half an hour and just as my vegetable tempura and chicken ramen arrives she drops this bombshell:

'I'm thinking about leaving Trevor,' she says flatly. 'It's not working.'

'You and Trevor are good together,' I say, 'you have your ups and downs like the rest of us but, you know . . .' I scramble around searching for the right thing to say '. . . you don't always get perfect.'

'I know that,' says Jenny. 'I think I'd even consider "nearly perfect" or even "just okay" but what Trev and I have isn't just okay, is it? It's not like what you and Izzy have.'

I don't say anything.

'I don't even think he loves me,' she adds.

'Of course he does.'

'No, he doesn't. He likes me, I think I'm not pushing the boat out too far with that one, but I'm not the love of his life, am I?'

She looks at me and then, without waiting for me to reply, carries on eating her noodles.

busy

Tuesday morning: Lee on the telephone

'Hi, *Teen Scene*, Dave Harding speaking.'

'All right, mate, it's Lee here.'

'How's it going?'

'Fine. Bit busy at the moment, I'm only just about managing to squeeze in a tea-break these days.'

There's a long pause, mainly because this is the longest telephone conversation I've ever had with Lee. He rarely calls me at home (I always call him) and I can count on a single finger the number of occasions he's called me at work.

'So?' I say, in the hope of prompting him to speak.

'I was just wondering . . .'

'Yeah?'

'If Stella had said anything to Izzy about me and her.'

'Like what?'

'Like . . . I dunno. Just stuff about me and her. She's been acting a bit strange with me recently. Just a bit off. You know, starting arguments for no reason and everything.'

'Isn't that just how Stella is?'

He laughs but it sounds forced. 'Yeah, I suppose so. But this is more pointed.'

'Do you think she wants to split up?'

'I know she thinks about it. I can just tell. It's the age thing . . .'

'It's not inevitable just because of the age thing.'

'Yeah, it is,' says Lee. 'Of course it is. We knew right from the start that this was never going to work out.'

'But you've lasted this long.'

'Yeah.' He sighs.

There's a long silence and I can just make out someone talking to him in the background.

'Listen,' he says, 'that was my boss. I'd better go and look like I'm doing something.' He adds, 'See you at the weekend probably.'

'Yeah,' I reply. 'See you at the weekend!'

ago

Wednesday evening at home: Stella on the phone
'Hi, Dave, it's Stella.'

'How are things?'

'Okay, you know. Overworked, underpaid. And how's the UK's number-one agony uncle?'

'He's fine,' I reply. 'This agony-uncle lark is a good laugh once you get going. I've read some classic letters this week. I'll have to bring them home and show you them at the weekend or something.' I pause briefly then add, 'If it's Izzy you're after she's at the gym, I think. It's her yoga class tonight. She shouldn't be too late though. I'll tell her you called, shall I?'

'Don't worry. I'll probably try her a bit later.'

There was a long pause.

'Dave?'

'Yeah?'

'Nothing. It's okay.' She pauses again. 'Has Lee said anything to you?'

'About what?'

'About him and me.'

'Why?'

She sighs heavily. 'It's just that I've been a real bitch to him recently and I wondered if he might have mentioned anything to you.'

'But you're always a real bitch to Lee.'

Stella laughs. 'Listen, Harding, I only let you get away with stuff like that because you're my friend's husband. The thing is, I *have* been a real bitch to Lee.'

'Why?'

'I don't know. I think I want us to split up but I'm too much of a coward to do the dirty work.'

'Are things really that bad?'

'Yeah, they're really that bad. You know as well as I do that Lee and I weren't meant to last this long. He was supposed to be a fling to help me get over Patrick.'

An image of Stella's old boyfriend comes back to me. 'He was a really nice guy, I remember.'

'I know. We were together two years.'

'What's he doing? I haven't seen him since you two split up. It's weird that the four of us used to go out together all the time, didn't we?'

'I bumped into him a while ago,' says Stella. 'He's married now. Two kids. They live over in Kentish Town . . . You two got on really well together, didn't you? He liked all the same music you did . . . I suppose that's what happens when people split up. You end up losing some good friends along the way.'

changes

Thursday: Trevor, in the Coach and Horses, Soho, after work, having clearly drunk too much

'Someone a long time ago once asked me what I thought love was,' says Trevor. 'I thought for a long time because it was a deep question and eventually I said, "A face". And they said, "What?" And I repeated, "A face, I think love is a face. A face that you see day in day out. You wake up in the morning, there's that face again staring at you from the pillow opposite. You have breakfast there it is once more hiding behind a packet of cornflakes. You kiss that face goodbye as you go your separate ways to work. Eight hours later you kiss that same face hello. The face tells you about its day at work. You tell the face about your day at work. You cook for the face, and it does the washing up from the previous day. And when you go to bed, you kiss the face once more and hope you'll see it in your dreams. You see a face that much you have to love it, I told her . . . Love it or loathe it.'

dial

To: izzy.harding@bdp.co.uk
From: dave_atch01@hotmail.com
Subject: Women and the messages they leave on men's answerphones.

Dear Babe,
Okay, I'm beginning to get into the swing of this writing for women lark. You're going to love this next column: it's funny, it's truthful and it's light-hearted. Some of it is actually true too.

love

Dave xxx

PS Is the last line a little too cheesy? I spent ages trying to come up with something better that didn't sound quite so 'Hey, baby, you're all right by me!' Feel free to improve at will.

After the Beep

Back when I was single the answerphone played an invaluable role in my life. I used it to avoid my mum, organise my social life and let people know how wacky I was (my outgoing message in the style of Michael Caine was a killer). And, of course, I used it to take messages

from . . . girlfriends. For the most part what the ladies
in my life left after the beep was quite endearing, like
Nina (message type: Rambler – give her a minute and a
half of blank tape and she'd fill it), or Sadie (message
type: Linguaphone Loon – garbled sentences delivered
with such speed she sounded like a learn-to-speak
Esperanto tape on fast forward).

There are, however, a few exceptions, women who
never quite grasped the four basic rules of boyfriend
answerphone etiquette. I'd come home and see the
machine's flashing red light and immediately my stomach
would tighten, palms sweat, and I'd feel sick and woozy
as my finger hovered nervously over the play button in
case it was them. Their problem? They just didn't understand that there are things a woman should never say or
do on a man's answerphone. Things like this:

Post beep style: The Locator
Rule broken: No multiple messaging of a grievous nature
is allowed. Ever.
Message 1: 'Hi, it's Cassie. It's eight thirty. Give me
a call when you get in.'
Message 2: 'Hi, Cassie again. It's ten twenty. Er . . .
give me a call.'
Message 3: 'It's twelve fifty-four. Where are you? I
called your mobile, I've called your best mate *and* your
mother. Where are you?'
Message 4: 'It's one thirty. You're with that tart from
Accounts, aren't you? I always said her skirts were too
short. Well that's it, we're finished!'

In the space of five hours Cassie had somehow managed
to work herself into such a frenzy she concluded I was

cheating on her (I was actually out with friends) and dumped me, informing me in such a manner that my answerphone knew before I did. What she didn't understand is that for men, especially in the early days of a relationship, independence is everything. We've spent most of our lives attempting to break free of our mother's apron strings, so the last thing we want is someone worrying about our every movement and making us feel like we're under police surveillance.

Post beep style: The Haunter
Rule broken: Always make it easy on us by never making us spell it out to you.
Message: 'Hi, this is Amy. Your answerphone must be broken because I've left three messages this week and you haven't got back to me on any of them! Give me a call.'

This was the last of four messages my mate Trevor found on his machine a few years ago the week after a one-night stand that he was busy trying to forget. He thought she'd understood the Code – that by not returning any of her calls he was saying quite clearly: 'Thanks but no thanks.' No amount of wishful thinking – 'Maybe the tape got mangled/the electricity in his flat has gone off/his dog must have attacked his machine' can change the fact that in the battle zone called Love there are no such things as broken answerphones, only broken promises.

Post beep style: The Clicker
Rule broken: Never scare a man half to death by making him try and guess who you are.
Message: Click.

There are few things guaranteed to annoy a man more

than pressing the play button on his machine only to hear
the click of a phone being put down. We don't take ourselves off to electrical stores, study the specifi-
cations of each and every model then spend forty quid
purchasing a piece of top machinery just for you to
ignore it. We buy a machine – we want messages! The thing
about Clickers is that they make us rummage through our
consciences for past misdemeanours come to haunt us.
For instance, in his student days my friend Lee had a
Clicker hounding him for weeks. At first he thought it was
Karen, a recently exed girlfriend stalking him, then he
thought it might be Lucy, his current girlfriend checking up on him while he was up to no good with her best
friend Kim. In the end, it just turned out to be his
mother refusing to have anything to do with 'new-
fangled technology'.

Post beep style: The Booty Call
Rule broken: Always think carefully about the consequences of your message.
Message: 'Hi, it's Melissa. I'm thinking me, you, a tub
of Häagen Dazs and those fur-lined handcuffs you bought
me.'

If there's a message to be saved for 'future reference' it's this one. It's loaded with the sort of long-
ing, mystery and immediacy we'd love to find in the woman
who left it – which is all well and good when you've got a
bachelor pad, or are sharing with some mates who will no
doubt be green with envy, but when you're living with
your parents, like my mate Lee was at the time, it can be
a complete nightmare. 'I hadn't made Melissa aware of my
domestic arrangements for obvious reasons,' explains

Lee. 'So you can imagine how horrified I was when I came in and my mum smirked at me, ''Oh, there's a message for you from someone called Melissa, dear. She sounds like a nice girl.'' '

We men know leaving a message after the beep can be traumatic. We know you want to leave something that says: 'Hi, I'm the sexy/witty/intriguing woman you've been seeing,' instead of: 'Remember the sexy/witty/intriguing woman you've been seeing? Well, I'm her tongue-tied twin sister.' But none of that matters, because as long as you're not leaving messages like the ones above you should always feel free to be you after the beep.

together

It's Saturday morning, over a week since Nicola and I went to Burger King, and I've vacillated between feelings of acute excitement and complete terror of being caught. No matter what I do Nicola is always on my mind. I've been rolling the situation around in my head thinking that there must be a solution to what's going on if only I can find it.

Nicola and I have been talking on the phone, trying to sort out another time when we can meet up next but it has been difficult. Today, though, I'm going to see her because Jenny, Stella and Izzy set off to Brighton for a day out early this morning. When I found out they were going I called Nicola to see if she could meet me. Ever since I've been feeling nervous and now I feel like a teenage boy on his first date. I've even bought a new pair of Diesel jeans and I'm wearing a dark-blue Evisu sweatshirt Izzy bought me and my favourite white shell-toe Adidas trainers. Kids are obsessed with designer labels and, though it might be shallow, I want Nicola to be one hundred per cent impressed with me.

I've arranged to meet her two streets away from her home and told her to look out for me in a white Mercedes convertible. When she sees me she waves and a big grin spreads over my face. I pull over, get out of the car and put the hood down – it's not the warmest day of the year but it's not freezing either.

'This car's wicked,' says Nicola. 'I didn't realise you were so cool.'

She's wearing a knee-length denim skirt, an Adidas track-suit top zipped right up to her chin and chunky-looking trainers. She looks like a miniature streetwise pop star and seems a lot more at ease than the last time I'd seen her.

'Where does your mum think you are?' I ask, as she climbs into the car.

'At drama club, and then I told her I'm going to the library.' She adjusts her seat-belt. 'So that gives me about five hours. Where have you told Izzy you are?'

'Nowhere. She's gone to Brighton for the day.'

She nods but doesn't say anything for a while. Neither of us is proud of ourselves for having lied to people we love.

She turns to me and says, 'I've decided I'm not going to worry any more.'

'You've decided, just like that?' I repeat.

'We've only met twice and . . . well, both times I spent too much time worrying and it's a waste of time, isn't it? This isn't *that* weird, is it? You're my dad. I've got every right to spend time with you if I want to. So I'm over all that being nervous lark. And I'm not going to worry any more.'

It's strange seeing these two sides of her personality: her shy side and her slightly more precocious side. Multiple personalities must run in the family. It's definitely stretching a point but I feel like at the moment I've got four: 'po-faced music journalist', agony uncle, husband and now father to a thirteen-year-old.

'Okay,' I say. 'No more weirdness. No more worrying.' I reach for the ignition key and stop. 'One thing, though.'

'What?'

'Have you thought about what we're going to do today? What do you fancy?'

'I don't mind,' she says.

'Cinema?'

She shrugs.

'Are you hungry?'

She shakes her head.

'The park?'

She shrugs.

'Come on,' I encourage. 'What would you really want to do if you could do anything right now?'

'I'd like to see where you live,' she says, almost inaudibly.

'Why?'

'Because I'm interested in your life.'

I think about her request and the attendant problems. First, the neighbours in the flats above and below might spot her. Second, if the two of us are going to sit in the flat for the next few hours I'm going to have to entertain her and I'm not sure how to entertain a thirteen-year-old without fast food. Third, there's the terrifying but unlikely scenario of Izzy returning early.

However, if this is what Nicola wants, I want her to have it. Of course she's curious about my life – I'm just as curious about hers. I want to know all about the thirteen years of her life that I've missed out on. I want to know what she was like as a baby and as a toddler, her first day at school, who her friends are. I want to know everything too but I'm aware of pressuring her. I just have to remind myself that I'll learn all about her in time.

'Are you sure that's what you want to do?' I say eventually.

'If that's okay with you. You won't get into trouble with Izzy, will you?'

'No, of course not.'

I start the car and as we head towards Muswell Hill I take out the Ministry of Sound album I've borrowed from the *Teen Scene* office and slip it into the car's CD player. And even though I can't stand dance music I turn the volume right up for Nicola's benefit and drive.

home

'That was *so* cool,' says Nicola, as I pull up outside my flat forty-five minutes later, having made a detour through Crouch End and Highgate so that she could spend more time posing in the car.

'Yeah, it was.' I point to the house where the flat is. 'This is where I live.'

She climbs out of the car, helps me put the hood back up, then follows me up the pathway. I don't have any plan ready in case I bump into anyone – whatever happens, happens.

'Are you thirsty?' I ask, as we go in.

'I'm all right for the minute, thanks.'

The cat strolls into the hallway from the kitchen and eyes her with a degree of alarm. 'This is Arthur,' I say, pointing to the cat who is now sat by the radiator watching me carefully.

Nicola kneels down and starts rubbing her fingers together to attract him. I can see he wants to go to her but he's not sure. He looks at me disdainfully, then takes the plunge and heads straight for Nicola and starts rubbing against her ankles. She strokes his head gently and suddenly he's purring loudly, entwining his tail around her ankles. She's made a new best friend.

'I take it you like cats, then?'

'Arthur's great,' she says. 'He's got really nice eyes. But we can't have one because Mum's allergic.'

'Well, you can make a fuss of Arthur for as long as you like. He doesn't get as much attention as he'd like from me and Izzy.' I open the door to the living room and Nicola follows, with Arthur at her heels. I turn on the TV and switch it to one of those teenage channels that have endless repeats of *Sabrina the Teenage Witch*.

Nicola doesn't even look at it; she's too busy stroking Arthur, who has now rolled on to his side exposing his belly.

I watch her for several moments without speaking. She seems fine. And this makes me happy. So I disappear to the kitchen and take my time over making myself a coffee.

errr?

'So, what do you fancy doing now, then?' It's half an hour later and even the cat is bored of being the centre of attention. 'I've got videos and DVDs we can watch – action films mostly and arty sub-titled nonsense – CDs we can listen to – a fairly eclectic collection although it doesn't feature any Ministry of Sound compilations whatsoever.' I point to the TV. 'We've got Cable TV, so you can flick through forty-odd channels, or we could . . .'

Nicola doesn't seem interested in any of the things I've suggested.

'You don't fancy any of it, do you?'

'Not really.'

'So what *do* you want to do?'

'I was thinking about this on the way over . . .'

'And?'

'I'd like to see photos of you.'

'Photos of me?'

'I want to catch up on all the stuff I missed.'

'Are you sure? I mean . . . won't you be a bit bored? I've got a PlayStation, you know, and some pretty good games too: *Colin McRae Rally 2.0, Tekken 3, Dino Crisis 2 . . .*'

'The photos will be fine. I really want to see them if you've got them.'

So that's what we do. I collect together every single photo

album in the flat, and the small suitcase filled with photos that lives under the bed and I bring them all into the living room. I show her all the black-and-white photos of my mum and dad, taken when they first arrived in England from the Caribbean; pictures of me as a baby, at school and university. I get out the wedding album too and tell her how beautiful Izzy was on that day. In the group family photos I point out Izzy's mum and explain to her why Izzy's dad isn't there. Nicola asks a lot of questions about Izzy so I dig out some photos of us taken when we first met, when we were still just good friends, and then I tell her how we got together.

story

Izzy and I had been friends since 1992 when we'd met on a year-long post-graduate journalism course at Cardiff University and become friends almost immediately. Initially I'd thought she was pretentious because she was obsessed with being cool: wearing the right clothes, listening to the right music and going to the right clubs. Nicola asked me what had changed my mind about her and I told her that my mind hadn't needed changing because as well as being gorgeous and cool, Izzy was an incredible person.

When we first got to know each other she and I had raging debates. 'I'm a man,' I used to tell her. 'I don't worry about relationships. If it's working I stay. If it's not working I leave. What's the point in carrying on with a broken relationship when you can just go out and get yourself a brand new one? Surely I've got enough on my plate with working at my job to come home after a hard day and have to work on a *relationship*!' This was why the majority of my encounters with women had lasted a total of six weeks. That, I'd discovered, was enough time for us to be passionate (weeks one and two), to fool ourselves into thinking we might be in love (weeks three, four and five), then have our first argument (week six), at which point I'd bail out.

My behaviour infuriated Izzy, who harangued me for the way I treated women. Especially when I ended a relationship because 'she likes me too much', 'she likes me too little' or my all-time favourite, 'she's got two Blur albums!' when the truth was I'd got bored.

Over two post-college years we'd meet up regularly to bitch about our separate love-lives in spectacular fashion. Usually this would involve Izzy calling me up to ask my advice about whichever guy she was seeing at the time. When she'd get bored of telling me about her love life, even though I would want to talk about music, she'd drag out whichever nightmare of a relationship I was in and tell me in no uncertain way why I was acting like a pig.

On the night we got together – 14 July 1995 – we had just such a session, which took place in the flat she shared with Stella and Jenny in Ladbroke Grove. I was freelancing for *Below Zero* and Izzy had just graduated from junior to senior writer on *Femme*. I'd just split up with a beautiful girl called Katrina because I felt she was getting a little too serious. Izzy said to me – and I remember this clearly, 'What are you afraid of?' And I said, nothing. 'So why do you act like such a . . .' she began, but she didn't finish her sentence because I kissed her and that was how it all began. That kiss led to another, and another, and with each one I realised I wasn't feckless: I'd just never found the right woman until that moment.

days

After that Saturday afternoon with Nicola something changes in our relationship. The strangeness disappears. We'll talk regularly on the phone and not just to arrange the next time to meet up – she'll actually call me when she's got nothing much to say. We'll have a disjointed, awkward conversation, where I'll ask her about her day and then she'll ask me about mine and then she'll tell me after five minutes that she's got to go because her mum has got her tea or something and I'll think to myself, Why did she phone? And then I'll realise that in her world when you like someone, you talk to them even when you haven't got much to say – in fact, you talk to them *especially* when you haven't got anything to say. Because the call isn't about communication as much as checking and double checking that your relationship is fine. Nicola has taken it upon herself to be caretaker of our budding friendship. She's made it her job to reassure me – a thirty-two-year-old man – that everything's okay. It feels like we both have a new, urgent mission to get to know each other before anything goes wrong. Over the following month we meet up once a week.

Week 1
Day: Tuesday late afternoon
My alibi: Meeting old college friend for a drink

Her alibi: Going to a friend's house after school
Place: the Prince Charles Cinema, Leicester Square

The Prince Charles shows a combination of arty films and films that were on release ages ago. At the moment there's a teen comedy season on so Nicola and I see *Ten Things I Hate About You*. We both like the film, but for different reasons. Nicola likes it because it's romantic and she fancies the male lead, Heath Ledger. I like it because it's stupid and makes no sense.

I tell Nicola that the film is based on Shakespeare's *The Taming of the Shrew* and that I studied the play at university. I can see she wants to believe me but she's sceptical. Her face is saying, 'How can a film as good as this have been written by boring old Shakespeare?' I don't argue. When we finish dissecting the film the conversation turns to our all-time favourite movies. Nicola's are *Titanic, American Pie, Men in Black, Austin Powers – The Spy Who Shagged Me* and now *Ten Things I Hate About You*. Mine are *The Terminator, Le Apartment, La Haine, Angels With Dirty Faces* and *Das Boot*. I think we're both a little disappointed that there isn't more crossover so I promise Nicola I'll get *American Pie* out on video and she tells me she'll ask her mum to see if the video shop has *Angels With Dirty Faces*.

Week 2
Day: Saturday midday
My alibi: None needed, Izzy is on a fashion freebie trip to Milan for two days
Her alibi: Drama club
Place: Yo Sushi! Poland Street, Soho

I tell Nicola I'm fed up with eating in burger places and that we need to branch out. The second we get to the sushi bar I can see she's really impressed. She likes the robot that goes around the restaurant carrying drinks and the conveyor belt on which the food goes round. Her least favourite thing is the sushi. I try to explain to her that eating raw fish is a healthy thing to do but she's not convinced, and when I give her a bite of a simple tuna roll she can't bring herself to swallow it.

Fortunately they have a number of non-raw-fish dishes and Nicola tucks into several plates of chicken and cabbage dumplings and a can of Coke. She asks me if I'm disappointed in her because she doesn't like sushi and I laugh and tell her, of course not, I'm disappointed in her because I got *American Pie* out on DVD and it was crap. She laughs and tells me that her mum's video shop didn't have *Angels With Dirty Faces* and she was glad because her mum told her it was in black and white and then she pulls a face as if to say, 'Can you believe it?'

Week 3

Day: Friday afternoon
My alibi: None needed – I take the afternoon off work
Her alibi: She's sprained her wrist falling down some stairs at school and convinces me it's okay to wag her games lesson because she wouldn't be doing anything anyway.
Place: South Bank, on a couple of benches outside the NFT facing the Thames

It's my suggestion that we come here as this is one of my favourite places: it reminds me of what a great-looking city London can be. The wind when it blows is quite cutting but the sun's out. Nicola tells me she's been here before with her mum to buy books from one of the many second-hand stalls. We sit watching people walk by for ages and Nicola spots a well-known TV soap actress with her dog. We talk about what it would be like to be her and decide we wouldn't fancy it. We have a late lunch of several chocolate bars and a shared can of Lilt. As we eat I ask Nicola how it felt to know she had a dad but not where he was or what he was like. She says she used to have dreams about me where I'd turn up out of the blue and live with them. She says she always imagined I did a regular job like her friends' dads. I ask her what she thought I'd be like as a person and she laughs and says she can't remember. I ask her to tell me three things I don't know about her and she thinks then says okay. The first thing she tells me is that when she was small she had a yellow blanket she carried around with her. I ask if she's still got it and she rolls her eyes and says no. She laughs when she tells me that sometimes she pretends she's a singer on *Top of the Pops*. I tell her I used to do that too. I ask her what's her favourite record to sing along to and she responds with a few lines of a Mariah Carey ballad that neither of us knows the name of. The last thing she tells me is that she's never kissed a boy properly though she's told her friends she has. She says she's had the chance but she hasn't really liked the boys who have wanted to kiss her. Moments later she tells me that she kissed a couple of boys last year at a party but that was without tongues and because of that, she explains, they don't really count as proper kisses.

Week 4
Day: Tuesday
My alibi: Spending the day in the library finding information on university courses
Her alibi: School closed because of burst water-pipes and she's told her mum she'll spend the day at a friend's house
Place: My car, listening to music, driving round north London aimlessly

We're driving along the Holloway Road when Nicola tells me that she wants to ask my advice. I ask her what about and she tells me about boys. For one desperate moment I think she's going to ask me about sex, but she spots the look of horror on my face and laughs a really cheeky wide-eyed laugh. 'You thought I was going to talk about *doing it*, didn't you?' she says grinning. I nod and she tells me that she's already had 'the talk' with her mum and that they've done sex education at school. She tells me that she's going to wait until she gets married and I ask her if that isn't a bit of an old fashioned thing to do. She shrugs dismissively and tells me about a girl called Petra Wilson who 'did it' last week with a boy she met at a party; Sophie Walker who's two years above Nicola has apparently had to take the morning-after pill twice this term; and Katie Snell in year eleven is pregnant and not only is the dad fourteen, 'he's *really, really ugly*', too. 'All the boys at school talk about doing it like it's *nothing*,' says Nicola. 'And some of the girls talk about it like that too. But it's not nothing, is it? How can something that can make babies be nothing? It doesn't even make sense. It's not nothing so I don't see why every-one's acting like it is. That's just stupid.' I tell her that she's made a good point and ask her if she's been influenced by

Britney Spears. She rolls her eyes and says no it's something she decided herself. She tells me about a boy she likes at school, called Brendan Casey, and tells me how she semi-stalks him sometimes. She asks me how she can get him to like her. I tell her just to be herself. She asks what he might be thinking about and I tell her that when I was that age I used to think about football and dying young. She asks me if that's what every teenage boy thinks about. 'I think it's just me,' I say. 'I was quite a morbid child, really.'

quiet

It's relatively easy for me to disappear unnoticed because Izzy is spending a lot of time at work preparing for her interview. She's coming home tired and going to work tired and I try my best to be supportive. I don't allow myself to feel guilty about lying to her because I can't begin to contemplate the enormity of what is happening in my life. Nicola, too, is happy to enjoy our time together although it must be hard for her to keep such a huge secret from her mum. 'It's too important to tell,' she tells me, when we're talking on the phone. 'I just have to keep it all in.'

Nicola is awakening new feelings in me. Everything she says interests me and I never cease to be amazed at how beautiful she is. I want to protect her and lay the world at her feet. In my head I create all manner of glamorous images of us culled from celluloid: Ryan and Tatum O'Neal in *Paper Moon*, Jean Reno and Natalie Portman in *Leon*, John Wayne and Kim Darby in *True Grit* – the adult male with the adolescent sidekick wise-cracking their way through a life of adventure. I don't know what any of this will mean for Izzy. But I do know that Nicola has changed my life beyond recognition.

house

It's parents' evening at Nicola's mum's school and Caitlin's told Nicola she wouldn't be home until nine. I know that all it would take is for her to come home early and I'll probably end up hiding in a wardrobe or on a balcony. But Nicola pleads with me to come and I relent. I want to see her home. I want to know about this part of her life.

I reach the Victorian terrace where she and her mum live at six thirty and she opens the door wearing jeans and a dark blue hooded top several sizes too big for her. I can't help but smile.

'What?' she says defensively.

'I was just looking at your top. Isn't it a bit big?'

'It's the fashion,' she replies.

Laughing, I follow her into the hallway and close the door behind me. It feels odd being here, as if I'm an intruder.

'Do you want a drink?' asks Nicola.

'No, thanks.'

'I'm having a cup of tea so . . .'

'Nah, I'm all right.'

She looks a bit put out. I think she'd been looking forward to playing host.

'Are you hungry?' she asks.

'Yeah,' I lie. 'Just a little bit. What have you got?'

'I can make you toast or beans and toast or egg on toast or cheese on toast.'

'You're very handy with the toaster, aren't you?'

She laughs. 'I can open a packet of biscuits too.'

'Biscuits sound okay. I'll have whatever you've got.'

'Mum went shopping on Monday and got some really nice ones. They were German or Belgian or something but we ate them all so we've only got the rubbish ones left. Do you like Digestives?'

'Digestives are fine.'

She looks up at me, her face is slightly pensive. 'They're not the chocolate ones.'

'Plain Digestives are fine by me.'

She lets out a sigh of relief. 'Have a sit-down in the living room,' she points to a door to the left of me, 'and I'll bring them through in a minute.'

personality

I go into the room as instructed and look around me. There's a TV and video in a corner, a large sofa along one wall and two armchairs. There are shelves in the two alcoves lined with hundreds of books, a piano with a violin case next to it and, opposite, French windows that look out on to a minuscule garden. I smile as I realise I'm double-checking my escape route.

Pictures of Nicola are scattered around the room, on the walls and on the mantelpiece, and I study them: Nicola as a baby lying in her cot; Nicola as a toddler in a bright blue dress; a slightly younger version of the Nicola I know with her mum and, at a guess, her grandparents in a garden; another of her on the beach holding a bucket and spade – she must have been six or seven in that one. Finally there's an official school picture of her at nine or ten in her uniform. Seeing these photos reminds me of when she came to the flat and looked through mine. I feel what she must have felt then: they represent a world of exclusion.

'Grub's up,' says Nicola, coming into the living room. She's holding out a plate of Digestive biscuits. The fact that she's bothered to present them out of the packet speaks volumes about her. But then again, I suspect the fact that I've noticed speaks volumes about me. Really, this girl can do no wrong.

I take one and she puts the plate on a side table next to her mug of tea. 'This is my house,' she says, gesturing to the room proudly. 'Do you like it?'

'Yeah, it's nice.'

'It's not as posh as your flat. I don't mean that horribly I just mean that, well, we haven't got as many nice things as you have but I like it all the same.'

'It's not what you've got, it's what you do with it. This place looks great.'

'Mum and I decorated in here last summer. Well, I helped her choose the colour for the walls – it's called Country Apple Blossom – and she did most of the work along with my uncles. I did paint my bedroom, though.'

'Really?'

'Yeah, do you want to see it?'

She's so excited that I can't say no, even though I'm wondering about my emergency escape route from upstairs. 'Go on, then,' I tell her. 'Show me your room.'

She grabs her tea and a handful of biscuits and leads me up the stairs. 'This is my room,' she says pointing to a large, flat multi-coloured foam rubber sign on the door that says, 'Nicola's room'.

'Really?'

She nudges me with her elbow. 'Yeah, really.'

Although she tells me she's painted her walls in 'Corn-flower Blue' I can hardly tell because there are so many posters. She gives me a guided tour of some of the highlights of her gallery of popular recording artists, which include NSync (because she likes their music), Steps (because she likes their dance moves), Robbie Williams (because she wants to marry him), Westlife (because she fancies two of them), Usher (because she likes the music and fancies him),

230

Mel C and Geri Halliwell (because they cover up a spot where she's torn the wallpaper), Limp Bizkit's Fred Durst (because Keisha likes them although Nicola finds them a bit loud), S Club 7 (because she likes their songs), Kurt Cobain from Nirvana (because she'd seen Brendan one Saturday morning on Wood Green High Street wearing the Nirvana stoned smiley T-shirt), Britney Spears (because the picture had come free in a newspaper) and Eminem (because Keisha had the album on tape and he swore a lot on it, which amused her greatly).

'My room's cool, isn't it?'

'Yeah, it is. I didn't realise you had this many posters. I'll have a look what's knocking about in the *Teen Scene* office because we've got loads, I'm sure.'

Nicola pulled a face. 'I don't put just anything on my walls, you know. I've got some taste.' She continued the tour, pointing out her favourite books, her favourite CDs, her favourite incense sticks and even her favourite cuddly toys – the only things in the room that remind me she's still only a kid. Only a few years ago these toys had been her favourite things in the world and even now it's obvious they still hold a strong attachment.

'I used to have hundreds,' she explains, pointing to the collection of soft toys that reside on the floor in the corner of her room by her portable CD player. 'But I gave a lot of them away because they were a bit babyish.'

'So what are these?'

'These are my favourites.' She points them out one by one. 'This one,' she waves to a teddy bear the size of a four-year-old, 'is Patrick. I've had him since I was really small. My gran bought him for me.' She points to his nose. 'Can you see how that patch of fur is worn?' I nod. 'I did that. Mum said I used to rub his nose to get to sleep. I did it every night for years.

'This one,' she points to a furry white gorilla, with a red face and beady eyes '. . . is Harry and he does this—' He has springs attached to his hands and a string attached to his head so that when he bounces up and down his arms wave in the air. 'Mum bought me him for my birthday when I was ten because I was really into wildlife and said I wanted a pet monkey.'

'Who's this one?' I ask, indicating a furry tiger. Its mane is slightly matted, its fur is worn: all in all it has seen better days.

'This one,' says Nicola. 'He's one of my favourites. I've had him since I was eight. You're going to think that I've made this up but his name is Dave.'

'Dave?' I repeat.

'I named him after you,' she says and smiles. 'I always knew you two would meet one day.'

whole

It's a few days later and I'm on my way home from work when I bump into Sean, an old friend of Izzy's who lives in Glasgow. Sean's wife Amy had a baby daughter, Amber, last summer just before Izzy got pregnant and I'm not even sure whether he knows what happened. Sean is in London for the day on business and on his way to a meeting with a client. He asks after Izzy and I ask about Amy and Amber. He says Amy's fine, then spends a good ten minutes telling me about Amber: her sleeping patterns, her favourite foods, how her ability to grab his fingers shows that she's destined to be a genius. The list is endless.

I hate myself for it but I feel jealous – not because he's got a baby and I haven't but because he's telling me how wonderful *his* daughter is but I can't do the same for mine. I want to tell this man, who isn't even a close friend, all the things that make me proud of Nicola: how pretty she is, how good she is at art, how her teachers say that some of her Key Stage 3 work is so good she might get a gold certificate. But I have to bite my tongue. He concludes, 'You and Izzy really should have kids. It really will change your world.' I kind of laugh and half smile because I know he doesn't mean anything by it. But his careless comment really stings and I look at my watch quite deliberately because I don't want to stand here with him any more. Before we go our

separate ways he makes me promise that Izzy and I will
come and spend the weekend with him, Amy and Amber,
and the first thing I do after leaving him is get out my mobile
and call Nicola.

plan

'Hello?' says Nicola brightly.

'It's me,' I say. 'Where are you?'

'Hi, Dave,' she says. 'I'm in my room listening to music. How are you?'

'I'm fine. Really good. What about yourself?'

'I'm a bit bored. I've got loads of homework and I just feel too tired to do any of it. I'd go to sleep but Mum said she'd be checking to make sure I did it. She was joking but you can't be too careful with my mum.'

'I was just wondering what you fancied doing next time we meet?'

'I don't mind, really. I don't think I'll ever get bored of driving around in the car.'

I laugh. 'I think I am.'

'How about a compromise? We could drive around in the car and listen to a CD of *your* choice. You're always telling me about those millions of albums you've got that I should listen to. Here's your chance.'

'I tried that one, don't you remember? I played you my favourite REM album *Automatic for the People* and you said it was "totally rubbish and boring".'

'But it *was* totally rubbish and boring,' Nicola giggles.

'That's as may be but it doesn't matter anyway because

I've got a plan. Maybe . . . we could go shopping for your birthday.'

I've been thinking about asking her if she wants to do this all week. I don't like to ask whether she and her mum have enough money but it's clear that it isn't overflowing. I want to do something for her – anything, really – and this is all I can think of.

'We can't go shopping.' She sighs. 'It's not my birthday until May and, anyway, how would I explain anything I get to Mum?'

'Two good points you've made there and I've thought about both already. How about we do this? We don't go ordinary shopping, we go window-shopping. You choose what you want right now and when it's your birthday we'll come back and get them. What do you reckon?'

'It sounds great. But what about you?'

'What about me?'

'What about all the presents I should've bought you? Birthdays, Christmas and Father's Day?'

Father's Day hasn't been a day to which I've ever paid much attention. I've always believed it's been created by the greetings-card industry to boost trade. Mother's Day is the real thing. The one you don't dare to forget. Father's Day is a cheap imitation, an excuse for your dad to do what he does every Sunday – sit in his favourite armchair and watch rubbish TV, but in cartoon socks and a bad-taste tie. But as I listen to Nicola talk I suddenly believe in Father's Day. I want my bad taste ties and cartoon socks.

'I don't need any presents,' I tell her. 'I'm fine, honest.'

'If we're going to do this,' she says adamantly, 'I want to get you something too. And I won't go unless you let me.'

imagine

Nicola and I meet as arranged and travel into the West End by tube. I've told Jenny I'm going to be working from home all day. Nicola has told her mum she's going to Keisha's house and she told Keisha to cover for her because she was secretly meeting a boy. Between us we have created a complicated web of necessary lies – which we were becoming exceptionally gifted in delivering.

The afternoon is a revelation to me of the inner workings of the teenage mind. Nicola takes shopping for gifts seriously: she drags me into accessory shops, sportswear shops, mobile-phone shops and even a sandwich shop before attending to her real delight, clothes shops. Her favourite is a large store near Oxford Circus. Here she tries on skirts, most of which look exactly the same to me but which I'm told have different detailing. She tries on tops, hats, shoes and all the time with a look of complete contentment.

As she picks through the rails, and throws them back with a dismissive huff if they're not quite what she wants, I look around me. There are girls with nose-rings, girls with purple hair, tall girls, short girls, girls with skateboards, hard girls, posh girls, rude girls, and girls whose jeans are so baggy I can't understand why they don't fall over – there are girls of every variety and yet they all have one thing in common:

they're wearing clothes that make them look older than their years. With some, it's only when I look carefully that I can see their baby features and the youth they're trying to hide. Even Nicola is at it. At one point she tries on a pair of hipster jeans and a crop top and asks my opinion. She could easily have passed for seventeen, and this saddens me because I don't want her to grow up so fast when I've only known her such a short time.

taste

In contrast to the earlier part of the window-shopping expedition my side of things is far more sedate. I take Nicola to the rock and pop section of the Oxford Street HMV Megastore, locate the M section and, within seconds, find what I'm looking for and show it to her.

'Van Morrison, *Astral Weeks*,' she says, reading the cover. 'Who's he?'

'Just a bloke who can sing a bit.'

'It's only six pounds ninety-nine,' she says. 'Is that all that you want?'

'The truth is I can't stand Van Morrison,' I tell her. 'It's nothing personal but I absolutely hate him and detest everything he's ever recorded.'

Nicola laughs.

'But Izzy – and this *is* her only flaw – likes him. At least, the early stuff. She had *Astral Weeks* on tape when I first met her and she played it all the time. She drove me up the wall with it and then she eventually wore it out or lost it and never got round to replacing it because she doesn't care much about music, these days, but every now and again I see her mooching about the flat and I think that if she had her *Astral Weeks* tape she'd be listening to it. I told her to buy another copy but she always forgets and I've thought about doing it myself but I never do.'

'Why?'

'I know this is going to sound pathetic but it's difficult to spend money on music I loathe.'

Nicola laughs. 'Oh, come on, Dave. You can't even do it for Izzy?'

'No. One year she asked me to buy *Abba's Greatest Hits* for her mum and I couldn't do that either.'

'Why?'

'Because it's Abba, isn't it? I would've gladly bought her mum *Blondie's Greatest Hits* or a five-CD boxed set of Nick Drake or even Madonna, *The Immaculate Collection*. But not Abba. I couldn't stand the thought of my hard-earned cash winging its way to Sweden to keep Benny and Bjorn in the luxury to which they have become accustomed. That's where you come in. You can buy *Astral Weeks* for me with *your* money and I can give it to Izzy, and I won't feel like I'm contributing to "The keep Van Morrison in even bigger Irish mansions fund".'

Nicola punches me on the arm. 'You're so annoying sometimes.'

It's an action that if I'd been a regular grumpy father teasing his regular moody teenage daughter, wouldn't have stood out at all from any of the actions of the hundreds of people in the store. But as I turn towards her I catch a glimpse of someone on the other side of the CD display rack. It's Izzy. I'm less than a few feet from her but she hasn't seen me. She's nearly close enough to touch yet she might as well be a million miles away. For a second I hope she sees me. In a way I wish that, right now, she would stare at Nicola, then at me, and make the connection. Then the deceit could stop. Then everything would be out in the open. I wouldn't have to find the courage to tell her about Nicola.

Life isn't that easy, of course. The choice is mine. All I have to do is speak and she'll recognise my voice and look up and it will all be over. *All* I have to do is speak. I stand frozen in time trying with all my might to do the right thing. But the right thing won't come. I duck down to the floor and pull Nicola with me then break into the coldest of cold sweats.

'What is it?' asks Nicola.

'It's Izzy,' I whisper. 'She's here. You've got to go. I'll call you later, I promise.'

Nicola heads for the exit without looking back once. Watching her walk away is the saddest thing in the world. I feel like I'm letting her down, as if I'm ashamed of her. I feel disloyal, but there's nothing I can do about it. I wait until I can no longer see her then prepare myself for what I have to do next. I decide there are two options: the first is to walk out of the store without looking back; the second is to make myself known to Izzy. It seems wrong to walk away from her, it seems like the easy way out again and I don't deserve an easy way out. So I take a deep breath, stand up and, as if nothing has happened, continue browsing through the CDs. In a matter of seconds she calls to me.

'Hey, babe,' I say, looking up. 'What are you doing here?'

She walks over and greets me with a kiss. 'I was just looking for a present for Stella. She seems a bit down so I thought I'd get something to cheer her up. What are you doing here?'

'I fancied a change of scenery and, well, you know me . . . I find it hard to walk past any record shop without having a look. Anyway, never mind me, what were you going to get Stella?'

'I don't know, really. Something she can chill out to. She's a bit stressed at work at the moment. Any recommendations?'

'Hundreds.'

Izzy nods thoughtfully then glances down at my hand. I realise for the first time that I am still holding the Van Morrison CD. 'Is that *Astral Weeks* I see before me?'

'Yeah, it is.'

'But you hate that album,' says Izzy incredulously. 'You once called it "the worst load of pseudo-soul-folk-blues-rock" you'd ever heard and said it was "a shocking waste of a pair of ears to listen to such rubbish".'

'I said that?'

'You know you did.'

'Well, a man can change his mind, can't he? Do you want it? I'm prepared to compromise yet more of my long-held principles just for you.'

'I'd love it.'

'Well, I'll get it for you. And what about Stella's present?'

'What do you suggest?'

I take her over to W in the rock-and-pop section and show her the cover of Kathryn Williams's *Little Black Numbers*. 'Get her this.'

'The girl who does our music page was raving about her ages ago.'

'It's the whole girl-with-a-good-voice-acoustic-guitar-and-a-string-of-broken-relationships thing. But it's done very well. Stella will love it.'

'Okay,' says Izzy. 'I'll get it.'

I take it over to the till, pay for it with Van Morrison, hand both CDs to her and she kisses me. 'What time will you be back at the flat?' she asks.

'The usual. What about you?'

She looks at her watch. 'I'll try not to be too late.' She kisses me again. 'I'd better get off.' She turns to walk away, then stops. 'Oh . . . I've completely forgotten to tell you the good news.'

'What good news?'

'You know Adele? As in Adele and Damian?' They are old university friends of Izzy's who are pregnant. They aren't division-one friends – more the kind that Izzy keeps in touch with in bimonthly phone calls which always conclude with the phrase 'we really should meet up sometime.'

'Adele had the baby last Saturday,' she says. 'A little girl. Madeleine Katriona Mason. Eight pounds six ounces.'

I watch her face for any signs of upset at this news. Neither of us has mentioned the miscarriage in such a long while that it feels like it never happened and yet when she tells me about Adele and Damian's baby I'm still a little uncomfortable. Izzy however appears to be completely fine.

'How's Adele?' I ask.

'Exhausted. It was quite a long labour, apparently. Eighteen hours. Her contractions kicked in early in the morning when they were in bed and then her waters broke and it was all systems go . . . Damian cried at the birth.'

'Well, I suppose you would, wouldn't you? It's an emotional thing.' As the words leave my lips I'm struck by their pertinence. How would *I* know that?

'They want us to go round and see them, if we can,' says Izzy. 'Tomorrow after work. Do you fancy it?'

'Do you?'

She nods.

'Okay, then,' I reply. 'We'll go.'

mini

We've just arrived at Damian and Adele's flat in a converted Victorian three-storey house in Finsbury Park laden with gifts: a huge array of aromatherapy stuff for Adele; a bottle of brandy for Damian; and a baby gym from the Early Learning Centre for Madeleine. I press the buzzer and we wait. Moments later Damian appears. He's usually impeccably dressed in designer clothes but this evening he's in an old pair of jeans, a Moschino T-shirt stained with what I suspect is baby sick, and bare feet. A few days' growth covers his normally clean-shaven chin. He welcomes us in and on the way up to the flat he tells us about how much sleep he's not been having. 'She woke eight times last night . . . and the night before she didn't go to sleep at all . . . and the night before that she slept three hours . . . and then the night before that . . .' we reach the front door and he opens it '. . . I'm not sure what happened. I don't know what day it is now.' He scratches his stomach absentmindedly. 'So how are you guys?' he asks, and leads us to the living room.

'We're fine,' says Izzy. 'Work's good for me.'

'And work's fine for me,' I add.

Damian smiles. 'Adele was saying you've left rock journalism to work in teen mags or something. How's that going? It sounds like fun.'

'Yeah, it is. Not as easy as it sounds but it's a good laugh.

Anyway, never mind what's going on with me and Izzy, we've come to see *you*. How are you, new Dad?' I shake his hand. 'Congratulations once again.'

'I didn't really do much except get in the way. Here,' he says, pointing to the sofa, 'you two take a seat and I'll make you both a drink. Adele's just trying to make herself look presentable – her words not mine.'

He disappears and leaves Izzy and me to look around us. I can't remember the last time I was in their flat but I'm sure they've done a lot of decorating in here. The room is pale green when before it was yellow, the old gas fire has been ripped out and replaced with an open hearth, and piled up in a corner are several half-unwrapped presents. I can make out a few soft toys and a large box with the Fisher Price logo. Lying across the back of a small armchair is a pair of lime-green dungarees. I recognise them immediately as the ones from babyGap. I walk over to them and pick them up, holding them up to the light like I'd done that day in the shop.

'They're cute,' says Izzy. 'But aren't they a little big for a newborn?'

'You're right,' says Damian, coming back into the room. 'My brother Gareth bought them. He's only nineteen and it didn't occur to him to read the size label, which says "twenty-four to thirty-six months". Still, she'll grow into them.'

We all look at the dungarees. But only one of us has to leave the room because of them. I announce that I need to use the loo, and when I return I'm back to normal, composed, the moment of shakiness gone.

me

'So, how does it feel to be a dad, then?'

'Great,' says Damian. 'Just as good as I thought it would. It's so weird now she's here. You know, it was like this huge build-up and then she was kicking and screaming in the real world. I still can't believe it, really.'

'That's it now, Damian,' says Izzy cheerfully. 'You're a dad for life. You've got it all to look forward to, especially with a girl. Before you know it she'll be a teenager, sulking in her room, fancying spotty teenage boys and playing music really loud.'

'I don't mind the loud music, it's the boys I worry about. I've already told Adele that Maddy won't be having anything to do with boys until she's well into her twenties . . . or, even better, her thirties.'

'As the only person in the room who used to be a teenage girl,' says Izzy, 'let me tell you for a fact, dear Damian, that there's not a dad in the world who can stop a teenage girl when it comes to boys so you might as well get used to the idea now. I'm not even sure that my dad was too keen on Dave to begin with but he warmed to him eventually.'

'Your dad thought I was really cool until you told him we were moving in together,' I say, laughing.

'It's true,' says Izzy. 'He even warned me that by shacking up with Dave I'd ruin my chances of him ever making an honest woman of me. He said, ''Why would he buy the cow when he can get the milk for free?'''

Adele enters the room holding the baby. She looks even more shattered than Damian and she's wearing a T-shirt, a towelling dressing-gown, tracksuit bottoms, and *Simpsons* socks. This casual look, like her husband's, is something of a new departure given that the last time I saw her – over a year ago when the four of us had gone out for dinner – she was wearing a very sexy black sleeveless Prada dress and spent the whole evening worrying about her hair.

Damian takes the baby from her, and Izzy and I give her a hug. Maddy snuffles in Damian's arms.

'Do you want to hold her?' he asks.

Izzy nods and takes her carefully from Damian's outstretched arms. I have to leave the room once more under the pretext of getting a glass of water.

date

It's eight thirty p.m. and Izzy and I are on the Northern Line travelling home. We are in the end carriage which is virtually empty. Izzy has been quiet for most of the journey, content to stare out into the darkness or read the small adverts above the windows; only occasionally do we speak and when we do our voices are hidden from the world at large underneath the rhythm of the train on the track.

'Do you know what March the nineteenth was?'

'No?' I reply.

'It was the day our baby would've been born if it had gone full term,' she says, matter-of-factly. There is no sadness at all in her voice. 'I worked it out months ago.'

'You shouldn't think like that.'

'I know.' She looks at me, her eyes searching. 'Do you think about it, though?'

I hold her gaze. 'Yes, of course.'

'I didn't think you did.'

'Why?'

'You don't talk about it any more. I know I didn't like talking about it either. But at least when it happened I could tell you wanted to talk. But now . . . nothing. It's like it never happened.'

'Would you like me to talk about it more?'

She focuses on the carriage window opposite. 'No . . . I

248

just wondered, that's all. Do you still want kids one day?'

I nod, and wonder where this is going.

'I do, too,' she says. 'What do you think it would be like to try for a baby?'

'Do you want to?'

She shakes her head. 'No. I'm just thinking aloud. I've been thinking about what it would be like to have sex with the intention of getting pregnant and whether it would be any different from, you know, what we're used to.'

'I'm pretty sure it would be the same.'

She takes my hand and squeezes it, then lets go. 'Are you sure? Of all the couples we know who have kids they all say they didn't plan them.'

'I had the same thought a while ago.'

'But don't you think that's strange? Why don't people want kids any more?'

'They do. People have kids all the time. Maybe it's just the type of people we know. A lot of our friends have got small flats or live in dodgy areas, or maybe they feel like they haven't sorted out their careers.'

'I suppose you're right. Perhaps we're all waiting for the perfect time . . . I think it's quite scary, though.'

'What?'

'Saying that you actually *want* to get pregnant. I mean they even call it *trying* for a baby. Some people just say, "We're trying," and everyone knows what they're talking about. *Trying*. The thing is if you try you can fail, but if you're just intentionally forgetful about contraception there's no failure if nothing happens, is there? In fact for most of our twenties it's the other way round: you're lucky, you had sex without contraception and you didn't get pregnant. Think about it: no more fiddling around with foil

249

wrappers; no more stuffing yourself full of dodgy chemicals; you can be free to make love without consequences. That's why I think most people don't admit to trying because that way they can't fail. But for the people who try and try and try and then fail; for the people who want and desire a child more than anything in the world; for the people on their third or fourth round of IVF treatment: for these people sex without consequences is the worst thing in the world, isn't it?'

She looks at me as if she's waiting for an answer. But I'm thinking about Nicola and the short conversation we'd had about sex. *'Everyone's trying to make out like sex isn't a big deal but it is.'* It's only now that I see that she's right. You can call it 'casual', you can call it 'safe' but it always has the potential to turn your world upside down.

I look at Izzy and respond to her question. 'Yeah, you're right. Sex without consequences can be the worst thing in the world.'

'You see,' she says, 'this is what I don't understand. Who in their right mind would want to join them voluntarily? I couldn't do that yet. I don't think I could face it, no matter how much I wanted a child.'

'But you're talking as if failure's a foregone conclusion.'

'I am?'

'Yeah.'

'I don't mean to. All I'm saying is that, right now, I don't have what it takes to face failure. Do you?'

'I don't know. I think it's one of those things where you often don't know what you can do until you do it, isn't it?'

'Do you think I'm a coward?'

'No,' I say. 'Of course not.'

'You can, you know. You can say what you want.'

'I know I can say what I want. And *no*, I don't think you're a coward. What happened was sad and horrible. Anyone would be a bit apprehensive.'

'I think I am a coward,' she says, so quietly that I can only just make out what she is saying above the sound of the train, and then, without looking at me, she says, 'Are you having an affair?'

'A what?'

'An affair. It's a simple question, Dave. Are you having an affair?'

It's as if I've just been roused from a dream. I turn to face her, my whole body rigid with fear. 'No, of course not.' I speak louder than necessary. The couple sitting closest to us in the carriage look at me and then look away. I lower my voice immediately. 'I don't understand what would make you ask me such a thing.'

This is a lie, of course. I understood precisely why she was asking me this question. I have thought dozens of times of the similarities between my situation with Nicola and an affair: the lies, the sneaking around and, most of all, the fact that I have fallen hopelessly in love with someone other than my wife. It *is* an affair – just not a romantic one. But it will be equally catastrophic and devastating when the truth gets out.

I watch the tears well up in Izzy's eyes and roll down her face. 'I'm sorry,' she says. 'Just ignore me. I shouldn't have said anything.'

'You should, if it's what you believe. You must know I'd never do anything like that.'

'I do.'

'Then why did you ask?'

'Because things don't feel right between us. They haven't

felt right for a long time. I don't know. I'm just being paranoid.'

'But why? Why would you think that of all things? I love you. I'd never do that.'

'It's my fault. I've been neglecting you. I feel like I'm working all the time. I don't deserve you.'

If there's ever been a moment when I should tell Izzy everything, this is it, but I don't have that strength of character. 'Don't say that, babe. Don't ever say that.'

'Why shouldn't I? It's true. We barely see each other any more, now that I'm so busy at work. And when we do see each other I'm always tired or in a bad mood or whatever. Love doesn't work like that.'

'Like what?'

'Like there's an endless supply of it that you can keep taking out time and time again. I feel like I'm taking from our relationship without putting anything in. I feel like I'm taking you for granted. What happens if we run out of love?'

I look at her and, for a second, she reminds me of Nicola on the day I first met her: she looks so lost, so badly in need of looking after that my heart goes out to her.

When we reach home that night she's looking more tired than ever so I suggest we go away for the weekend but she says she doesn't want to run away any more. She wants to stay at home. I say okay, but only as long as we make it special.

I turn off both our mobile phones, unplug the land line, the fax, the computer, the TV and video, close the curtains and we go to bed, determined to shut out the world. We don't leave the flat all weekend. Instead we talk and sleep and look after each other like a latter-day John and

Yoko. We might not have brought peace to the world but by the time Monday morning comes round it seems a nicer place.

aged

To: izzy.harding@bdp.co.uk
From: dave_atch01@hotmail.com
Subject: Dave's Male Man column

Dear Izzy,
Here's my new column. Let me know if you need me to make any changes.
Hope it makes you smile.

love

Dave XXX

PS I'll sort out dinner tonight. I'm going to make my very special Harding heavy-on-the-garlic lasagne.

Getting Older
The fear of getting older has for a long time been considered an oestrogen owner's concern. It was women who worried about the ticking of their biological clocks, who were 'creative' when talking about their age, and worried about being left on the shelf. Men, like fine wine and good cheeses, were supposed to get better as they aged. The getting-older man was supposed to have

made it. He'd be like Sean Connery in *Goldfinger*: cool, accomplished and self-assured. Women would find him irresistible, twentysomething men would find him intimidating, and everyone would be envious of him. That was how it was supposed to be. That was how I wanted it to be. But now, at thirty-two, I too am getting older and I'm not so sure.

So what happened? A number of things. First the previous generation who should've been turning forty in the potting shed of their garden, surrounded by small children and tax returns, have decided to grow old disgracefully. This group, composed of confirmed bachelors, childless divorcees and the serially monogamous, are behaving like twentysomethings. This is not only against the natural order of things but quite upsetting too. Most getting-older men I know are in relationships and like it that way. The thought that one day all the security that our partners offer could be taken away, leaving us to relive our twenties, is truly terrifying. So now we getting-older men not only have to worry about finding and keeping Ms Right, we have to face the prospect that failure will result in us spending the next decade driving sports cars, dating teenage girls and wearing leather trousers. A nice idea in theory but cheesy in practice.

Second, now that for women weekly sessions with a therapist, a yogi *and* a *tai chi* master are the norm we men, having so little to complain about in our relatively uncomplicated lives, have decided to join the party. Now we worry about our weight, we worry about our love lives, and we worry about worrying. Getting-older women, on the other hand, are having a great time. The media have created a new buzz word 'middle youth' to describe them. These women are more likely than men to instigate divorce proceedings if their partners aren't up to scratch and, to top it all, they're reaching their sexual peak just as the average guy is slipping into something of a trough.

My greatest fears about getting older focus on achievements in life. The first of which being the list: What I can no longer achieve that I used to be able to achieve very easily. The edited highlights alone make for grim reading. I can no longer beat my mate Lee in a sprint (he is twenty-five, skinny and unhealthy, and until recently I'd always beaten him). I can no longer stay up all night (I went to a glamorous club in central London a while ago and fell asleep while young girls in fluffy push-up bras danced around me – it was only ten past midnight). I can no longer make love all night. (Thankfully my wife and I are always so tired from work that she probably wouldn't want to even if I could.)

Of course life isn't going to come to a halt just because I'm getting older. I know I'm not going to swap my Air Max trainers for a pair of slippers, but what I fear, and what I suspect all men fear, is change, no matter how gradual, no matter how subtle. But change is a fact of life, so you can either fight it and fail or, like Millennium Woman, accept it and grow. Alternatively, like most things in life there is a middle ground: while I might rage against the dying of my Nikes there's a part of me that's secretly looking forward to getting older.

PART FOUR

(March–June 2001)

When your heart is broken, your boats are burned: nothing matters any more. It is the end of happiness and the beginning of peace.

Ellie Dunn, in Bernard Shaw's
Heartbreak House

best

I'm driving back to Wood Green with Nicola in the passenger seat. My current alibi is that I'm out looking for a new set of headlight bulbs for the car. Nicola's is less specific: she's on half-term holiday and she's told her mum she's out with friends. We have been driving around north London aimlessly all afternoon because that was what Nicola wanted to do today and I was happy to make her happy. Because it's raining we've had the car roof up but we've still had a good time listening to music. We've even found some common ground: she played me *Remedy* by Basement Jaxx, an album I ignored when it was released because I don't like dance music. But it's actually quite good and we listen to the title track on repeat for ages.

Over the past month life seems to have become more balanced. Izzy and I are making a conscious effort to spend time together. In fact, once I've dropped Nicola off I'm heading home to get changed and go out with Izzy for the evening. She's booked a table at a new restaurant in Knightsbridge, which allegedly has a three-month waiting list for dinner reservations. This is the first time she's flexed her muscles as the boss of a magazine.

As I pull up at a set of traffic lights Nicola turns off the CD in the middle of 'Red Alert' and I look at her anxiously. 'I was listening to that.'

'I'm sorry,' she says. 'I have to ask you something. Remember ages ago when I told you about the boy at school I liked?'

'Brendan?'

'There's a party tonight. And he's going to be there. And . . . well, I think I'm going to try to pull him.'

'Pull him?'

She nods. 'I don't know if he wants a girlfriend, though. He's always with girls but he never has them as girlfriends.'

I'd much preferred this boy Brendan when he was an object of Nicola's unrequited fantasies. I'd known boys like him at school. In fact I'd *been* a boy like him at school.

'Are you sure you like him that much?' I ask her.

'Yeah. Of course.'

'So what's this "not sure he wants a girlfriend" business, then?'

She shrugs. 'Well, he might not, might he?'

'But isn't that what you want? You know, to be his girl-friend?'

'Yeah.'

'So why just settle for letting him kiss you, then?'

'Because I *want* to kiss him.'

As the traffic lights change to green I try a different line of argument. 'Does he do a lot of kissing, this Brendan?'

'Loads of girls like him. And, yeah, he does get off with quite a few.'

This is all I need to hear. 'I don't think he's the one for you,' I tell her.

'Why?'

'Because you're better than that.'

'Better than what?'

'Better than letting some fifteen-year-old waste-of-space

kiss you if he's not going to be your boyfriend. You have absolutely got to be the prettiest girl at your school and . . . well . . . I think you deserve someone better.'

'But I don't *want* someone better,' she says moodily. 'I *want* Brendan.'

Nicola sulks and even though I'm old enough to know better I sulk too. I keep my eyes on the road, sigh a lot, turn the car radio on and listen to Radio 4, which really annoys her. We don't speak to each other again until I drop her off at our usual point two roads away from her house.

'I'm off,' she says, picking up her bag and opening the car door.

I suddenly feel guilty. 'You can't go like this.'

'Like what?'

'Like this – you in a mood with me just because I've said something you disagree with.'

'But I *like* Brendan.'

'I know you do, sweetheart. All I'm saying is that boys . . . well, they can be a bit crap, really. Not all of them . . . just some of them . . . so . . . I don't know . . . Just . . . look after yourself and don't trust them as far as you can throw them. I'm only saying this because I want what's best for you and I'm proud of you . . . and, well, you make me laugh, which is no bad thing.'

'You make me laugh too . . . sometimes.'

'So, are we friends again?'

'Okay.' She looks at me. 'I'd better go. I'll call you tomorrow and let you know how the party went, okay?'

'Okay.'

'See you later, then?'

'Yeah,' I reply. 'See you later. I love you, you know.' I

hadn't intended to say that but it's true and it feels as natural saying it to Nicola as it does to Izzy.

'I love you, too,' she says, and climbs out of the car.

I watch her walk down the road and disappear, and then my phone rings.

survival

'Hi, Dave, it's me.'

It's Izzy.

'What's up?'

'Bad news. I think I'm going to have to cancel our plans for tonight.'

'Why?'

'It's Stella. She's in a right state. I think she and Lee have split up for good.'

According to Izzy, Stella had decided to call it a day with Lee during an argument about whether to go to the cinema or not. Lee had wanted to go and Stella had wanted to stay in. Stella said, why didn't he go on his own and Lee had said that was what he was going to do. She said, well, if he was so keen to go out without her why didn't he just take his things and leave? So he did just that. She was in floods of tears and Izzy was going over to Stella's to make sure she was all right.

'I'm really sorry, babe,' says Izzy. 'I'll make it up to you, I promise.'

'It's fine, honestly,' I reply. 'There's no problem. Being on twenty-four-hour call for your mates is just one of the things that go with the territory when you're an agony uncle . . . or aunt.'

She laughs. 'You should still go out, though. You should

do something nice. I'll feel bad if I think you're just sitting in on your own on a Thursday night.'

'It's okay, I'll stay in.'

'And do what?'

'Do what I did before I met you.'

'What? Eat bad food, watch crap telly and go out with desperate women?'

'No,' I reply. 'I'm going to play music. *Loud*.'

do?

It's nearly midnight and I've been playing my all time favourite songs, track by track, *in the living room*, which I'm never allowed to do, with the volume turned loud enough to annoy the neighbours. CD jewel cases are scattered all around me, albums lie out of their sleeves and like a demented DJ with an audience of one, I'm showing absolutely no sign of waning. I'm just about to follow up the seven-inch single of 'Seven Rooms of Gloom' by the Four Tops in deliberately eclectic fashion with '50 Dresses' by Animals That Swim, with an eye to following that up with 'Everyday' by Angie Stone and then perhaps 'Sliver' by Nirvana when my mobile rings. I think about ignoring it but it might be Izzy.

'Is this Dave Harding?'

It's a teenage girl's voice. But not Nicola's.

'Who's this?'

'You don't know me. My name's Keisha. I'm a friend of Nicola's.'

I'm worried. 'What's wrong? Isn't she meant to be at the party with you? Has something happened?'

There's a long pause. I can hear music in the background. I feel sick with nerves.

'Not really . . .'

'What do you mean "not really"? Has something happened at the party?'

267

'That's where we are now. The thing is . . .'

'The thing is *what*?' I'm losing my patience with this girl.

'The thing is . . . *Nicola's really drunk*.' Keisha starts to cry. 'She's really, really drunk and she's throwing up every-where and she won't let me take her to her mum's and I can't take her to mine because my mum and dad will kill me if they find out we've been drinking.' She's sobbing her heart out now. 'She said to ring you.'

'But she's all right? She's not in any danger?'

'She's okay,' sobs Keisha.

'So why doesn't she call her mum?'

There's a long silence.

'Her mum doesn't know she's here. My mum doesn't know I'm here either. We're supposed to be staying at each other's houses and we'll both get in big trouble if our parents find out.'

'Tell her I'll be right there as soon as I can.' I sigh.

'Are we going to get into trouble, Mr Harding? Are you going to tell our parents?'

The fear in her voice reminds me of my own youth when the worst thing in the world that can possibly happen to you is getting into trouble with your parents. I can't help but feel for her.

'No,' I say softly. 'Just give me the address of the party and I'll sort everything out.'

I end the call then look around the living room at all my records and CDs. My party for one is over. I think about what to do next then dial Fran's number.

'Fran's phone.'

It's a man's voice. I assume it's the legendary Linden.

'Hi, is she there?'

'Who's this?'

'Can you tell her it's Dave from work? It's a bit of an emergency.'

Linden semi-grunts and seconds later Fran is on the line. 'Dave, it's midnight,' she says. 'Where are you?'

'I'm at home. Where are you?'

'I'm at Linden's in Tufnell Park. I can't believe you've just spoken to him. What did you think of him? Ignorant pig, isn't he?'

'Listen, I've got an emergency and I need your help.' I tell her everything Keisha had told me. 'I need you to come with me and put them up at your place. I know it's asking a lot but—'

'Don't be ridiculous, Dave,' she interrupts. 'Of course I'll help you out. And don't worry about her either, she'll be okay. I've been there – a third of a bottle of gin when I was fourteen. Threw up like a fountain. I've never touched gin since. But we'd better get over to this party quickly just to make sure. You call a cab, pick me up here in Tufnell Park and we'll sort everything out.'

'But what about you and Linden?'

'What *about* me and Linden?'

'Well, I've just disturbed you, haven't I?'

Fran laughs. 'Yeah, well, he shouldn't be such a crap boyfriend, should he? Anyway, you're a *friend*, Linden's a *boyfriend* and in my book friend beats boyfriend every time.'

knock

'Is this the one?' asks the cab driver, as we pull up outside number 55 Rowheath Road.

I peer out of the window. Several dozen teenagers are standing in the front garden smoking and the music is loud enough to make the cab windows vibrate. A number of couples are kissing and groping by the front door.

'Yeah,' I tell him, exchanging glances with Fran.

'So, what's your plan?' asks Fran, as we get out.

'I'm going to go in there and sort out Nicola. That's my plan.'

Fran grabs my arm. 'But you're angry.'

She's right. I *am* angry. I'm angry because it hadn't even occurred to me that she hadn't asked her mum's permission to go to the party. I'm angry because she's been drinking alcohol. I'm angry because, for the first time in our relationship, I'm going to have to act like a real dad. But mostly I'm angry because the thought of anything bad happening to her makes me feel more vulnerable than I'd ever thought possible.

'She's not even fourteen yet,' I say to Fran. 'Anything could happen to her in the state she's in.'

'If you go into that party and let her know you're angry with her you'll regret it,' says Fran, 'Just think before you act, Dave. I know you're worried and, of course, she's been really stupid. But out of all the people in the world, who has she called to help her?' She jabs me in the chest with her index finger. 'You. This is your chance to score some points with her. There's going to be no need to shout at her, believe me. She'll be mortified that you've even seen her in this state. And you can guarantee that once tomorrow morning comes round she'll have sworn off the booze for the foreseeable.'

'Who's the agony uncle, you or me?'

'You,' says Fran. 'I'm just your sidekick for the evening.'

useless

As soon as the kids smoking in the garden spot me and Fran they throw away their cigarettes and disappear inside, in no doubt that we are responsible adults come to stop their fun. In the hallway we disturb a host of people snogging. For no other reason than my own amusement I tell them I'm an off-duty policeman and that I'm searching for a Nicola O'Connell. Within two milliseconds I'm pointed in the direction of the bathroom by a boy called Devon, whose twenty Benson and Hedges and Bacardi Breezer I confiscate. Along the landing, propped against the bathroom door and looking thoroughly dejected, is a pretty girl with dark brown hair. She's wearing a dark blue asymmetrical top and jeans and is holding a mobile phone in her hand. I ask her if she's Keisha. She nods and asks if I'm Nicola's uncle. I wonder briefly whether 'uncle' was some sort of teenage euphemism (for what I don't know) but then realise that even drunk, Nicola has probably had the foresight to make up a plausible lie about who I am.

'Yeah,' I tell her.

Keisha and I both look at the bathroom door.

'Is she in there?' I ask.

Keisha nods again, sorrowfully.

I knock on the door. 'Nicola, it's me, sweetheart, Dave. You can come out now. Everything's going to be okay.'

She doesn't answer.

I look at Fran, who shrugs and looks at Keisha.

'What exactly is she doing in there?' asks Fran.

'Crying mostly,' says Keisha. 'And being sick.'

'And she's locked the door?'

'She only did it when you arrived. It was her idea to call you in the first place, but I think she's sobered up a bit and when she saw you getting out of the cab she got a bit upset and locked herself in here.'

'How much has she had to drink?' asks Fran.

'I dunno. She had a bit of everything, really. She didn't like lager, though. I think that's what made her throw up. She's never been drunk before. She only did it because Emily got off with this boy she fancied.'

'Would that be Brendan Casey?' I ask.

Keisha nods. 'You know him?'

'Of him.'

There's no joy to be had in being right about Brendan Casey. None whatsoever. I've half a mind to go and find him so we can have this out, man to man, but what am I going to say? You're in big trouble, son, because you declined to get off with my daughter? But I only care about Nicola.

'Are you sure me and Nicola aren't going to get in trouble?' asks Keisha. 'My mum will go mental if she finds out.'

'No, you're not going to get into trouble,' I tell her. 'Fran and I just want to make sure that the two of you are safe tonight.' I look at the bathroom door once more. 'How about you go downstairs with Fran while I have a quick chat with Nicola?'

'I'll see you in a minute, then,' says Fran, and follows Keisha downstairs. 'Best of luck, Dave.'

'Yeah,' I say. 'I'll probably need it.'

hidden

'It's just you and me now, Nicola,' I say, to the bathroom door. 'Are you going to talk to me?'

Silence.

'I understand how you must feel but I'm a bit worried. I just want to know that you're all right.'

'I'm all right,' says Nicola eventually. Her voice is small and shaky.

'Good. I'm glad and . . . I'm glad you felt you could call me up when you needed help.'

She starts to cry.

'Have I said something to upset you?'

'No,' she sobs. 'It's just me.'

'What's just you?'

Silence.

'Are you all right in there?'

'I feel really stupid. I shouldn't have called you out. Now you'll never trust me again.'

'I don't think that at all. I promise. We've all done stupid things in the past, haven't we? I know I have.'

'I feel really bad, Dave.'

'You will, sweetheart, you've had a lot to drink.'

'No, not that way. I feel really bad about you coming here. I've messed everything up, haven't I? You've had to tell Izzy about me because I've messed up. I saw her through the window. I didn't want her to see me like this. I've got sick all over my top. I bet she hates me already.'

There's genuine worry in her voice. It hadn't even occurred to me that she might come to these conclusions. All thoughts of being angry leave me.

'That's not Izzy who's with me,' I say gently. 'That's a friend of mine – Fran. She works on *Teen Scene*. You've probably seen her in the mag a few times.'

'So where's Izzy?'

'She's staying at a friend's house. I've told you about my friends Stella and Lee, haven't I? Well, they've split up. Stella's a bit upset so Izzy's gone to look after her. Just like I'm here to look after you.'

There's a long pause and then she opens the bathroom door. She looks a bit rough but I can see she's okay. Regardless of the sick on her top I put my arms round her and squeeze her tightly while she sobs her heart out. It is, without a doubt, one of the proudest moments of my life.

Fran offers to let the girls sleep on the floor at her place, as long as they go straight home first thing in the morning, and soon all four of us are in the back of the black cab on our way to Fran's flat in Brixton.

Overwhelmed by the evening's events Nicola falls asleep on one of my shoulders and Keisha on the other.

morning

It's a quarter to ten the following morning and I'm at *Teen Scene*. I called Fran this morning before I left the flat to make sure the girls were okay and she told me everything was fine. I've got two phone interviews to write up with two near-identical boy bands (neither band said anything at all of interest), the pop-gossip page to pull together, yet more Love Doctor mail to work my way through and my next column for *Femme* to tidy up and e-mail to Izzy. I'm about to begin work on one of the interviews when Jenny comes into the office.

'Morning, Dave,' she says.

'Morning, Jen.'

She comes over and leans on the edge of my desk. 'I take it you've heard about Stella and Lee?'

'Yeah.'

'What do you think of that, then?'

'It's a bit sad but it was kind of on the cards, really, wasn't it? Izzy spent the night round there because she was so upset.'

'I might try and call her later, find out how she's getting on. Have you spoken to Lee to find out how he is?'

'No.'

'Why not? Do real men not call their mates when they split up from a long-term relationship?'

'Lee's all right, but you know as well as I do that this'll be the last we see of him. Stella's our main friend and Lee was her boyfriend. The law states that when a couple splits up it's a case of last in first out when it comes to friendships. Stella was our friend before Lee, *ergo* we no longer see Lee.'

Jenny sighs. 'It's harsh but I suppose you're right. So what would we do if you and Izzy ever split up? Who would get custody of the friends then?'

'We're not going to split up. So thankfully that conundrum will never have to be solved.'

later

At ten thirty Fran walks into the office. She's half an hour late.

'I know,' she says, following my gaze to the office clock. 'It's that stupid Victoria Line.'

'Victoria Line?' I say. 'Oh, *please!*'

Fran laughs. 'I don't think Jen believed me either when I called her this morning to say I'd be late but she was cool about it. She knows I work late all the time . . . I'm so terrible at lying. I mean, who's ever been trapped on a tube train for over an hour? I really do have to think up some better excuses.'

'What time did you get to bed? Nicola and her mate weren't a pain, were they?'

'Not at all. They were great. I'd forgotten how fun the world is when you're thirteen. Everything's amazing – living on your own without your parents is amazing, even having washing-up in the sink that backdates to the Bronze Age is amazing. They're sweethearts. Barely made any noise at all even this morning.'

'And they got off okay?'

'They were watching TV when I left. Kay, my flatmate, said she'd look after them because she's not at work today. I left them the money you gave me for them to get a cab back to Wood Green so I'm sure they'll be fine. Do you want me to call the flat and check?'

'No, don't worry. I'll call Nicola later this afternoon and make sure she's okay. Thanks again for looking after them, Fran. You really helped me out, you know.'

'No problem,' says Fran. 'It was my pleasure.'

Seconds later my mobile rings inside my coat pocket.

'Hello?'

There's a slight pause. 'Is this Dave Harding?'

It's a female voice with a soft Irish accent.

'Yeah,' I reply, 'who's this?'

As the words leave my mouth I realise how redundant the question is.

'This is Caitlin O'Connell,' says the woman at the end of the line, 'Nicola's mum. I think you and I both know we've got a lot of catching up to do.'

you

It's early evening and I'm just coming out of Wood Green tube station to meet Caitlin for the first time in nearly fifteen years. I open her front gate, ring the bell and wait. After a short while I can just make out a figure approaching through the glass in the front door. I hold my breath, the door opens and there before me is Caitlin. There's no bolt of lightning, no choir of angels singing or even a round of applause for this momentous occasion. Instead we stand there, wondering how it's possible to have created in Nicola a permanent connection between us and yet know so little about each other's lives. We're two strangers brought together after all these years because on one night out of all the thousands of our lives we slept together.

I'm not even sure how to greet her. A handshake seems too formal, a kiss too intimate, even a simple 'hello' is ridiculous. There's nothing in the guidelines of human interaction to prepare either of us for this encounter, so instead we continue to say nothing, taking in each other in a curious although restrained manner. Seeing her in the flesh brings memories of her back with perfect clarity. Seeing her there right in front of me unlocks all the memories of her all those years ago that I'd thought I'd lost forever. Her jet black curly hair is tied back from her face and she's wearing small oval glasses and a touch of makeup. Her face has aged but in an invisible manner that's hard to pinpoint. She's wearing dark blue jeans, a zip-up hooded top, stripy woollen socks and no shoes. I ask myself if she looks like the mum of a thirteen-year-old girl. She doesn't. She looks more like Izzy, Jenny and Stella – young enough still to be irresponsible and old enough to know better. Instinctively I ask myself if I still think she's attractive and the answer comes back, yes, she is. Very. But leave it there.

'Come in,' she says.

I nod and smile, and she retreats inside the house. I follow after her. As I stand in the hallway she asks me if I want a drink of any kind and I tell her no thanks and so she leads me through a door on my left into the living room at the rear of the house. The TV is switched off and the house is silent. I wonder where Nicola is but Caitlin reads my mind and her eyes flit up to the ceiling. 'She's in her room,' she explains. 'I thought it would be best if we talked first between ourselves before we bring her into it.' She offers me a seat on the small sofa while she sits down in an arm-chair opposite.

'Right,' she says. 'Where exactly do we begin?'

out

Caitlin had called Keisha's parents at nine this morning to surprise Nicola with a shopping trip to the Bluewater Centre. When she discovered from Keisha's mum that neither Nicola nor Keisha was there they quickly realised they'd been lied to. A call to Keisha's friend Emily's parents revealed that Emily had come home early from a supposed sleep-over at Keisha's because of an argument with Nicola. An interrogation of Emily revealed that the girls had been to a party. Caitlin got the number for the house where the party had taken place and had spoken to a Mrs Felicio, who informed her that her house had been ruined by the party thrown by her son Mario. Most alarmingly, she told Caitlin that no one had stayed overnight. At this point Caitlin became so frantic that she called the police. Ten minutes later Nicola walked through the front door.

Initially Nicola stuck to her sleep-over story, but when Caitlin told her she'd spoken to Keisha's mum, she admitted going to the party but refused to say where she'd spent the night for fear of getting me into trouble. Eventually, however, the whole story came out but not without a fight. Nicola told her she'd spent the night at a flat in Brixton. Whose flat was it? A friend's. Which friend's? My friend Fran's. Where were this girl's parents? She lives on her own. How do you know her? Through another friend. How old is Fran? She's

282

twenty-five. That was when Caitlin exploded. She asked Nicola again how she knew Fran and Nicola, in tears, had told her, 'She's a friend of my dad.'

herstory

Caitlin's in tears while she's telling me this story and I feel about as low as it's possible to feel. I can't believe I'm responsible for upsetting her like this.

'I'm sorry,' she says, wiping the tears from her face with a tissue. 'It's been such a terrible day. When I didn't know where Nicky was I was so terrified that something had happened. It's been such a strange day. Possibly the strangest of my life.'

She bites the corner of her lip and half smiles. It's pure Nicola.

'D'you know,' she continues, 'this morning I woke up in bed I thought, It's a nice day today, I'll go and pick up Nicky, we'll do some shopping, maybe see a film in the afternoon and it'll be a really relaxing day. And now here I am, less than twelve hours later, sitting here in my living room with you . . . my child's father.'

So there it is. The answer I've been looking for all this time and it's the king of anticlimaxes. Had she told me I wasn't Nicola's father I'm not sure it would've made the slightest bit of difference to me.

'Listen,' I say, 'I know I've done everything wrong. This is all my fault.'

'No,' she says, looking across at me. 'It's not your fault

and it's not my fault. It's *our* fault. We both created this confusion. We're both responsible.'

I nod half-heartedly.

'It was about a week after the girls and I came back from Corfu that I realised I was late,' she continues. 'I tried to put it to the back of my mind because, well, I reasoned that as we only slept together once I was being paranoid. But then after another week I went to see a doctor at my local surgery and had a test. I remember every single second while I waited for the results as if it were yesterday. I was just there hoping with all my might that it would be negative. I told myself that I'd been stupid and I'd never be that stupid again, if only I could have my future back and everything get back to normal. When the doctor told me it was positive I cried and cried. I was so scared. Absolutely terrified. All I could think was how I'd messed everything up.'

Suddenly I feel this all-encompassing sadness, as if I've been taken back to that time. I imagine Caitlin going through all this on her own at seventeen years old and can barely believe it. I'd known girls at school who had got pregnant at fifteen and sixteen and I'd never given them a second thought because they were always the ones whom everyone expected to have kids before they left school. They were the tough girls who thought they could look after themselves. The ones who shocked us were like Caitlin: when news spread around the playground that they were pregnant no one laughed because everyone knew it could so easily have been one of them.

next?

'Did you always know you were going to keep the baby?' I ask her. (What prompted the question was my recollection of a girl at sixth form college who had an abortion after her boyfriend had got her pregnant at seventeen. What was strange was that all these years later I can't recall this girl's name, can't picture her face, or anything else about her; no matter what she's ended up doing with her life, whatever she's achieved in later years, she will always be in my mind 'The Girl Who Had The Abortion'.)

'No,' says Caitlin. 'But I don't regret for a second that I did.'

'No, of course not. Nicola's great. You should be proud of her.'

'I am.'

'I know I haven't acted like any kind of responsible adult during all this,' I tell her. 'I mean, Nicola's thirteen and, well, you're her mum and you're legally responsible for her and who am I? No one, really. It's just that, well, this has been a really strange situation and I just want to say that none of this is her fault.' I laugh. 'Well, her going off to the party was definitely her fault but the rest of it – her contacting me – that was just her being curious. Her not wanting to hurt your feelings. It's not her fault. It's mine. I should've insisted that she tell you straight away but . . . I didn't and I'm sorry.'

'When Nicola told me I was angry with you. Very angry. I

was scared, too, because I didn't know anything about you and your life now. I didn't know what sort of man you were. She could've easily got herself into trouble . . . but I suppose her being so trusting of you was my fault too.'

'Why?'

'She's always asked about you. Even when she was really small. And I've always wanted her to know that it wasn't because you didn't love her that you weren't with us. You weren't there because you didn't know. I always tried to show you in the best light. I told her about everything you hoped and dreamed about doing in your life. I suppose I turned you into a bit of a hero. But I wanted her to be proud of you. So, like I say, it is partially my fault. Still, I hated the fact that she'd been lying to me all this time, that she's capable of keeping such a big secret from me. It just seems wrong. I'm her mum, the closest person to her in all the world. She should have been able to tell me anything.'

'She can,' I tell her. 'She just didn't want to hurt you. She didn't want you to think she loved you any less just because she wanted to meet me. And you have to admit that if she had told you she would've been dealing not just with all her own feelings about meeting me but her feelings of guilt about you.'

'Is that why you haven't told your wife?' says Caitlin sharply.

I don't reply. I deserve what she has said. It must've sounded like I was justifying Nicola's lying to her, which I was.

Caitlin apologises immediately. 'I'm sorry,' she says. 'That was completely uncalled-for. This is just so difficult.'

'But you're right, though,' I tell her. 'That *is* one of the reasons why I didn't tell Izzy.'

2.4

Caitlin is laughing softly to herself. When I look at her for an explanation she explains, 'I'm sorry, you're going to think I'm mad. I was just about to ask you how you are. Isn't that weird? All this stuff to talk about and I'm acting like I've just bumped into you in the street . . . but, well, how *are* you?'

'A good question,' I say. 'And my answer is that I've definitely had better days than this.'

'Me too.' She exhales deeply as if she's trying to relax. 'Nicola's told me all about you. Well, you know, all the important stuff. I can't believe you're an agony uncle! She showed me the picture of you in *Teen Scene* and I just had to laugh.'

'It's an odd thing for a grown man to be doing, but it's just a job, really. When you're a journalist you have to be prepared to do the odd weird thing like that to make a living.'

'But didn't you want to be in a band?'

'I've wanted to be a lot of things in the time that's passed since we met. I ended up writing about music, though. This is terrible, but I can't even remember what you wanted to be.'

'A teacher. And that's what I am . . . How long have you been married?'

'Three years. Although we've been together six.'

'Congratulations.'

288

'What about you? Are you seeing anyone?' I'm asking out of politeness rather than a desire to hear an answer I already know. If I didn't ask it would feel as if I was openly acknowledging her failure to find a partner – a failure which I presume in part is down to the fact that she has a teenage daughter and therefore in part my fault.

'I'm single,' she says, 'but out of choice rather than circumstance. I suppose I've always been a bit commitment-phobic.' She stands up and picks up a magazine from the coffee table in the corner of the room. It's a copy of *Teen Scene*. 'I didn't know what to make of it when Nicola told me how she'd found you. In fact, I didn't believe her until she showed me your picture in here. It all sounded too far-fetched for words. I mean, first there was you as an agony uncle on a teenage girls' magazine but then there was Nicola managing to spot it was you. What were the odds of her recognising a picture of you in a magazine from a single old photograph? I'm not sure that even I would have recognised you. It was one night. A long, long time ago.'

Our eyes meet briefly and we both look away. There's a long uncomfortable pause.

'Can I ask you a question?' I ask.

She nods.

'Did you ever try to find me?'

'No,' she says. 'Over the years I've thought about a million different ways I could've contacted you. I could've written to the hotel you were staying at or found out the tour company you'd booked through. I knew which university you were going to and what subject you were studying so I could've addressed a letter to your department. I could've looked up all the Hardings on the electoral register living in Streatham, but at the time I didn't do anything. During my pregnancy I had way too much to deal with to find you. After Nicola was born in May, I had too much to deal with in being a new mum and then it was university, teacher training . . . The list of excuses was endless. The thing is, every single one of Nicola's birthdays has always been a reminder of my failure to find you.'

focus

'So what do we do now?'

'What do you want to do?' asks Caitlin.

'I want to be part of Nicola's future because there's nothing we can do about the past. Sometimes I'm not even sure who I am to her or what role I could play in her life but what I do know is this: she's part of *my* life now. I don't know what I'd do without her.'

'She already loves you – I could tell from the look on her face when she thought she'd got you into trouble that she thinks the world of you . . . And she really liked your friend whose home she stayed at last night. Sounds like they had a right party this morning.'

'What's her punishment going to be?'

'I haven't thought about it yet. I can't punish her for seeing you, that wouldn't make sense, and I already know she regrets lying to me about the party. She's a good girl normally. I think maybe we'll just put this behind us and start anew. No lies and no secrets.'

Even though it's late Caitlin and I continue talking, filling in all the gaps. In a short space of time our conversation becomes both frank and honest. Caitlin tells me more about her last relationship and the moment she realised it was unlikely she'd ever find what she was looking for. The reason, she tells me, is simple: 'While I'm prepared to compromise on my own behalf I absolutely refuse to settle for anything less than perfection when it comes to Nicola.' I wonder whether given her circumstances I would've been able to make such sacrifices in the name of love.

Then she suggests we tell Nicola that everything is okay and she leaves the room to call her down from her bedroom only to discover her sitting on the bottom stair. Caitlin explains to Nicola in front of me how we've sorted things out between us and that everything is going to be okay now. I am dumbstruck by the momentous realisation that this is the first time that all three of us – father, mother and daughter – have ever been in the same room. I wonder if we're a family and if so what kind? And if we aren't then what exactly are we?

This question is my companion on the Tube on my way home. When I get home I still have no answer to it but what I do know is this: I have to tell Izzy the truth. I have to tell her everything.

don't

I can hear Izzy in the kitchen but I don't go in and say hello straight away. I head to the spare bedroom and search for the record where I'd hidden Nicola's letter. I take out the photo and put it into my back pocket. When I enter the kitchen Izzy is loading the dishwasher.

'Hey,' she says, and flashes me a huge smile. She stops what she's doing and comes and puts her arms round me. 'I didn't hear you come in. How was your day, sweetheart?'

'Fine. How was yours?'

'Don't get me started.' She presses her lips lightly against mine. I return the kiss with more force, and then I do it again and again until I've manoeuvred this simple greeting into a full-blown bout of passion. All the time I keep wondering if this just might be our last kiss.

'Wow,' she says, as she pulls out of the embrace. 'What was that about?' She smiles mischievously. 'Whatever it was I'll have some more, please.'

She kisses me again but this kiss is different. The moment has gone. The passion has evaporated. All that remains is guilt.

'What's wrong, babe?'

'You'd better sit down. I've got something to tell you.'

She can tell I'm serious and her face is filled with concern. Without speaking she sits down on the stool next to the sink. 'Whatever it is you can tell me, Dave. You know that, don't you? It's not Mum, is it?' Tears are already rolling down her cheeks. 'Nothing's happened to Mum, has it?'

'No.'

'It's not your parents?'

'No,' I reply. 'No one's sick. Everybody's fine.'

'Then what is it?'

I reach into my back pocket and hand her the photograph of Nicola.

'I don't understand,' she says, looking at it. 'Who's this?'

'My daughter.' For a moment neither of us speaks. There doesn't seem to be anything to say. She knows this isn't a practical joke. And there are no misunderstandings to be had either. All the escape routes out of this situation are closed. 'Her name is Nicola,' I continue. 'She's nearly four-teen. I met her mum, Caitlin, when I was eighteen. I was on holiday in Corfu. We spent one night together and I never saw her again. I got a letter a few months back when I'd first started doing the problem page at *Teen Scene*. It was from the girl in the picture. I've been in regular contact with her since then without her mum knowing. This morning her mum found out.'

All that was missing was 'The End'. Only I could distil a saga like this into a few hastily thrown-together sentences. I look at Izzy and I can tell she wants to cry again but the reality of the situation has shocked the tears from her. I know I have to give her more details – anything that might make her understand my point of view and so, without prompting, I tell the story again, right from the beginning, and as I speak the same question keeps recurring in my mind: *Why didn't I tell her from the very start?*

love

Izzy listens without interrupting. Once it becomes clear that I've finished talking she stands up and picks up Nicola's photo from the kitchen counter. 'I stopped taking my pill three weeks ago,' she says.

'What?'

'I stopped taking my pill three weeks ago.'

'Are you saying you're pregnant?'

'I don't know. Yet.'

'I don't understand. Why didn't you talk to me? Surely you could've talked to me about . . .'

'I wanted the decision taken out of my hands. It sounds stupid when I say it aloud but that's how I felt. I just wanted to get "accidentally pregnant" again. I didn't want us to have to try to have a baby and have it fail again.'

'And what does all this mean after what I've told you?'

'I don't feel anything,' she says, without looking at me. 'I'm numb.'

'You must know that I didn't do this to hurt you. I acted stupidly. I acted carelessly. I acted hurtfully. But I never did any of it to hurt you.'

'So that's okay?' she says sharply. 'You didn't mean to hurt me so the fact that you have makes it all right, does it? Whether or not you inflicted this pain on me on purpose the result is the same. After dealing with all the hurt of the miscarriage, now I have to deal with this: the fact that you have a daughter with another woman; the fact that you've been skulking around, telling me lies all this time. How dare you try to deny me the right to be angry with you? How can you stand there and tell me you're sorry? It's meaningless. And if that is meaningless what else have you said to me that's meaningless? You promised to love and cherish me for ever – was that meaningless? You promised you'd share everything with me – *the good and the bad*. Was that meaningless too? How can you stand there and say something like that? Something that will completely and utterly destroy my peace of mind? I hadn't thought it possible to feel so betrayed.' She walks out of the room, grabs her coat and bag from the hallway and opens the front door.

'Where are you going? You've got to stay. We've got to work this out.' I catch up with her on the landing outside the flat and grab her arm. 'Don't go. Just don't go, please.'

She looks at me in a way she never has before – with a mixture of hurt and hatred. '*Don't touch me!*' she spits. 'Don't you *dare* touch me again.'

listen

It's late afternoon on Monday and I'm at work. I could've stayed at home and moped around the flat. I could've spent the day in bed. But I don't feel I have the right to fall apart. All I've earned is the right to go to work, keep it together and suffer in silence. So that's what I do.

I haven't heard a word from Izzy for two days now – the entire weekend. I've called her mobile but it's switched off, I've called Jenny and Stella, and both deny knowledge of where she is or might be. I even called her at work this morning and her assistant told me she was working from home today.

Because I can't talk to her in reality I talk to her in my head. I tell her I'm sorry a million times. I tell her I want everything that has happened to be in the past. And then I tell her I want us to make a new future – and what better way than with a baby? Her being pregnant seems to be the answer to everything. But I want to know that this is the right thing. I want to be sure. I want the kind of answer I give the readers of *Teen Scene*. They write to me looking for solutions to their predicaments and I oblige by giving them not just any answer but *the* answer, reducing their options from many to one so that they know exactly what they should do. I grab a handful of Love Doctor letters from my postbag, open them and begin to read.

The first was in a plain white envelope with small, neat, feminine handwriting:

Dear Love Doctor
I've been going out with my boyfriend for two
months. It's great in so many ways: he makes me
laugh, he's always attentive and buys me presents
all the time. The only problem is his jealousy. He
gets annoyed if any of the boys in my class even
look at me let alone talk to me. This is really
getting me down. What should I do?
    Anonymous (15), Inverness

I pick up a second letter, a pale blue envelope with unmistakably teenage handwriting in silver ink:

Dear Love Doctor,
About a month ago my boyfriend cheated on me
with a girl at a party. I was devastated but carried
on going out with him because I thought I loved
him. Last week, however, I was at a party and I
ended up kissing a boy who wasn't my boyfriend.
Now I have a double dilemma: do I tell my
boyfriend that I cheated on him? Or do I dump my
boyfriend and go out with the boy I kissed at the
party? He's phoned me several times since that
party and says he wants to go out with me. I'm so
confused. What should I do?
    Buffy the Vampire Slayer fan (16), Nottingham

I pick up a third letter, a cream-coloured envelope with a cartoon fieldmouse in the corner chewing a blade of grass.

The handwriting is much the same as the previous one but this time the ink is a silvery green.

Dear Love Doctor,
I think I'm in love with my maths teacher. He's
quite young, only in his twenties, and has only
just joined my school. I don't know what it is but
there's definitely a connection between us. I find
myself staring at him in class all the time and
sometimes I even catch his eye and he doesn't look
away immediately. Do you think there is any
chance that things could work out between us?
A Janet Jackson fan (14), Cornwall

I compare the letter in my hand to the previous one. They have exactly the same handwriting. I check the postmarks on the envelopes. The first says Cambridge, even though it's supposed to have been from Nottingham, and the second says Cambridge even though its writer apparently lives in Cornwall. The *Buffy the Vampire Slayer* fan (16) and the Janet Jackson fan (14) are both some bored teenage girl in Cambridge who likes *Teen Scene*, *Buffy the Vampire Slayer* and Janet Jackson but doesn't have any problems with her life and needs to make some up to feel like a valid human being. If I'd been in any other frame of mind, this would have made me laugh but now it depresses me.

I'm wasting my time doing this job and I'm wasting my talents. The readers of *Teen Scene* don't have real problems – *I* do. I wake up my computer, which had long since gone to sleep, open my e-mail and begin a note to Jenny. I tell her that I'll write agony-uncle columns for another two issues but after today I won't be back in to work at *Teen*

Scene. Then I write one to Fran, who, thankfully, is out of the office on a 'make over your life' competition shoot. I tell her thanks for everything and that I'm sure we'll bump into each other some time in the future. I press send on both e-mails, tidy my desk, pick up my bag and walk out of the office.

pop

I'm sitting on a bench in the gardens at the centre of Soho Square. The weather, although not warm, is okay for the time of year – pleasant enough to attract a number of people with nothing better to do than sit down and waste a few hours looking at the sky. I dig into my bag for my personal stereo. When I was younger I listened to music at every opportunity: on my way to and from work, at work, and in those spare moments at home when Izzy had gone to bed and I'd stay up until four listening to album after album on my headphones, cocooned in a world I understood. I want that feeling right away. I put on my headphones, close my eyes to the world outside and press play, but even in music there's no escape because every song on the tape has a link to Izzy – songs she loved, songs she hated, songs she tolerated, songs that made her cry and songs that made her happy. And, for some reason, this makes me happy too. Even in music she's there at my centre. Being lost in music means being lost in her.

tape

Song 1: 'Safe From Harm', Massive Attack. The first song I listened to after Izzy and I had our first ever full-blown no-holds-barred row.

Song 2: 'Debris Slide', Pavement. A song from the days when we were just friends and I tried to convince her that it was the future of rock 'n' roll by playing it to her at every opportunity.

Song 3: 'I Forgot To Be Your Lover', William Bell. A sixties soul record I discovered in my dad's collection. I called Izzy up at two o'clock in the morning to play it to her over the phone – in my defence, I was drunk.

Song 4: 'Everybody In Here Wants You', Jeff Buckley. Another song I played to Izzy over the phone when I first heard it. I insisted that she should fall in love with it immediately. And she did.

Song 5: 'Don't Believe The Hype', Public Enemy. We had this on repeat on the CD-player the day we decorated the living room in the flat. Izzy said it helped us paint faster.

The tape lasts ninety minutes.

if

When the tape ends I decide to go home. I head towards Oxford Street and as I walk I check my phone for messages. There are three: one from Jenny, telling me she refuses to get another agony uncle until she's spoken to me, and two from Fran, asking my whereabouts. None from Izzy. I dial Fran's number at work.

'Hello, *Teen Scene*.'

'Hi, Fran, it's Dave.'

'I got your e-mail. Were you really going to say goodbye like that?'

'I didn't want to make a big fuss.'

'Are you sure you won't come back to *Teen Scene*? I was talking to Jenny about it and she said she was going to try to persuade you to stay. There's no need to go.'

'I know. It's just that . . . this is going to sound stupid but I got two Love Doctor letters today and they were so obviously made up by the same girl that it just . . . well, it kind of depressed me. I mean, what's the point?'

'The point, Dave, is that you're mad for thinking that two letters from one girl count for anything. You help people. The girls who read the column feel better about themselves because they've written to you. That's got to be a good thing, surely?' I don't reply. 'I get the feeling something's gone wrong,' says Fran.

'You could say that.'

'Is it what I'm thinking?'

'Yes.'

'How did she find out?'

'I told her.'

'Oh. And she's . . .'

I finish her sentence for her. 'Left me? Yeah.'

'But she's coming back?'

'I don't know. I haven't seen her since Friday night.'

'You shouldn't be on your own,' says Fran. 'I'll be finished here in a few minutes. I've got a couple of things to put through that Tina's been nagging me for all week and we'll go for a drink or something to eat. I'm not going to take no for an answer. I'll meet you downstairs at the Phoenix on Charing Cross Road in half an hour, okay?'

'I can't. I'd be terrible company.'

'I don't mind. We can just sit, if you want to.'

'No, really.'

'Well, when will I see you again?'

'I don't know. I don't know when any of this will be sorted. And I just won't be thinking straight until then.'

'So why don't you come back to *Teen Scene* until then?'

'I don't know. It's not really me. I've been thinking I might go back to music journalism full time.' I laughed. 'I don't think I'm cut out for the world of relationships.'

'So that's it, I'm not going to see you again?'

'Of course you will. I just don't know when.'

'Come for a drink,' Fran pleads. 'It'll be the world's smallest leaving party. Just you, me and too much alcohol.'

She makes me laugh so I say okay. 'I'll meet you from work and we'll go for a drink,' I tell her.

I switch off my mobile, put it back into my bag and nearly

walk straight into a couple heading the other way. I'm about to apologise when I realise I know them. Only they're not supposed to be a couple. It's Trevor and Stella.

-ish

'Dave,' says Stella immediately, 'I can explain.' She looks at Trevor. '*We* can explain.'

'I know this looks really bad,' says Trevor. 'We're together, Dave,' he explains. 'We have been for a while. Everyone's going to find out soon anyway.'

'How long has this been going on?' I ask.

'A while,' says Stella. 'Before I split up with Lee if that's what you're asking.'

'So, why were you so upset when you and Lee split up?'

'Because even if I didn't want to be with him, I did still love him.'

'Oh,' I say. 'Does anyone else know?'

'No,' says Stella, and then there's a long silence.

Secrets, I think. Everybody's got them. Even me.

'No offence,' I say to them both, 'but I'd never have put you two together. I don't know, we've all been friends for such a long time but it never occurred to me that something like this could be going on.'

'It came as a surprise as much to us,' says Stella, 'but one day Trevor and I just clicked. I couldn't believe I hadn't realised how great he was.'

'I felt really guilty at first,' says Trevor. 'I still do, but Jenny was never right for me and I was never right for her. We were together out of habit, really. I'd have moved out a long

306

while ago but . . . I'm not brilliant at breaking bad news. I know I have to tell her soon but now never seems to be the right time.'

'It's true,' says Stella. 'When this all comes out I know it's going to cause a lot of hurt – especially to Jenny as she's my friend – but we just couldn't help ourselves.'

'I feel like we're finally getting serious about life,' says Trevor. 'Serious enough to start looking at houses that we might be able to afford . . . Houses with gardens and okay schools in the area.'

'You're not . . . ?'

'No,' says Stella. 'Not yet, anyway. But it's part of the plan. We buy a place, maybe we get married, but by next year we want to have a kid.'

'Isn't this all a bit fast?' I ask. 'What's the rush?'

'It isn't too fast at all,' says Stella. 'That's been the problem all along. I used to think I had all the time in the world to do everything I wanted. But what's the use of having all the time in the world if you're always wasting it on things that don't mean a thing?'

10/10

This morning some CDs arrive in the post from various music PR companies. Normally I just bundle them all into the spare bedroom to work through when I can be bothered but today, as I'm not going in to work, I decide to listen to them. I'm usually cynical when it comes to CDs – all the staff at *Louder* were unless it was an artist we really liked. Basically we'd act like kings with a court jester, dropping the promo CD or tape into the stereo and giving it a short amount of time to prove itself before being consigned to the pile marked 'Crap', never to be played again. You have to do this kind of thing when you're a music journalist simply because of the sheer volume of stuff that you get sent. Not every album can be judged like this – some are 'growers' and in my time I've consigned a fair number of multi-platinum or critically acclaimed albums to the 'Crap' pile but that's just the way it goes. What I really love, though, is the rare moment when you put on an album by someone you've never heard of expecting to skip through the tracks in moments only to be blown away, and this morning that happens. I put on a CD called *Small Moments*, by an Irish singer called David Kitt, lie in bed and listen to it. It's simple stuff – a bedroom recording-studio operation: one guy with a guitar and a few bits of rudimentary electronic gadgetry but it works perfectly. It was – to put on my music journalist head – a twenty-first century Nick Drake. I love it. It lifts my mood and transports me to another place. I listen to the whole album on repeat until midday. In the middle of 'Another Love Song', the album's high point, the bell rings. I pick up my jeans and T-shirt from the floor, throw them on and answer the door. It's Nicola in her school uniform.

'Nicola,' I say, surprised.

'Hi,' she says.

'What are you doing here? Shouldn't you be at school?'

'I wanted to see you. I've been worried about you. Why haven't you called me? I've left about a million messages on your answerphone.'

This is true. She has been ringing all weekend. Big, long, rambling messages, and I haven't returned a single one.

'I'm really sorry, sweetheart,' I tell her. 'Honestly. It's just that something came up and everything dropped out of my head.'

'I was worried. I thought something bad had happened to you.'

'I'm really, really sorry. I should've remembered.'

'Didn't you get my other messages?'

'Yeah, I did, but I had a lot on my plate.'

She looks hurt. 'So you ignored them?'

'I didn't do it on purpose, Nicola. It was . . . just . . . well, I had a lot on, okay?'

'But I left loads of messages . . .'

'I know.'

'Don't you want to see me any more?'

'Of course I do.'

'Then why didn't you call me? I thought my phone was broken. We've never gone this long without talking since I've known you.'

This isn't true but that's not the point. I should've returned her calls. I know it's a hateful thing to do. But standing there in the communal hallway of my house being lectured by a thirteen-year-old girl is the last thing I need when my wife has left me. The absolute last thing. And before I know it I've lost my temper with my beautiful girl.

'What do you want from me?' I snap. 'I've already told you I'm sorry. What more is there?'

The look of horror on Nicola's face brings me to my senses. If I'd wanted to hurt her my mission is accomplished. Within seconds floods of tears are streaming down her face and all the time she's just looking at me, unable to believe I can act in such a terrible way. I can't believe it either.

'What have I done wrong?' she asks. 'I only wanted to talk to you.'

'I'm sorry,' I tell her. 'I'm so sorry.'

'What have I done?' she repeats. There's real pain in her voice. 'Why don't you like me any more? What can I do to make you like me again?'

'It's not you,' I tell her. 'Of course I love you. I'm sorry. You're all I've got.' I throw my arms round her and hold her tightly, unsure if I will ever let go.

control

We talk, my daughter and I, about everything. It's hard to tell her the truth but I want to be honest with her. I tell her about Izzy leaving, I tell her about the miscarriage, and I even tell her that Izzy might be pregnant, although I half expect her to get even more upset. But she doesn't. She's really *grown-up* about it. She listens carefully, and when I finish she tells me not to worry. She says that whatever it is I need to do to get Izzy back she'll help me. She tells me that everything will be all right. And the strange thing is, I believe her.

So, after she leaves to go back to school, I make my way to the spare bedroom and turn on my laptop, slap a fake smile on my face and begin my next 'Male Man' column. Two hours later I've finished it. Eight hundred words of 'What your boyfriend might be thinking' that makes me sound like the world's most perfect partner. It made me feel good writing this piece. I'd hit rock bottom and now the only way is up.

forever

To: izzy.harding@bdp.co.uk
From: dave_atch01@hotmail.com
Subject: My Male Man column

Dear Izz,
The show must go on eh?

Dave XXX

Weddings

Madonna was once asked why, if she knew Sean Penn had
wanted to marry her for a long time, she didn't ask him
earlier. She replied, 'It's one thing to have to read
a man's mind. But it's another to have to read it back
to him.' That pretty much sums up the differences
between men and women when it comes to marriage: women
know everything and men know nothing. And in this game
knowledge is power. Proposing marriage has never been
men's strong point. Quite often we can be happy with
our partners, yet the idea of marriage will not have
crossed our minds. It's nothing personal, girls. Pro-
gress within a relationship has never been our pri-
ority. With us, the fact that the relationship exists
at all is sufficient sign of commitment. However, as

312

time moves on and our partner's hints become less subtle, we finally see the benefit. In the end the grooms enjoy the wedding more than the brides – even if they never say so. I said to my wife on our wedding day, 'If you'd pitched this wedding lark to me as a massive party where we get all our family and friends round and just drink too much I would've asked you to marry me ages ago.'

The planning of a wedding will always be a woman's job. Women will, of course, pretend that it is a joint effort. But we men know different. I tried suggesting something out of the ordinary for ours – wearing jeans and T-shirts to the ceremony – just for a joke, and received a look that in my wife's facial lexicon meant, 'Don't. Just don't.' But, seriously, if wedding arrangements were left to men we'd plan the whole thing when we woke up and we'd turn up late at the wrong church wearing yesterday's boxer shorts and a Manchester United top. The reason why women excel at wedding arrangements is that for them the small things in life are as important as the big things, if not more so. And detail is everything when it comes to weddings. To this day our local florist occupies the number-one slot at the top of my wife's personal hate list (way ahead of fascists and men who leave the toilet seat up). Why? Because despite the strictest of instructions on the big day, her wedding bouquet arrived with a white ribbon on it instead of a cream one.

It's not just your own wedding that requires planning: attending other people's requires military-style planning too, especially when it comes to purchasing gifts. My wife and I are so good at it we have a system: she does it all. It took us a while to work out that this was the best way to do things but after the last time I did the present shopping and returned with three CDs, a PlayStation but no wedding present she gave up. Now she shops on her own and seems to derive as much pleasure from it as shopping for herself. First she has to survey every store within a fifty-mile radius before she can 'short list' a number of 'maybe' gifts. Second, she has to revisit her chosen stores and spend at least five minutes touching each of the preferred gifts (in her contacts my wife has 20/20 vision and yet her dependence on her fingertips never ceases to amaze me). Third, she has to narrow it down to two potential presents, both of which she buys, takes home then returns to the shop where they were bought the following day to buy a third item.

And that, in a roundabout way pretty much sums up how men feel about weddings. On the surface we might seem unfocused and uninterested but, metaphorically speaking, deep down we know, having walked around the shopping mall of life, we have found the perfect gift for ourselves, which is, of course, you.

rules

Two days later Izzy arrives at the flat late in the evening. She looks tired and drawn. We walk into the living room in silence and then, as we sit down on the sofa, she opens up the conversation: 'I'm not pregnant.' Neither of us speaks for a moment and I take the opportunity to let the disappointment soak in. Realistically I think we'd both known it was unlikely that she was going to be pregnant. In this day and age even a self-confessed former po-faced music journalist has enough amateur fertility expertise to know that it can take up to three months after coming off the pill for a woman's hormone levels to get back to normal. Three weeks, then, was always pushing it a bit.

'How do you feel?' I ask her.

'I don't know . . . but I suppose maybe it was for the best. They weren't exactly the best circumstances for a child to be conceived, were they?'

I don't answer her question and instead ask one of my own. 'Where have you been?'

'I went to Mum's.'

'How is she?'

'She's fine. It was good to spend some time with her. She helped me get a lot of things into perspective.'

'Are you coming home?'

There's a pause and then she asks, 'Do you want me to?'

315

'I love you,' I tell her.

'That was never in question,' she replies.

'So *are* you coming home?'

'You haven't answered my question yet,' she says.

'Of course I want you to come back,' I tell her. 'This is your home.' There's a long silence. I prompt her again. 'So?'

'What?' she replies, as if her mind is somewhere else.

'Are you coming home to stay?' I ask.

'That's up to you,' she says. 'I've tried hard to see things through your eyes. I can understand that you didn't know how to tell me about Nicola, how the news about this girl had hit you so hard that you hadn't been able to think straight.' She pauses, as if losing the thread of her thoughts. 'I can even understand how you might have thought you were protecting me from the truth. But I don't need protection as much as I need honesty. I mean, what else might there be in your life that I don't know about?'

'There's nothing more.'

'I know, but that's the fear I've got to live with now.'

'I see.'

'Do you? Do you really?' She doesn't wait for a reply. 'How do you think it made me feel to know that you couldn't talk to me about this? We're supposed to be there for each other. No matter what, you should know that I'm always going to be on your side. *Always*. No matter what you do I can't stop loving you. That's how love works. Did you think I was just going to turn round and say, "That's it, I don't love you any more"? I love you without condition, Dave. Yes, what's happened has hurt me and yet despite it all I continue to love you with a strength I didn't know was possible. I love you because you are part of me. I love you because loving you is like loving myself. I know that, despite all that has happened, you are a good man. And I won't . . . I can't give you up . . . There's one thing, though . . . I suppose it's the biggest thing of all. I've tried and tried to get my head round Nicola. But I can't. She's your *daughter*. She's part of you and someone from your past. And I just can't seem to get over it, no matter how much I love you. This beautiful girl is everything I wanted *us* to have . . . I can't stop you seeing her. I don't even *want* to stop you seeing her. She's part of your life. But I don't ever want to meet her. I just can't. And, well, I need to know you can accept this before I agree to come back. I'm not going to change my mind. This will just have to be the way it is.'

I tell her I understand and finally she allows me to take her in my arms. And I hold her tightly and tell her that I'm going to make it all up to her. This isn't the way I wanted things to turn out, though. It isn't meant to be like this.

gift

A few days later an invitation arrives from Damian and Adele
to the christening of baby Maddy. I tell Izzy we don't have
to go, that we can send a present instead. But she says it's
something we have to do, that it'll be all right. So eventually
we find ourselves sitting in a pew in a church in Totteridge
where Adele's parents live.

At eleven o'clock on the dot, the vicar gives a short sermon about love, understanding, and the imparting of knowledge. He advises Damian and Adele to bring up little Maddy
in a manner that's both true and right and then he
announces that everyone should move to the baptismal
font. The congregation shuffles to the back of the church
and stands in a semicircle, while Adele passes a sleeping
Maddy to Damian, who passes her to the vicar, who calls
for the godparents to step forward. He dips his hand into
the water and sprinkles a few drops on Maddy's head.

Afterwards everyone moves on to a pub round the corner
called the Cricketer's Arms. Izzy and I try to chat to Damian
and Adele but they're forced to work the room like a Hollywood celebrity couple.

'This is all a bit strange, don't you think?' says Izzy, as we
stand at the bar. 'Everything's changed so much in such a
short time . . . It seems like change happens faster the older
we get,' she continues. 'I used to be scared of change, you

know, but it can be *good*. It means you're moving on, moving forward. I was thinking about work and how I loved my job when I began and now . . . well, it doesn't feel half as important to me as being with you.'

I take her hand. 'I know what you mean. That's exactly how I felt about *Louder*. It was my dream job but when it closed I knew it wasn't everything. There's so much more to life.'

Izzy nods thoughtfully. 'We both live in a world where everything that's seen as important is to do with being the latest, the most fashionable, the most *must-have*. I can't begin to count the number of times I've bought some item of clothing not because I liked it but because I knew there was a waiting list as long as my arm for it.'

'Or the number of times I've proclaimed some band or other to be the most important band since the Beatles or the Stones only to get bored before they've even released an album.'

'I remember when we were just friends and you'd always try to brainwash me into liking whichever band you were championing at the time,' says Izzy. 'You'd give me promo tapes by the dozen, call me up and play music down the phone at me and then drag me to some grotty pub to hear the future of rock and roll.'

'But that's the way you're supposed to feel about music,' I tell her. 'You're supposed to feel like every new band you hear could be bigger than the Beatles. Now, though, every new band seems like it's just a bunch of kids recycling my record collection, and although they probably are, I don't think that's the point. Maybe I'm out of touch.'

'I know what you mean. I can't stay at *Femme* for ever. There will come a day, in the not too distant future, when

I'll have to graduate from the world of feisty young women to a more sedate women's mag or a nice interiors mag. I can see it in some of our contributors now. They're the best writers I know but their stuff is starting to sound hollow because they're not living it like their readers are. Do you know what I'm saying? It's like *Femme* readers are out every Friday night with a bunch of mates doing vodka shots, and for us, these days, a Friday night is just you, me, the TV and the sofa. I can fake it for a while longer but pretty soon I'm going to get bored of it.'

She sips her drink. 'I've been doing a lot of thinking about my dad dying recently. I never tried to see any good in it. It was always easier to see it as the most terrible thing ever. Devastating. To think that it had ruined my life. And then recently it occurred to me that ever since it happened it's like I've been looking at it the wrong way. I had the most wonderful dad in the whole world. His love made me who I am today. What more could I want? There are people in the world who have never experienced that kind of love and they're the ones who have the right to be bitter about life, not me. Imagine if my dad had never been there and I'd never had his love. I wouldn't be me at all. I'd be someone else. Maybe someone you could never have fallen in love with. Sometimes we spend too much time wishing life wasn't the way it is. Sometimes, I guess, you just have to be grateful for what you've got.' She lets out a nervous laugh. 'And here endeth the sermon.'

Time

Workwise, things get back to normal relatively quickly. I take on some freelance shifts in the *Sound Scene* office in Bayswater, and while it's not what I want to be doing I reason that it will do for now. Izzy, meanwhile, has a lot on with running the magazine and preparing for each round of interviews for the editor's job. As for our relationship, it's hard to say what's going on but I know it's not normal. Izzy is in denial about Nicola. If I'm on the phone she makes a point of not asking who I'm talking to, if I go out she won't ask where I'm going and when I come in she won't ask where I've been. In short, she no longer asks the everyday questions in case she can't handle hearing the answers. When I try to talk to her about Nicola she won't be drawn. When I try to talk to her about what's happening to us, she won't discuss that either.

choice

It's Friday evening, two weeks later, and I'm on my way to Nicola's house to join her, assorted family and friends to celebrate her fourteenth birthday. I've spent weeks wondering what present I can possibly buy her that might make up in some small way for all the birthdays I've missed. I thought back to our window-shopping trip all those weeks ago and called Caitlin to find out Nicola's dress and shoe size then returned to Nicola's favourite shop. I saw items that looked vaguely similar to the ones we'd seen that day – but every time I picked anything up I wasn't sure. I didn't want to get her a present that she'd thank me for then leave at the bottom of her wardrobe. I wanted her jaw to drop. I wanted her to feel like I'd got the right present for her because I knew her so well.

After that I thought about giving her money – the ideal gift for any teenager – but I knew that, under the circumstances, it just wouldn't be right. I thought about music but, like clothing, it's so much down to personal taste and easy to get wrong. Other gifts I crossed off the list included: a new mobile phone, makeup, perfume, a car (grasping at straws here), a PlayStation 2, concert tickets, signed autographed stuff from any number of the bands I've interviewed, and a new pair of trainers. In the end I went back through all of the things I'd rejected, selected two items and carefully wrapped them in shiny dark blue foil.

here

'Dave!' says Nicola, on opening the door.

'Hey, you,' I give her a kiss, and hand her the two presents but hold on to the bottle of wine I've also brought.

'Thanks.' She kisses me again. 'Mum says I have to wait until everyone's arrived before I can start opening the presents. Two of my cousins haven't turned up yet and they're always late so it could be a while.'

'Fourteen, eh?' I say, sounding middle-aged.

'Do I look older?' she asks.

I look at her before I answer. She's obviously wearing a number of her birthday presents because everything looks brand new: a pair of indigo bootcut jeans, a pair of relatively high-heeled strappy sandals and a tight black top with the word 'Babelicious' marked out in diamanté studs. Her trademark corkscrew curls are down and although she's wearing 'going out' makeup, she doesn't look like she's plastered it on. She *does* look older. But she looks beautiful too.

'Yeah,' I say, with a big smile. 'You do. Can I come in now?'

Nicola laughs as she realises we're still standing on the doorstep. 'Yeah,' she says.

She ushers me into the living room where one of her dreadful club-mix CDs is playing just loud enough for her friends to be entertained but for the adults not to have to yell at each other. The room is fairly packed – there must be at least thirty people in there. Nicola asks if I want a drink and I tell her I'll help myself. She says her mum's in the kitchen sorting out the food.

'Dave!' says Caitlin, as I enter the kitchen. She's in the middle of putting a tray of something into the oven. Another woman, uncovering a platter of sandwiches wrapped in cling film, turns round and looks at me, then looks at Caitlin and smiles.

'It's good to see you again,' says Caitlin. 'I'm really glad you could make it.' She closes the oven door, wipes her hands on a tea-towel. She looks a lot different from the last time I saw her, more glamorous. Like Nicola, she's wearing her hair down and it frames her face perfectly and she's not wearing her glasses. Bizarrely she's wearing bootcut jeans, strappy sandals with heels and a tight black top with 'Babeli-cious' across it.

'I feel like I'm seeing double,' I tell her.

Caitlin laughs. 'You mean the outfit? Us O'Connell girls like a little joke. Every now and again Nicola and I pretend we're sisters instead of mum and daughter. I had the jeans and the shoes already and the top is apparently a very early or very late Mother's Day gift – even though I had to pay for it myself.'

I hand her the bottle of wine. 'Thanks,' she says. 'We're drinking the really cheap stuff at the minute so this'll be a nice change.'

I can see that Caitlin's friend is angling for an introduction. Something about her seems familiar but I can't place it. Eventually she drops all pretence of subtlety and says, 'I'm Colleen, Caitlin's best friend and Nicky's godmother.' She holds out her hand. 'Pleased to meet you.'

'I'm Dave,' I say, shaking her hand.

Caitlin laughs. 'She's not backward in coming forward, is she? Dave, meet Colleen. Colleen, meet Dave. The funny thing is, Dave, you've met her before.'

'You don't remember me, do you?' says Colleen. 'I was with Caitlin on that holiday. I got off with your mate Jamie.'

It all comes back to me. 'Of *course*,' I reply. 'Wow, it's good to see you again.'

'She's been dying to speak to you ever since she heard we were in touch,' says Caitlin.

'Why?'

The two women exchange secretive glances.

'It's a long shot,' says Caitlin, laughing, 'but Colleen's kind of hoping that you're still in contact with Jamie and that he's single.' With that they burst into fits of laughter.

'You want Jamie Earl's phone number?' I ask.

'He was really cute!' says Colleen, laughing. 'He had an arse like a ripe peach.'

'I haven't spoken to him in ages,' I say, when I can control the laughter that erupts at her description. 'But the last I heard of him he was living in Bournemouth working in the hotel trade. I've got his parents' number so by all means give him a call.'

'Excellent,' says Colleen. 'Mission accomplished, so I'll make sure all the guests have drinks – and leave you two alone.' Still chuckling, she grabs two open bottles of wine, one white, one red, and exits the kitchen.

'You'll have to forgive her,' says Caitlin, wiping down one of the surfaces with a paper towel. 'She's just split up with her fella for about the fifth time in as many years and it's sending her a bit funny in the head.' I smile but don't say anything. 'I take it you sorted out what to buy Nicola in the end?' she asks.

'Nearly,' I reply. 'Couldn't make my mind up.'

'Whatever you've got her she'll love it. She's quite good like that.'

'It's nice to know I have her pity if I need it.'

'I didn't mean it like that!'

'I know.'

'She's been really nervous about you coming tonight. The clothes, the hair, the makeup, it's all for you.'

'For me?'

'This afternoon she told me she wanted to look perfect for you. I told her you wouldn't mind what she looked like but she wouldn't have any of it.'

'She looks beautiful.'

'She does. There's a couple of lads from her school here and they're all gobsmacked by her.'

'Not Brendan Casey?'

'He's old news now, apparently.'

There's a long silence.

'I'm really sorry your wife couldn't come.'

'I'm sorry too,' I say. 'It's just that she's acting editor at the moment and things are . . .' My voice trails off. It's obvious Caitlin doesn't believe me. 'She didn't want to come,' I correct myself.

'I kind of guessed that,' says Caitlin. 'It can't be easy for her. I'm not sure I wouldn't be the same if the tables were turned.'

'But what's the solution? I can't extricate Nicola from my life. She's in there now, part of me . . . just like Izzy's part of me.'

'It must be difficult being the one stuck in the middle.'

'You don't understand,' I reply. 'It's more complicated than that.' And, taking a deep breath, I tell her about the miscarriage.

'That's so sad,' says Caitlin, when I finish. 'No wonder she doesn't want to meet Nicola.'

'But what can I do? I don't want Izzy to feel this way. And I don't want Nicola to think any of this is her fault. But now that things are out in the open she's going to think it's strange Izzy hasn't met her.'

'I don't want to be presumptuous, but . . . genuinely, and I mean this with my whole heart, is there anything I can do? I feel really terrible at how things have turned out. I feel bad for not trying hard enough to contact you when I knew I was pregnant and that Nicola's never had a father in her life until now. I just feel that if there's something I can do to make things even a little bit better I'd do it.'

'Thanks. It's really good of you to say that. But the truth is I don't think there's anything either of us can do. At the end of the day this is something only Izzy can come to terms with. I hope with all my heart that she will but I have to accept that there's every chance she won't, and that she has every right not to.'

12"

It's now nine o'clock, everyone has arrived and Nicola has begun to open her presents. In the last hour or so I've been introduced to Caitlin's three brothers, David (the youngest at nineteen, studying law at UCL), Aidan (twenty-five, works in the City) and Paul (thirty and in computing), her sister Eloise (thirty-eight, the oldest of the family and mum to Nicola's two fifteen-year-old cousins), and a whole host of friends. Everyone makes me welcome, and it would have been the perfect evening if Izzy had been there. I feel her absence like my own heartbeat – a constant reminder of what you need to survive. It doesn't feel right being here without her. It feels disloyal. I decide to leave early.

'I think I'm going to have to get off,' I say to Caitlin, who's standing next to me watching Nicola unwrap her presents. She looks at me, concerned, but doesn't try to persuade me to stay, for which I'm grateful as I already feel like I'm letting Nicola down.

'Are you going to take some birthday cake with you?' she asks.

I refuse with a smile. 'I'll just say goodbye to Nicola.'

She taps Nicola on the shoulder, whispers in her ear, and Nicola announces to the whole room that she's going to take a break from opening presents for a moment to spend some time with her dad who has to go. I've never heard her refer to me as her dad before in anything other than the biological sense; I'd certainly never heard it said so proudly, like it was some sort of new must-have fashion item.

'I still haven't opened your presents yet,' she tells me. 'I was going to save them until last.'

I laugh. 'I don't think you should go that far, Nicola. They're not going to be that good.'

She ignores me and picks them up from next to the sofa where they'd been left, loops her arm through mine and leads me into the hallway.

'What are we doing?' I ask, as she closes the door.

'Having some time on our own.' She sits down on the stairs and I join her.

'Which one do you want me to open first?' she asks.

'I don't mind.'

She looks at them both. 'I'll open the bigger one,' she says. 'What is it? Will I guess?'

'I don't think so. I don't really know why I'm giving it to you. I'm pretty sure you won't like it.'

She looks up at me, right into my eyes, until I'm gazing in hers. 'Whatever it is, I'll love it.' She opens the wrapping carefully and takes out a twelve-inch single. 'It's a record,' she says.

'I know.'

She reads the cover. 'Maybe If I Wear Your Jacket', the Parachute Men. 'Is it any good?'

'It's my favourite record. Ever.'

She looks at it again. 'Your favourite record ever? You mean out of all the thousands of CDs and records you've got, this is the best?'

I smile. 'I wouldn't say it's the best, but it is my favourite.

It's the one that reminds me just what music can do when it's done well.'

'Is it famous?'

'Not really.'

'Is it worth loads of money?'

'I strongly doubt it.'

She thought for a moment. 'And this is your favourite record in the world?'

I nod.

'Have you got another copy of it?'

'No. That's the only one I've got.'

She starts to cry.

'What's wrong, sweetheart?' I ask gently.

'You've given me your favourite song,' she says.

I wipe away her tears with my hands, put my arms around her and give her a hug. 'I'm giving it to you because I want you to have it.'

'But it's your favourite. I can't take it. You haven't got another.'

'I want you to have it, sweetheart. That way two of my favourite things will be together.'

'But we haven't even got a record player.'

She starts to laugh and I laugh, too, because it hasn't occurred to me that in this day of mp3s, compact discs and mini-disc players there are homes without record decks. 'I'll buy you one. Next birthday.'

'This is the best present in the world. The best. I promise you I'll look after it. I promise.'

'I know you will. Anyway, never mind that.' I gesture to the second present on the stair below her feet. 'You've still got one more to open.'

'What is it?'

'Open it,' I tell her, 'and find out.'

She picks it up. 'It's very light.'

'Yeah, I know. Anyone would think it was made of paper. But open it carefully.'

I watch as she follows my instructions.

'It's money,' she says, her eyes wide with surprise.

'One hundred and forty pounds,' I tell her. 'Ten pounds for each year. I didn't really want to give you money . . . it seemed a bit . . . well, you know. But then I thought about that day we spent window-shopping and I know that, like me, you're someone with very particular taste and I knew I'd only get it wrong.'

'You wouldn't,' she says quietly. 'Whatever it was I'd like it.'

'Even if I'd bought you a pair of acid-wash jeans with purple sequins?'

She laughs. 'I'd love them because you bought them for me. I wouldn't be caught dead wearing them outside, of course, but I'd probably put them on every time you came round to the house.'

'That's very kind of you. But you're sure you're not offended by the money?'

'Of course not.'

'And you're not allowed to spend it all at once,' I warn. 'Make sure you give it to your mum to look after. You can get into a lot of trouble with all that.'

'Okay, okay,' she says. 'But there are a lot of things I can buy with it! Like . . . something for you. You wait until it's *your* birthday. You won't know what's hit you.'

CD

When I get home Izzy's sitting in the living room. She has brought some work with her from the office: folders, papers, magazines and memos surround her. Her laptop is balancing precariously on the coffee table next to her. She doesn't look up when I come in, just continues shuffling through the papers in her hands. It's a gesture designed to let me know that she doesn't care where I've been, even though she does. It's a gesture designed to prick my conscience and make me feel more guilty than I already do.

'You all right?' I ask. 'How was work today?'

She looks up briefly then looks away. 'It was okay,' she replies. 'You?'

'Fine. Nothing much to report.'

'No, there never is.'

It's a small comment, nothing to write home about, really, but it speaks volumes about the state of our relationship. I now see that although I've tried my best to be patient and understanding it hasn't worked. Izzy simply can't come to terms with Nicola's existence and there's nothing I can do about it. I can see that it's eating away at her and tearing her up inside. And I realise it isn't fair that I'm putting her through this.

'I think maybe it would be best if I moved out,' I say quietly.

'Is that your answer to what's happening?' she says. 'To run away from your marriage?'

Her choice of words, her tone, her body language, everything is designed to provoke rather than bring about peace.

'It's not an answer,' I tell her, 'but I think that if I stay here, the way things are going there won't be much of a marriage left.'

She takes a deep breath as if about to speak – but instead she bites her lip. There's no anger left inside her, only fear – a fear that I feel too. No matter how long we spend apart, the situation that has caused the problem will remain: Nicola will still be my daughter from a relationship with another woman. And if Izzy can't accept this, what can we do? I think about us splitting up for good. Three years of marriage, six years of relationship reduced to rubble. The promise of a lifetime together reduced to however long we can fool ourselves that what's happening isn't happening.

'I don't want you to go,' she says.

'I know,' I tell her, 'but you know I have to.'

'Where?'

'Where what?'

'Where will you go? I'll worry about you if I don't know where you are.'

'I don't know. I could stay at my parents', I suppose.'

'Don't,' she says urgently. 'Please don't. I don't want them to know what we're doing to ourselves – what a mess we're making of everything.'

'Listen, don't worry, I'm sure I can go to a friend's house somewhere. I can go to Phil Clarke's.' He's a PR I know from my days at *Louder* who's the kind of friend I can go months without seeing and still be able to pull up at his front door

333

at midnight and sleep on his sofa without him making a big deal about it.

'You can't do that,' she says, half smiling. 'He lives in New Cross, doesn't he? New Cross is as dangerous as it gets.'

I smile. She has a point.

'Why don't you go to Jenny's?' she says. 'I'll give her a call and sort it out.'

'Are you sure she won't mind? I mean, isn't she still upset about her split with Trevor?'

She doesn't speak but I can see that she's shocked at the reminder of how easily our friends' relationships have fallen through and how we might be next.

'I can always try Fran in Brixton,' I suggest. 'I'll have to give her a ring and make sure it's okay, though.'

She nods and that's that. She's back to her normal self. We've gone from a sullen row to a normal caring couple in minutes – only I was leaving and she's helping me to do so. I call Fran and she tells me it's okay. I pack a large sports bag with a few days' worth of clothes, grab some tapes and CDs, throw the lot into the back of the car and she starts to cry.

'This is the right thing to do,' I tell her.

'I know,' she says. 'It is. It's difficult, that's all.'

'You need time.'

'We both do . . . but what if you decide you don't want to come back?'

'That won't happen.'

'But what if it does?'

'It won't,' I tell her.

'How long are you going to stay away?'

'I don't know.'

'I'll miss you,' she says.

'Listen,' I tell her, 'we'll speak on the phone.'

'But I need to see you. *We* need to see *each other* ...
This is how people split up, Dave, this is how they lose the
love between them – distance. We can't let that happen.'

'We will see each other. We can go for dinner or something. And we can talk and try to sort this mess out. But you
know we can't carry on living together like this because if
we do there won't be any chance of saving us at all.'

'Are we splitting up?' she asks.

'No,' I tell her.

'So what are we doing?' she asks.

'I don't know,' I reply. 'I think we're doing what we've got
to do.'

dinners

Over the weeks that follow my leaving I see Nicola every week without fail and sometimes more often. She and I expand our repertoire of places to go all the way from Burger King and McDonald's to Pizza Hut and Bella Pasta. Sometimes we go to the cinema, sometimes we just watch TV round at her house but Nicola's favourite thing in the world remains sitting in the passenger seat of the Mercedes with the roof down and the music turned right up. Running parallel to this, Izzy and I meet up once a week to talk about what we're going to do.

low

Week one: Tuesday evening, Spiga, Wardour Street

Starter

It's eight o'clock and Izzy has just arrived at the restaurant, straight from work. She's wearing charcoal-grey wide-legged trousers, a fitted white shirt with three buttons undone and a denim jacket. Her hair is tied back. In short she looks beautiful. 'How are you?' she says quietly.

'I'm okay,' I reply. 'How about you?'

'I've had better days.'

'You look great,' I say.

'I miss you,' she replies.

'I miss you too.'

There is a long pause.

'How are you getting on at Fran's?' she asks.

'I'm on her sofa. It's okay as sofas go.'

'And how's life at *Sound Scene*?'

'It's okay,' I tell her, 'but I don't think I'll be there much longer. I've had some good news.'

'What?'

'You remember Nick, my old editor at *Louder*? He called yesterday to say that he was back at BDP working on the launch of a new magazine. He wants to talk to me.'

'I've spotted him in the building a few times but I didn't know anything about the project. Congratulations. Is it another music mag?'

I shrug. 'I don't know.'

Main course

It's now eight thirty-three and we have yet to say a word about our separation, Nicola or how we're going to sort things out between us. Neither of us wants to bring up the topic when there's no obvious solution, so instead we talk about everything apart from the thing that's keeping us apart.

'I've got my final interview for the job tomorrow,' says Izzy.

'How have they gone so far?'

'Okay,' she says quietly. 'I mean, I've given it my best shot. The only thing is experience, isn't it? By the time they make their minds up I'll only have had five issues' worth of experience at editing a national women's magazine.'

'But you're brilliant at it. At least, I think you are.'

She smiles. 'Thanks.'

'You'll get the job. I'm sure.'

'I wish I had your confidence. It's just that I hear all these rumours about who they've approached and what they might do. The latest one is that they're going to bring someone over from BDP's sister companies in the US or Australia. It would make a lot of sense, too. It's rare that you're ever appreciated where you are. They probably think I'm too stuck in the old management ways and that someone else from another continent could give a fresher perspective. If I'd had any sense I would've left *Femme* a while ago and kept job hopping until I reached the top.'

'But you didn't because you loved the magazine you worked on. Surely that's got to count for something?'

'No,' she says. 'Not really.'

Dessert

It's now nine fifteen and Izzy and I have long since finished our meal. We have talked about work, the flat, mortgage payments and our friends, but we still haven't spoken about us.

'Would you like to see the dessert menu?' asks the waitress.

Izzy shakes her head. 'Not for me. Dave?'

'Not for me either,' I tell the waitress.

'Coffee?' asks the waitress.

Izzy and I both decline.

'Just the bill, please,' says Izzy.

'I'll get this,' I say, as the waitress walks away.

'It's okay,' says Izzy. 'You can get it next time.'

The waitress returns with the bill and Izzy pays on her credit card. We put on our coats in silence and step out into busy late-night Wardour Street.

'We didn't do much talking, did we?' I say, wondering what it's going to be like to have to leave her. 'At least, not about the things we were supposed to talk about.'

'No,' she says. 'We didn't.'

'Maybe next time, eh?'

'Maybe next time.' She leans forward and kisses me full on the lips. I kiss her back.

'I love you,' she says.

'I love you too,' I tell her.

And with that we turn in opposite directions and walk away.

measure

Week two: Thursday evening, Kettner's, Romilly Street

Starter

It's just after seven thirty when I arrive, and Izzy's already sitting at the table. She stands up to kiss me hello and then we sit down.

'How are you?' asks Izzy. 'How did your meeting with Nick Randall go?'

'Really well. It looks like I'll be back working in the same building as you pretty soon. He's been working on a dummy issue of a new mag ever since *Louder* folded and apparently it's been green-lighted and they're looking to launch in the next two months.'

'What kind of magazine?'

'Guess.'

'Music?'

'No, it's not music.'

She laughs. 'It's not teenagers, surely?'

'No.'

'Not a women's magazine.' She smiles. 'Don't tell me I'm going to have my own husband as a rival.'

'The exact opposite,' I reply, laughing. 'Men's lifestyle. Like *GQ* and *Esquire*. A few hundred glossy pages of interviews with models, film stars, features about ridiculously expensive cars, sandwiched between dozens of ads for high-performance cars, aftershave and electrical gadgets.'

Izzy laughs. 'That's fantastic! I mean, we'd both heard the rumours that BDP were looking in to this market but I never thought it would happen. I'm thrilled for you. What do they want you to do?'

'Nick's going to be executive editor, they're getting in some guy who's worked on men's lifestyle mags before to be the actual editor and they want me to be his deputy. The money's good and we have their assurance – for what it's worth – that they're going to keep the sales targets modest and as long as we make them within twelve months they won't pull the plug.'

'What's it going to be called?'

'*First Class*.'

'Dave Harding, deputy editor of *First Class*,' says Izzy. 'Well done. So, no more Love Doctor?'

'Jenny wants me to carry on the column and I've checked with the boss and he says it's fine.'

'So you're still the solver of love dilemmas?'

'Yeah,' I say. 'For what it's worth, that's me.'

Main course

It's now eight fifteen and I've been trying to summon the strength to bring up the topic ever since we sat down to eat. 'I think it's time we talked about Nicola,' I say.

'You're right,' says Izzy. 'Where do we begin?'

'I don't know. How do you feel about her?'

'If I'm being totally truthful – and I know this will sound horrible – I wish she wasn't part of our lives and that you'd never met her. I wish we could have our old lives back.'

'But that's not possible.'

'I know, but that doesn't stop me wishing, does it?'

'No,' I reply. 'I suppose not.'

'The strange thing is, I know that if Nicola had always been in your life – that if you'd known about her and told me when we first met – it wouldn't have been a problem at all. Loads of people have children from previous relationships.'

'So what's the difference?'

'It's hard to say. Some of it's to do with the shock, some of it's to do with the way you lied to me, but it's mostly to do with the miscarriage. I wanted to give you a son or daughter and it didn't work. But now you've got this beautiful teenage girl who's part you and part some other woman. And that hurts.'

Dessert

'Tell me about Nicola,' says Izzy. 'Tell me how you feel about her.'

It's now nine thirty and we've barely touched the food.

'I think she's amazing. I can't talk about her in terms of ifs or maybes. I can only talk about the way things are. So I can't say that I wish she didn't exist because she does. I can't say I wish I'd never met her because I have. And I can't change what happened fifteen years ago. Yes, things are messy. Yes, none of this has turned out the way I would've liked in a perfect world, but I don't live in a perfect world. Neither of us does.'

'You don't have to tell me that,' says Izzy. 'I wake up every day and you're not there. I come home to an empty flat because you're not there. I sit alone in the home we made feeling desperate for you to hold me and tell me everything's going to be all right. And I can't help but feel that the one reason you're not there at the centre of my life is Nicola. And that hurts. It hurts more than anything in the world because even though it might not be the case, it feels like you've chosen her over me.'

'I haven't. There is no choice. She's part of me. You're part of me too. It's like . . . I don't know . . . asking me to choose between my heart and my lungs.'

'I know,' she says. 'But the thing is, *you* are my heart and my lungs. You're everything to me. And what hurts is that I know I used to be everything to you.'

'Would you care for a dessert?' asks the waiter, approaching our table.

'Not for me, thanks,' I reply. 'How about you, Izzy?'

'No, thanks.'

'Just the bill, please,' I say to the waiter. Izzy slips on her coat and stands up. 'If you hang on a sec the waiter will be back with the bill and I'll walk out with you.'

'It's okay. I'd rather leave on my own.'

'Why?'

'Because saying goodbye to you is too hard,' she says, and then picks up her bag and walks out of the restaurant.

in

Week three: Atlantic Bar and Grill, Glasshouse Street

Starter:

It's nine thirty on a Friday evening. We meet in the bar beforehand. I'm wearing a black Paul Smith suit Izzy bought me for my birthday last year. Izzy's wearing a pale blue shift dress and heels, and looks too beautiful for words. We kiss hello as usual and make small-talk, and as we stand at the bar I look at our reflection in the mirror and wonder if we look like a couple to the people around us. We chat aimlessly for a while, catching up on each other. Izzy still hasn't heard whether or not she's got the job and is beginning to worry that no news is bad news.

In return I tell her that my first week at *First Class* went okay although I was certain I'd bump into her in the lift or the lobby but it never happened. We both seem to be keeping such odd hours at work that it's unlikely it will. I tell her how it's taken me a few days to adjust to the world of men's fashion, electronic gadgets, cars and, of course, good-looking women. I tell her that Fran's handed in her notice at *Teen Scene*. She's heard of a job going at *Fashionista* that she's going to apply for and if she doesn't get it she's thinking about travelling for a year with some old college friends.

Main course

'Can I ask you a question?' says Izzy. It's now ten fifteen, and we are in the middle of our meal.

'Of course.'

'Over the past few weeks we've talked a lot about Nicola. But neither you nor I have said a word about her mum, Caitlin. I have to admit I'm jealous of her, Dave, and I think that's one of the reasons why I'm finding all this so hard. You have a bond with this other woman – a living, breathing bond, a bond you love, and I'm afraid . . . of losing you to her.'

'There's nothing to be afraid of. You won't.'

'Deep down I know that. But what about when I'm not feeling quite so logical? When I'm not feeling quite so sure of myself. Whether you like it or not, the three of you are a family: Mum, Dad, and a kid. I'm the one who's surplus to requirements. It would be so easy for something to happen between you because then your life wouldn't be messy any more – everything would be tidy. You'd be with the mother of your daughter. There's no point in denying it.'

Everything Izzy says makes sense and I'd be lying if I said it hadn't occurred to me. Part of me – the part that has come to love Nicola – wants to make the world perfect for her, make up for everything she's missed out on, and right at the top of the list is a proper family. Izzy's right. All of our lives would be much tidier if Caitlin and I were to get together. But life isn't that tidy. I don't love Caitlin, I love Izzy, and no matter what she does or says that won't change.

Dessert

'Dave?' says Izzy, as she settles the bill at the end of the evening. 'I know this might sound strange but, well, do you remember the photo you showed me of Nicola?'

I nod.

'Do you think you could bring it with you next time we meet? I'd like to keep it for a while, if that's all right. It's just that . . . I don't know . . . I'd just like to see it again.'

'I'll make sure I bring it next time,' I say.

She smiles awkwardly, then says, 'I want you to know that whatever happens between us, I really am trying my best, but this is so hard though. Sometimes I feel like I'm never going to get over it.'

out

Week four: Tuesday evening, Bertorelli's, Charlotte Street

Starter

It's just gone seven thirty when Izzy arrives. The table was booked for seven.

'I'm really sorry I'm late,' she apologises. 'Did you get any of my messages I left on your mobile?'

'I couldn't get a signal. I thought it was probably something to do with work. What happened?'

'All the usual suspects: being behind schedule, advertising headaches, legal stuff. You name it I think I've probably had to deal with it today.'

'Still no news about the job?'

'I spoke to the publishing director after a meeting today and she reassured me that they'll have made a decision by the end of next week at the latest. So that's it. Seven more days and I'll be out of my misery.'

'You really don't think you're going to get the job, do you?'

'No. I'm not being modest either. I know I haven't got the experience. Everyone in the office thinks I'm this really confident person but if you'd seen me today, Dave, you'd have been able to tell I was *this* close to falling apart.'

'But you didn't, did you?'

'Not today but there's still tomorrow.'

'It won't happen, I guarantee, because you're good at your job. And I'm willing to lay down hard cash to prove it. I bet you five hundred pounds that by next week you're editor of *Femme*.'

'I wish I believed in me as much as you do.'

'It doesn't matter, does it?' I tell her. 'Because I've got enough belief for both of us.'

Main course

We talk all through dinner – sometimes about work, but mainly about our friends. I tell Izzy that Fran's got an interview at *First Class* for the position of full-time staff writer. Eventually we begin talking about Nicola again when I bring up the subject of the photograph and hand it to her. She stares at it for a long time.

'Are you all right?' I ask.

'I'm fine. I was just wondering . . . did you ever doubt that Nicola was yours?'

'In the beginning, yes.'

'If I'd seen this photograph I wouldn't have doubted it for a second. There are elements of you in her face, especially her eyes – and that smile is pure you.'

There's a long silence, then Izzy slips the photograph into her bag and we don't talk about Nicola or our problems for the rest of the meal.

Dessert

For the first time we have dessert and share a *crème brûlée* and I feel suddenly that there's renewed hope between us. That no matter what it takes we'll find a way to make things work. I pay the bill and we walk out of the restaurant together. Izzy decides she's too tired to get the tube so we decide to head over to Charing Cross in the hope of finding a cab. As we walk hand in hand through the noise and clamour of Leicester Square it feels like old times and I don't want to let her go. 'Do you have to go home?' I ask her, as we both try to hail cabs. 'We could go somewhere else for a drink or something.'

It's the 'or something' that let's me down. I can see in her face that she knows exactly what I'd like to happen.

'As much as I want to, Dave, you know it's not a good idea. It's crossed my mind a million times tonight, but being attracted to each other isn't our problem, is it? And sleeping together won't solve everything. We can't gloss over this problem, no matter how much we might want to. We have to face it head on.'

I look across the road, see a black cab with its light on and hail it. The driver turns on his indicator and pulls across the road to us. He winds down his window and Izzy tells him she wants to go to Muswell Hill. 'Are you getting a cab too?' she asks me.

'I'll get the tube.'

'What are you doing your next column on?' she asks, as she gets in.

'I don't know. I haven't thought about it yet. I've been toying with the idea of something about men and their relationship with their cars.' Izzy pulls a face. 'Okay, what have you got in mind?'

'Well, as we can't do what we want to do, I was about to suggest the next best thing.'

'Which is?'

'Eight hundred words on what makes a man sexy.'

allure

To: izzy.harding@bdp.co.uk
From: dave_atch01@hotmail.com
Subject: This month's Male Man

Dear Izzy,
I was up all night working on this.
Not much of a substitute but at least it pays well . . .

Dave XXX

What Makes a Man Sexy
When Rod Stewart posed the question back in the seventies, 'Do ya think I'm sexy?' my guess is that as a man, and especially a man sporting leopard-print Spandex trousers, he already knew the answer. This is the strange thing about men: no matter who we are, or what we look like, we all think we look sexy – all the time. First thing in the morning. Slouching on the sofa. Picking spinach from between our teeth. We are gorgeous. It's not an ego thing, or self-delusional mania either. It's simply that the self-assurance required to believe we are sexy is handed to us at birth. And when you think about it this makes total sense.

From the beginning of time until now, it's been a matter of fact that men pursue women and women (occasionally) allow themselves to be caught. Now, when you know from day one that nine times out of ten it is you who will suffer the embarrassment that comes with a declaration of love declined; that it is you who will offer your heart and soul on a plate to Sally Beale (my kindergarten love) and that it is you who will have the aforementioned minxtress laugh in your face, then, of course, you have to believe you're sex on legs. It's a survival mechanism. Without it, you (or rather, in this case, I) would still be licking the wounds of that particular rejection today. And herein lies the rub, because no matter how sexy we men think we are, unless we can convince womankind of this fact, we're basically on a hiding to nothing.

For example, I feel my best attributes are my eyes, shoulders and smile, yet when I asked my wife what she found sexy about me, the first thing she said was my forearms. Now, I pay no attention to my forearms whatsoever (but I do work on my eyes, shoulders and - oh, the shame of it - my smile) so how can she find them sexy? The sheer subtlety, randomness and elusiveness of what women find sexy is so frustrating.

A straw poll of female friends served only to further my confusion. My friend Stella once told me she adored Russell Crowe's fingertips in *Gladiator*. My friend Jenny informed me that the smell of her boyfriend's unaftershaved neck has her pulse racing. My friend Fran confessed she'd fixated on a man simply because of the way the light caught his skin the first moment she saw him. The sheer range of celebrity-men women found sexy was astounding too. Among names such as George Clooney and Will Smith were Danny De Vito, Tony Blair and Bart Simpson. Such information is all very poetic and/or democratic, but not a lot of practical use to men who wish to make themselves sexier.

So for me, when I want to feel sexy, I have to forget about what women want because I have no idea, and opt for what I like: my black three-button suit, a black V-necked T-shirt and if I'm really working it, baby, my trusty sunglasses that my wife bought me. Gorgeous? Well, nearly. Deep down, I suspect that not having the faintest clue why any woman finds me sexy is perhaps the sexiest sensation of all.

feeling

It's Thursday the following week and I'm on my lunch-break, which means that I'm at my desk at *First Class* working on my next Love Doctor column. As I go through the letters I think about Stella, Lee, Trevor, Jenny and finally, of course, my own predicament with Izzy. All these people with all these problems – and I can't do anything about any of them, least of all myself. The only people I feel I can help are my *Teen Scene* readership.

I've begun to feel protective towards them and I'm taking my role more seriously than I'd ever imagined I would. So, no matter how mad, deranged, or strange the letters I get, I do my best to read every single one and if I can't reply to them all, I know they feel better for having written down their troubles, put them in an envelope and mailed them to me.

Dear Love Doctor,
I'm cheating on my boyfriend with his best friend.
I've been with my boyfriend for eight weeks and
things were really going well between us but then
a few weeks ago I was at a party and I ended up
kissing his best friend. The kiss was great and I
have seen him three times since. I love both boys

and don't know what to do for the best. But I hate lying and this whole situation is making me depressed.

A Jennifer Aniston fan (14), London

Dear Jennifer Aniston fan,
It sounds to me like you're a little confused. It's always the way – you wait ages for a bus and then two come along at (roughly) the same time. So what are your options? You can (a) get on one and then get on the other (b) walk or (c) get someone to give you a lift. What you can't do is get on both buses at the same time because (a) it's physically not possible, (b) it's expensive (you'd have to buy two tickets) and (c) it's not nice to either bus. If you don't make a choice there's every chance that you'll be found out and it could be ages before any buses come your way in a long while.

Dear Love Doctor,
I went out with a boy for three weeks and I really liked him, and then for no reason he just suddenly changed. He wouldn't talk to me at school, he wouldn't take my phone calls at home and he tells his friends that he's not my boyfriend any more. What have I done wrong to make him act this way?

An MTV fan (15), Inverness

Dear MTV fan,
I'm sorry to be the bearer of bad news but it sounds to me that you have just encountered what

I call 'the bad boy break-up'. This is where a boy
decides for whatever reason that he no longer
wants to go out with you but, lacking the courage
to tell you, he acts like a loser in the hope that
you'll 'get the message'. The best thing you can do
is be dignified about it. Have nothing to do with
him whatsoever because at the end of the day
you're worth a million times more than he is. If,
however, you feel the need to be a little less
dignified spread a rumour around school about
him having bad breath and being a terrible kisser!

Dear Love Doctor,
I don't normally write to agony uncles but I have a
problem that I really need help with. I've been with
my girlfriend for two months and we get on really
well. She is my best friend. Recently we have been
spending all our time together and it's got to the
stage where I want to tell her I love her. The only
problem is I don't know how she feels. What if she
only 'likes' me – will she be put off and think I'm
too keen?
   A PlayStation addict (16), Liverpool

Dear PlayStation addict,
I don't normally answer letters that begin 'I don't
normally write letters to agony uncles' but in your
case I'll make an exception. It's a tricky question
you've posed: when is the right time to say those
three little words 'I love you'? If you feel it but
don't say it you feel awkward, and if you say it
and she's not giving you the 'I love you in return'

*you could look pretty stupid. Both actions have
their merits – but given a choice over looking
stupid and feeling awkward I'd take stupid. It takes
a brave man to get out there but if you get the
okay the rewards to be reaped are bountiful.*

one

I type the full stop after 'bountiful' and wonder whether that's the right word for the *Teen Scene* readership. My phone rings.

'*First Class*, Dave Harding speaking.'

'Dave, it's me.'

It's Izzy.

'How are you?' she asks.

'I'm fine. And you?'

'I'm okay too. I've got some good news to tell you.'

'You've got the job?'

Izzy lets out a huge scream down the phone. 'You're talking to the new editor of *Femme*! The MD and the editorial director told me less than half an hour ago.'

'Are you sure? You know what warped minds those magazine people have.'

'You'd better believe it's no joke.'

'I'm really pleased for you. You deserve it.'

'Dave, I miss you. I know we've got a lot to sort out and I know it's not going to be solved overnight but I just want you to know that I *do* miss you.'

'I miss you too.'

'Are you doing anything tonight? I've just booked a table for seven o'clock at Berwick's in Berwick Street. Will you come?'

'Of course I'll come. Just the two of us?'

'No, some of the girls from work will be there too . . . that's okay, is it?'

'Yeah, of course.'

'Are you sure?' she asks. 'I just sensed some reticence.'

'It's nothing. It's just that . . .'

'It's just what.'

'Tonight's the night we usually go out.'

'We can do it tomorrow.'

'Yeah, of course.'

'I tell you what, why don't you come round to the flat tomorrow evening and I'll make you dinner? But for tonight, let's forget everything that's happened and just enjoy ourselves. Okay?' She laughs. 'I'm editor of a top-selling women's magazine. And I'm going to turn it into the best magazine I possibly can. I have to celebrate!'

Her good humour is infectious. She's right. Sorting out the mess we've made of our lives can wait one night.

away

It's six thirty-five at the end of a working day and I've just emerged from the gents' toilets having changed from a Hawaiian shirt, jeans and trainers into a black suit, black T-shirt and shoes. The *First Class* office is empty: we finished putting the first issue to bed somewhere around three o'clock this morning and everyone's taking the brief respite in the schedules to enjoy themselves by slacking off early – apart from me and the magazine's latest recruit, Fran Mitchell. Apparently she was head and shoulders above the six young male journalists the editor interviewed and he gave her the job on the spot. Fran is now the only thing preventing the *First Class* office ending up like *Louder*'s and I'm glad she's around.

'Will you look at you?' says Fran, smiling mischievously. 'Are you ready to rumble or what?'

'What? This old thing? I just threw it on.' I laugh. 'It seems a bit strange, getting dressed up to have dinner with my wife and her mates but . . . you know.'

'I think it's sweet. I don't think you know this, Dave, but you're an easy man for a girl to fall in love with. You think you're this big, hard, serious music journalist then you end up writing for a girls' teen mag and writing cutesy bloke articles for a women's magazine. You're it – the perfect mix of manliness and sensitivity, the kind of guy who could make mad-passionate-caveman love to a woman and still be able to talk about "feelings" and all the rest of that crap we're supposed to go wild for.'

'Oh, come on, Fran,' I protest. 'You of all people must know that none of this is real. The stuff in the magazines isn't me. It's what Izzy tells me *Femme* readers want to read. It's what *Teen Scene* readers want to read. It's all fantasy.'

'But it's a fantasy I'd love to believe in and . . . well, better a fantasy than everyday reality.' She stops and laughs. 'And before you start getting all weird, I don't fancy you at all – although I admit I might've had an incredibly small crush on you in the early days, but you've no need to worry about me jumping on top of you any time soon because I won't. You love Izzy, don't you? You think the world of her. She's the one woman in the whole universe who makes you happy and you're hers exclusively.'

'And?'

'That's it. In a way I'd love to know what it feels like to be Izzy. I'd love to know how it feels to be loved like that. You worry about her, you talk about her all the time, you're proud of all her achievements, and this thing with Nicola has shown you're terrified of losing her. She means everything to you. Not just in a we-share-a-life-together way but in a deeper, more fundamental sense.' She giggles. 'Listen to me, I'm rambling like a right idiot now . . . but the fact remains that even though I love Linden with my whole heart – I know that he'll never feel about me the way you feel about Izzy. Not because he's malicious, or hateful but because I'm not even sure he knows what love is.' Fran looks at her watch. 'That's about as much of a pep-talk as you're going to get from me. You'd better be off if you're not going to be late.'

'Yeah,' I say, 'you're right.'

We both say goodnight to the cleaner, head out of the office and wait for the lifts. When one arrives a couple of female writers from *Metrohome* and the editor of *Fashionista* are already in it, deep in conversation. As we descend to the ground floor Fran and I smile wryly at snatches of conversations about haircuts, boyfriends and the previous night's episode of *Ally McBeal*.

away

As I walk along Oxford Street towards Berwick Street and
the restaurant it starts to rain so I speed up and try to get
myself into a positive frame of mind. This is Izzy's night and
I don't want to spoil it by being miserable. I want her to
have a good time. I want to celebrate her victory with her
and I'm even prepared to don the Love Doctor hat for her
workmates one more time, if that's required of me. I just
want her to be happy.

As I open the door into the restaurant my eyes immediately search for her and her friends but I can't see them.
The restaurant's packed with couples chatting over candle-
lit dinners. Izzy's never late for anything and I begin to
wonder if I've got the wrong date, time or, even worse, that
something's happened to her. I tell the waitress that I'm
supposed to be meeting my wife and some of her friends
and that the table's booked for seven under the name of
Harding. She runs a finger down a long list of names in the
restaurant's reservation book.

'The Harding party has already arrived,' she tells me. 'But
the table was booked for six not seven.' I can't believe I've
got the wrong time. Izzy's going to be livid. 'Shall I show
you to the table?'

I sigh resignedly, and follow the waitress through the
restaurant to the table at the rear and finally realise why I

hadn't spotted her when I came in. I'd been looking for a large group of women, but she isn't with a large group and she isn't on her own. Sitting at the table with her is Nicola.

Izzy stands up, puts her arms around me and kisses me. Then Nicola stands up and kisses me too. 'Izzy and I have got loads to tell you,' she says.

'I don't understand,' I reply.

'I decided it was time,' says Izzy, looking into my eyes, 'for all this to stop. I was tired of feeling angry, tired of feeling sorry for myself, tired of missing you. And I wanted to meet Nicola. So I called her last week – I knew her mobile number was on the back of that photo you gave me – and I met up with her and her mum. And that went so well I asked her to join us for dinner tonight – and she said yes, and then we both kind of came up with the idea of meeting early without you so we could have another little chat on our own without you getting in the way. The whole come-and-celebrate-with-the-*Femme*-girls line was a fib.'

'Izzy is *so* nice,' says Nicola excitedly. 'Do you know she can get free perfume just by ringing up perfume companies?' She corrects herself hastily. 'She's not nice just because she can get free perfume. She's nice because she's, well, she *is* nice.'

'Why, thank you, Nicola,' says Izzy. 'A free bottle of Gucci Envy will be winging its way to you in the post.' She looks at me. 'But she's right, you know, we have been getting on like a house on fire. Nicola's impossible – and I do mean *impossible* – not to like. You should be proud of her, Dave, really proud.'

'I am,' I tell her. 'I'm very proud of both of you.'

Izzy kisses me again and then we sit down at our table, the waiter brings over the menus, opens a bottle of wine and together we begin our very first dinner for three.

Don't miss Mike Gayle's bestselling novel
MY LEGENDARY GIRLFRIEND
a hilarious novel for anyone who has ever dumped, been
dumped or lived in a dump

'A funny, frank account of a hopeless romantic'

THE TIMES

'The male Bridget Jones'   EXPRESS

'Full of belly laughs and painfully acute observations'
INDEPENDENT ON SUNDAY

'Touching and funny'   MIRROR

Meet Will Kelly. English teacher. Film fan.
Pot noodle expert. Ex Boyfriend.

Still in love with The One, Will is desperate to discover
if there can be An-Other One. In his decrepit flat where
he can't even manage to cook spaghetti hoops without
setting off the communal smoke alarm, his lifeline is the
telephone. Will realises that with a single call, friends can
either lift him from the depths of depression or completely
shatter his hopes.

There's Alice (who remembers his birthday), Simon (who
doesn't), Martina (the one-night stand), Kate (the previous
tenant of his rented hovel). And of course his Ex, Aggi –
the inimitable Aggi. His Legendary Girlfriend.

Or is she?

Two men, three women and a donkey called Sandy . . .
basically it's your classic love hexagon.

Hodder & Stoughton Paperbacks

Don't miss Mike Gayle's bestselling novel
MR COMMITMENT
A wickedly observed novel for anyone ever faced with the
question: To live together? Or not to live together?

After twenty-eight years of shirking responsibility Duffy's
finally realising that he can't extend his adolescence
forever. His low-paid temping job is threatening
permanency. His gradually receding hairline is depressing
him greatly. And if that's not enough his long-suffering
girlfriend, Mel, wants to get engaged.

Trips to IKEA, dinner parties with married couples and talk
of babies, however, are giving Duffy cold feet. He doesn't
have many worldly goods to share – apart from the remote
control for his TV, the beers in the fridge and his record
collection – but can he really put his hand on his heart and
say 'I do'? He knows Mel's the one for him, so why is it
he'd feel happier swapping 'Till death us do part' for
'Renewable on a four year basis'?

But the choice is: all or nothing.

So after a lifetime of Mr Irresponsible does Duffy have
what it takes to become Mr Commitment?

Hodder & Stoughton Paperbacks

Don't miss Mike Gayle's bestselling novel
TURNING THIRTY

'Mike Gayle has carved a whole new literary niche out of the male confessional novel. He's a publishing phenomenon'
EVENING STANDARD

'Delightfully observant nostalgia . . . will strike a chord with both sexes'
SHE

'A warm, funny romantic comedy'
DAILY MAIL

'Gayle's chatty style sustains a cracking pace'
THE TIMES

'Thirty means only going to the pub if there's somewhere to sit down. Thirty means owning at least one classical CD, even if it's *Now That's What I Call Classical Vol 6*. Thirty means calling off the search for the perfect partner because now, after all these years in the wilderness, you've finally found what you've been looking for.'

Unlike most people Matt Beckford is actually looking forward to turning thirty. After struggling through most of his twenties, he thinks his career, finances and love life are finally sorted. But when he splits up with his girlfriend, he realises that life has different plans for him and Matt temporarily moves back home to his parents.
Within hours, his mum and dad are driving him up the wall just like the old days. Feeling nostalgic and desperate for sanity, he decides to get in touch with his old school mates. So, one by one, he tracks down the rest of the magnificent seven – Gershwin, Pete, Bev, Katrina, Elliot and Ginny, his former one-off girlfriend. Back together after a decade apart. But things will never be the same for any of them because when you're turning thirty nothing's as simple as it used to be.

Hodder & Stoughton Paperbacks